The Symbionts of Murkor

Gary Tarulli

To My Wife

Forever Young

CONTENTS

Symbiont - An organism living
in symbiosis with another

1 THE WORST OF ALL POSSIBLE WORLDS

SHE HAD BEEN FORWARNED, but a handful of holographs and a terse description offered by a disgruntled mining tech who had toiled on the planet were insufficient preparation for how grim it appeared, even at a great distance. Murkor "was toast," the tech took perverse delight in saying, its surface incinerated and nearly all life eradicated by a 40000 kph chunk of rock. Almost uninhabitable, what remained for humanity to plunder had earned the distinction of being called the worst of all possible worlds.

Looking starboard, Commander Jennifer Ellis glimpsed the last unimpeded view of the planet's orange dwarf star, inferior to Earth's Sol in size and magnitude. Murkor was the eighth distant planet of eight, the only body in the system with a surface density capable of supporting a person's weight. It had nothing to recommend itself other than isolated pockets of a vital mineral—and that, too, was disadvantaged by the processing required to render it transportable to the nearest inhabited system. Astrobiologists hoping to find

1

extremophiles had detected only a handful of organisms, with none more interesting than a dull brown splotch resembling a primitive lichen. Based on their cursory research, Murkor was considered no threat to humans and substantially ignored. That changed, Ellis thought with regret, because of Earth's need for one damn mineral.

Doubts that her prospective assignment was intended as a decidedly unique and unpleasant form of punishment vanished into the vacuum of space. As gravity drew the shuttle downward, she reflected on the weight placed on her shoulders and the unwritten orders she was determined to resist, no matter the personal cost. If, that is, her command could survive that long. Velcroed to her utility belt was a packet of encrypted files describing the troubles looming at Zenith, the mining base that would be her final destination. Reeking of Coalition's self-serving agenda, they were full of half-truths and errors, the verbose bull shit expected of bureaucrats and politicians. In her experience (and in personal practice), truth and accuracy typically meant brevity.

The month-long journey from Varian to the remote Orion Spur had been a constant struggle against tedium and lethargy, although zero-gravity yoga meditation had certain benefits. Floating up from the exercise pod, she sat next to the only other person onboard, the captain of the Coalition C5-Class shuttle. He was a space-hardened veteran who looked as battered as his ship, the psychophysical effects of prolonged and repeated interstellar travel having exacted their toll. It had suited her fine upon discovering he was also a man of few words. When asked his name, he had simply said, "Pilot," leaving her unsure if that was a name or a title.

The man's prematurely aged look prompted a comparison to her face, which reflected off the shiny surface of the control console. There were a few temporary lines on the forehead from concentrating on the difficult task ahead. Permanent wrinkles, crow's feet, spoked outward from the corners of her eyes, perhaps caused by a lifetime of grueling training and exercise regimens. Or were they from laughing or crying at human folly, frequently others, and on one tragic occasion, her own? Collectively, they made her appear older than thirty-three Earth years. The trade-off was that they also gave the impression of hard-earned experience, a valuable attribute when commanding. Otherwise, the almost gaunt face staring back at her sported a clear complexion, a small, upturned nose, and sharp cheekbones. Pleasant enough features framed by straight, dirty-blonde hair that had been close-cropped to be less bothersome in zero-g. Superficialities. Almost unimportant. What would it reveal to the uninitiated about her? That this was a facade, a mask hiding something troublesome deeper within? Dig deeper. The eyes express and reveal more. What was that saying? 'Mirrors to the soul?' And if you refused to believe in the soul? Her orbs were merely hazel.

Musings to pass the inner space of non-relativistic time.

Pilot was the first to break the long silence with an oblique reference to a topic they had avoided during the lengthy journey.

"It's a long way from the Varian System just to drop off a solitary passenger and a few supplies."

"No choice," Ellis replied.

"There is always a choice," Pilot responded, frowning.

"That might be so," Ellis answered, unsure if Pilot was commenting on what he knew of her assignment on Murkor or, slim chance, making a much broader philosophical affirmation of free will.

Silence resumed. Attention had to be paid, for the deep-space approach to Murkor was known to be a hazardous one. The shattered planet was encircled by a debris field made of countless particles of glistening ice (once the planet's ocean) and objects sufficient in mass to obliterate a ship.

"There are alternate ways to slip through that cloud and enter orbit," Pilot said, studying the visible line of the field's outer edge. "The direct approach, which is much faster, is also the riskiest."

"Direct approach would be my preference, though I will defer to your better judgment," Ellis said, adding, "Don't misconstrue my meaning. I'm in no particular hurry to arrive."

"No one ever is," Pilot replied. The matter decided, he donned a miniature headset linking his thoughts to the ship's navigation and propulsion systems, thereby eliminating two hundred milliseconds of muscle reaction time and facilitating near-instantaneous course corrections. Suddenly, simulations of the debris field's larger objects and the vectors to avoid them hovered in the air. On the periphery, despite his best efforts to suppress the distraction from his mind, was the faintly glowing image of a massive class C-40 supply ship.

Ellis immediately recognized it as the *Trillion*. The waiflike image had a sobering effect. Everyone knew the sad story. The massive supply ship had a catastrophic hull breach and disintegrated above Murkor's surface while attempting to navigate the space she was about to enter. A crew of thirteen souls, never recovered, was now a tiny part of the field that had destroyed them.

"I knew her captain well," Pilot said, the apparition fading in and out of view. "Well enough to know what happened was no way in hell a miscalculation on his part."

"Sorry," was all Ellis thought fitting to say.

"Still want to proceed on this heading?"

"If it's all the same to you," Ellis said.

"Good. I love a challenge."

"They say if you live to hear the impact, it's a good thing," Ellis said, and regretted, knowing it wasn't true.

"Yeah, they say a lot of foolish things."

The first disconcerting sound, a muffled *thunk*, caused the holo image to burst into colorful life.

"That reminds me," Pilot said. "*Seat…Mold.*" Responding to the command, his seat began to reshape until it had securely ensconced the entirety of his torso, leaving only arms and head free. "I suggest you do the same, Commander," Pilot advised, a note of caution entering his voice for the first time.

"For safety?" Ellis scoffed. "Seems pointless."

"Mostly for someone else's convenience," Pilot answered, visualizing a course correction. "It's easier for a recovery team to locate human remains when attached to a big chunk of a ship. That's if anybody's crazy enough to—"

A jarring interruption blared out from the ship's brain, its mindstor:

Shield loss twenty-seven percent. Repowering commenced.

Pilot glanced sideways at Ellis, seeing no emotion when he expected to see alarm.

There was a second thunk, louder and sharper this time, then a high-pitched sequence of pinging sounds, a short, unnerving lull—followed by an impact that vibrated the entire ship.

Shield loss thirty-one percent...correction. Shield loss fifty-seven percent...repowering...forty-nine...correction...shield loss seventy-one percent.

A bank of red lights warned that shield strength was diminishing despite constant repowering. Another impact would compromise hull integrity.

"We have no intention of joining you, Max," Pilot said, visualizing a course vector that sent his ship into a gut-wrenching six g-force yaw.

Ellis understood that Max referred to Maxwell Hendrickson, the distinguished captain of the *Trillion*. He and a crew of twelve were drifting out here somewhere.

Moments later, the planet-side edge of the debris field came tantalizingly into view.

"We're almost through," Pilot said, believing Ellis needed reassurance, unaware that her thoughts had already gravitated elsewhere.

"I understand there is a well-equipped gym at Zenith," she said.

Pilot again glanced over at his passenger. Upon discovering she wasn't joking, he laughed and said, "I'd be interested to see *you* wear this imaging headset."

"You'd probably think it's malfunctioning." As part of her military training, she had donned a device similar to what Pilot was now using. While most wearers could not prevent the formation of stray images, she could do so easily and for a long duration. Another minor benefit of the yoga meditation she practiced.

Leaving debris field...shield loss sixty-one percent. Returning to full power.

"It appears, Pilot, that your ship shall remain intact," Ellis said. "Well done." The compliment had been earned. Compared to the audible impacts the shield sustained, numerous were too small to be heard, and countless had been avoided.

"Hell, the ship handled most of it," Pilot answered, obviously pleased by the recognition of a complex skill acquired through many years of experience. "But I have managed to prove a point—again. The loss of the *Trillion* wasn't Max's doing. He was a far better pilot than I am."

"You've been to Murkor before?"

"This transit makes it two times too many. I'll spin the ship to give you a better look."

When Murkor came into full view, Pilot tried offering up a description. "What does it look like to you? A scuffed, misshapen baseball?"

"I see a blackening, decomposing orange," Ellis said.

"That's good," Pilot said in appreciation, "though we're being way too flattering."

"The sight does take your breath away."

"Quite literally when you're exposed on the surface," Pilot said.

Captivating their attention was a distorted sphere transected by narrow mountain ranges: The seams and ridges inspiring Pilot's baseball analogy. Violently torn asunder and then stitched back together by the forces of time and gravity, Murkor's surface had the garish look of a freshly autopsied cadaver. At an altitude of three hundred kilometers, the mottled "skin" resolved to show the midnight-black of solidified lava fields interspersed with broad patches of sallow yellow and orange where vast oceans had existed. Large portions of the surface were obscured by a dirty shroud of particle-laden gases billowing into the upper reaches of the stratosphere. Pitchforking within this murk were jagged streaks of blue lightning—electromagnetic discharges similar to those seen in the clouds above erupting volcanoes on Earth.

"With such a foreboding landscape, you can see how the story started," Pilot said, mesmerized by the planet's hideous appearance. "Have you heard it?"

"Which one? It's haunted?" Ellis said dismissively. "Or there lurks an undetected lifeform? Nearly every planet I've been to has a similar mythology, the modern-day equivalent of werewolves, vampires, and things that go bump in the night."

"True enough," Pilot said. In his many years as a shuttle pilot, he had heard his fill of such stories. Murkor's was the most convincing. "Nevertheless, I have no intention of staying longer than necessary."

"I'll keep that in mind. Let's make one complete orbit before we land at Zenith." The opportunity to study the terrain from altitude was an advantage that would disappear with Pilot's return to the Varian System tomorrow. Thereafter, only ground transport would be at her disposal.

"Altitude?"

"One hundred kilometers. Lower, if you can manage."

"I can manage. The ship should compensate for the planet's wobble."

The shuttle descended through the thermosphere. Areas that, at a distance, showed as pockmarked blemishes were eruptions from the planet's bowels. Fumaroles, the geologists had named them. Resembling gigantic open-topped termite mounds, many were vomiting a yellow-green fume which, rising and mingling like so many polluting smokestacks, contributed a blanket of haze into the atmosphere.

Flat surfaces were now distinguishable as plateaus where molten rock had once flowed, slagged, and solidified, creating a broken terrain of lava lakes, pahoehoe lava, and escarpments. At the foot of some escarpments were yawning mouths—the openings to a vast network of lava tubes. Ellis took a hard, second look. Residing deep inside a small fraction of these formations was a substance common to Earth, but it could ignite a conflict here.

Ellis could see why navigating the uneven terrain by ground vehicle was treacherous. Nevertheless, overland excursions were, out of necessity, routine. Correction: *Commonplace*. Nothing in such a hostile environment should ever be viewed as routine. To consider it so would be to court disaster.

Having completed one circumnavigation of the planet, Pilot transitioned the shuttle into a lower glide path. On the fringes of a bleak and barren lake of hardened lava, rising like a mirage in the shimmering heat haze of an Egyptian desert, squat a modest-sized pyramid. Ellis immediately recognized the structure as Nadir, the location of the opposition, Unión de Naciónes de la América Latina.

"You have to ask yourself," Pilot mumbled aloud, "why establish a base here? It defies reason."

"Do they have a defensive system?" Ellis asked, avoiding the question.

"Not to my knowledge."

"Take us in for a closer look."

"Your definition of 'close?'"

"Let's not rouse them. Five hundred meters should suffice."

Pilot closed the distance and banked his ship, affording a better view of a ten-meter-high four-sided pyramid squatting at the end of a long line of fumaroles emitting puffs of acrid smoke. The outlying terrain was pahoehoe lava and escarpments containing an inordinately large number of lava tube openings. Makes sense, Ellis thought.

The base showed advancing signs of wear. Metal alloy and palladium glass panels, once lustrous materials, had been etched to a dull patina—the effects of windblown pumice and corrosive gases. Several of the highest panels appeared to be improperly fitted. Assuming the base's occupants knew of the defect, this development had to be disconcerting. Tenuously clinging to the structure's apex was a bent metal mast, likely a weather monitoring or communications spindle. How it survived the harsh conditions was anyone's guess. Repairing it would almost be impossible. Two large vehicles were located at the base of the structure. One, dust-covered, had seen better days.

Ellis could now confirm that at least one item in the intelligence reports was accurate. The Unión base had been hastily constructed and poorly maintained. Very little intel, however, was available concerning the interior or its occupants. Given its outward appearance, it was ill-equipped, but no matter its shortcomings, Nadir was established here first. Unión had not only discovered Murkor but had the wherewithal and foresight to conduct ultrasonic mapping of the planet's subsurface— thereby locating and claiming the majority of precious subterranean water. It was a remarkable achievement that Coalition politicos and military brass were now lamenting.

"They must be a tenacious lot," Ellis said, intending it as a compliment given the structure's poor appearance.

"Would you expect otherwise?" Pilot responded, a trace of annoyance entering his voice.

"Let's move on," Ellis said, ignoring the question. "How far to base Zenith?"

"By air, exactly one hundred kilometers."

As Nadir disappeared in the gloom behind them, she reflected on the illogic of establishing permanent bases on Murkor. The enormous distance to Varian, the nearest inhabited planet, rendered routine commerce impractical and uneconomical, the valuable mineral anecrecium being the sole exception. What had compelled humans to come here initially was easier to explain. *Curiosity.* A trait that had served the human race well. If we weren't unrelenting snoops, Ellis thought, we would still be brandishing clubs or extinct as the dinosaurs.

"There it is. Coming into view now," Pilot said, scowling. "Your Coalition assignment. For what it's worth."

It was hard to miss the cynicism. Ellis was going to question the cause when two geodesic domes loomed up like giant blisters upon the barren landscape: The latest generation of organo-tech utilized in Zenith's creation or, more accurately, its growth. The base's two hemispheres—the larger was a third the size of an enclosed football stadium—had been grown in place (geneticists used the term *in situ*) from a genetically altered organic material that had repeatedly bifurcated and differentiated to create an impervious exterior shell and a significant portion of structural elements.

Components such as the rigid frames of couches, desks, and tables had been 3-D printed in place. Repeated runs by supply ships, such as the ill-fated *Trillion,* supplied the bulk of interior appointments. At great expense, the enclosed space had been rendered utilitarian and exceedingly comfortable for a sizable contingent of adults. With a full working chef's kitchen and separate areas designated for exercise and entertainment, Zenith was as opulent inside as impressive outside.

As the ship approached off-angle, hundreds of cerulean hexagonal facets, like so many jewels, refracted the sun's dim light sequentially. At regular intervals, a crimson glint revealed an identically shaped observation port.

"Nadir's wealthy neighbor," Ellis commented.

"Shall we set down?" Pilot said abruptly, wearing a second scowl.

"Soon," Ellis responded. "Plot in a mapping course. I want an overview of the area that comprises Zenith's exclusion zone."

The two opposing bases' one-hundred-kilometer Exclusion Zones (EZs), specifically the availability of the resources beneath them, were the source of contention. Nadir's zone had an abundance of water, as did Zenith's anecrecium. Anecrecium requires water for processing. The tension this disparity could produce became evident when the Interplanetary Mining Corporation (IMC), operating under the auspices of the Coalition of Canadian and American Nations, reluctantly and belatedly came to understand that the lack of water would upend an otherwise immensely profitable venture. Zenith, it seems, should never have been built.

Ellis knew that IMC worshipped the bottom line and Coalition politicians did not like being publicly humiliated—reasons why she was expected to play a disruptive role here.

The potential for strife on Murkor can be traced to its Earth-based origins when universal communication and rapid travel fostered the development of ever-larger geo-political and social groups. Nation-states expanded and organized. Superpowers emerged. Coalition was formed from the unification of Canada, much of the former United States, Iceland, Greenland, and half of the Caribbean islands. A decade later, Unión was created through the uneasy merger of Mexico, Cuba, and the countries of Central and South America.

Competition for the shrinking supply of natural resources and hardships caused by decades of environmental calamity ended the fragile coexistence between these superpowers. A beneficial relationship characterized by cultural exchanges and trade degenerated into social and economic disruptions. Cold war and rising tensions followed.

When Unión established a small base on Murkor, it became incumbent upon Coalition, taken by surprise, to follow suit. Although late to the party, they arrived in the grandest of fashion. Given the considerable expense involved, however, the public began to view the undertaking as a flagrant misuse of public funds. With the tragic loss of the *Trillion* and her crew, the word "boondoggle" came back into vogue. Soon after, the word began adhering to certain politicians who, finding no easy inoculation against the vocal criticism, tried to disassociate themselves from having fronted Zenith's cost while still supporting IMC's mining operation. It made sense. As the base's principal authority, they reaped much of the profit that would justify its enormous cost to the public.

Only it was not going as planned. The viability of the mining operation was in serious jeopardy due to the lack of an essential compound for mineral processing. It was the one compound, water, that Nadir had in relatively abundant supply.

Ellis was forced to accept a harsh reality as she studied the unwelcoming landscape rushing below. A calculated and cynical decision had been made: Send a bitch to handle the problem. Hurl her angry sorry ass out to the last inhabited planet with orders to relieve Zenith's ineffectual commander. Take control of Nadir's precious subterranean water by instigating a dispute in any way she deems appropriate. The beauty of it? This far out, Coalition culpability might be obscured. Other than orders to relieve Zenith's commander, the purpose of her mission was not logged in the official record. If it all turned to shit, she would be hung out to dry.

"That pretty much covers it, Commander."

For a moment, Ellis imagined that Pilot had read her thoughts. "Say again?"

"We've seen everything there is to see."

"Right. They'll be expecting me." Then, almost to herself, "They'll expect a lot *from* me."

"Yeah, right. To do Coalition's bidding."

"Is that what you've heard?" Ellis said.

"That, and more."

"And this information you're privy to—you believe every word of it?"

"When it has the ring of truth to it," Pilot answered.

"And what is this 'truth' telling you?"

"You're here to stir up trouble. It won't be difficult. A base full of IMC employees, mostly miners, mostly men, non-military. Disgruntled because things aren't working out quite as they planned."

If Pilot had something pertinent to say, it would be worth hearing. Having spent years traversing a sizable chunk of the spiral arm, he would have acquired a unique perspective. "And this affects you—how?" Ellis asked. "When's the next time you'll be within twenty light-years of this quadrant?"

"You're a fool if you believe what happens here won't spread. Only the politicians who sent you don't get hurt. To them, it's just a calculated game. The pieces fall, the players are untouched."

"So, you think you have me figured out," Ellis said.

"Do you know what the Latinos call us now?" Pilot persisted. "*Chancros*. It means 'canker' in Spanish."

She knew the derivation. Canadians were Canucks; Americans, Yanks. When the two countries merged, so did the two words, morphing into "Canks" and "Cankers." It had become as offensive as *beaner*, broadly disparaging anyone of Hispanic descent. Two slurs helping to populate the hundreds found littering the human lexicon.

"And what is your solution to Zenith's problems?" Ellis asked.

"Do nothing."

"Nothing?"

"I've been to colonies on eighteen planets. Four moons. Five floating space habitats. I've managed to see just about every culture you can imagine. Do you know what people universally have in common? What they want?"

Ellis shook her head and waited.

"They want to be left alone. They want to get on with living their lives. Earn a good living. Start a family. Enjoy a good meal. Breathe fresh air—"

"—consume fresh water," Ellis inserted, calling attention to Zenith's lack of the vital compound.

"Has Zenith run out of drinking water?" Pilot asked, seizing on the remark. "Last I heard, the shortage only affects their ill-conceived mining operation."

"Zenith has twenty-four disgruntled IMC miners who would probably advocate using force to obtain that water."

"Exactly why a sensible person should be worried."

Neither spoke as Pilot deftly navigated the shuttle to a soft touchdown near the larger of Zenith's two hemispheres. They passed through a portal that opened in the structure's sleek façade.

Ellis left her seat to retrieve the few personal articles she brought with her. Looking back into the ship's body, she noticed that Pilot, believing he was alone, had donned the same headset he had worn while navigating through the debris field.

She'd have to think long and hard to conjure up an image one-tenth as heartwarming as the one he was now contentedly viewing.

Floating in space was the delightful image of Pilot, an attractive middle-aged woman, and two smiling children, one holding a small poodle.

She felt a sudden, deep pang of regret. Years ago, she had forever stolen the pleasure of conjuring a similar image from someone else. Erasing the pain of that memory was the one thing that motivated her. If Pilot (who had otherwise shown a keen sense of judgment) had questioned her sad expression, he might have discovered how badly he had misjudged her.

There was a whoosh of pressurized air, and the shuttle's door opened.

"Commander Ellis, I presume?" came a booming voice. "Of course, of course. I'm Commander Frank Trenchon. Welcome to Zenith."

2 NADIR

"UNSAFE" WOULD NOT BE the first words that would come to mind if the six inhabitants of Nadir were to vocalize their reaction to the all-too-frequent breakdown of electronic components and mechanical equipment. The constant danger at Nadir was real, but in the crew's day-to-day existence, expletives such as 'mierda,' 'hijo de puta,' or 'la pucha' was more commonly used.

'Creature comfort' had unfortunately fallen victim to the prohibitive cost of deep space construction. A pyramid was more economical but not ideal for a domicile due to the living area lost to the structure's radically sloping sides. There was an unsettling feeling of confinement caused by the meter-high knee walls used to partition where a person could not stand. The resulting smaller space was used as an accessible chase for power, communication, and ventilation conduits.

Habitable areas were divided into three progressively smaller levels. Level One, by far the larger, was oddly chopped into six sleeping quarters, a communications hub, a cramped galley-type kitchen (used for food storage and assembly—preparation being at a minimum), and an equipment closet serving as the nerve center for the entire structure. An adjoining compartment housed the mechanical workings of the Environmental Support System, the ESS, a complicated and equally temperamental carbon dioxide scrubber/oxygen recharge system. Crammed into the same area was the unit's brain, the Nexus.

Level 2 was intended as a "community" space—the overcrowding of several competing functions, including research, conference, entertainment, and dining. Ceiling-mounted retractable curtains created a small measure of patient privacy during medical exams. In a nod to the psychological benefit of allowing a trapped animal to peer outside its cage, viewports were incorporated into two opposing walls. One faced a lava field, the other a more animated but no less depressing view of fumaroles belching gases high into the sky. Diminished by the gloomy atmospheric haze, the sunlight struggling through the dirty glass gave the interior the aura of a tomb. A few fading decorations could not prevent the place from looking insufferably drab. The primary color (other than the blue flashes from magnetic storms) was the iridescent orange of "caution" signs plastered to the gray, fiberform walls.

If there were any doubts in the minds of Nadir's occupants that their habitat was only an excuse for Unión to stake first claim on the planet, they were dispelled by the makeshift exercise room crammed into the pyramid's pinnacle. Here, the obnoxious, bizarre sounds of erupting fumaroles were most pronounced, an annoyance that could have been prevented had the structure's acoustics been given the attention it deserved.

The room's present occupants were Comandante Andrés Garcia and Sargento Carlos Alvarez. L3 was Carlos's favorite location, trumping the galley kitchen. Twenty-four years of age, he was the youngest and the most negatively affected by a sedentary lifestyle. He had waged war against the lack of physical inactivity by augmenting the room's two aerobic and resistance-type exercise machines with a sturdy bench and free weights of his own fashioning: Six strong fibermesh storage bags filled with chunks of lava and various metal objects considered unessential to the base's safe operation. Pairs of forty, fifty, and sixty-kilogram bags were created using counterbalance scales. When attached in varying combinations to the ends of a metal rod, it allowed for lifting seven specific increments ranging between eighty and three hundred kilograms.

Although unwieldy at times, it produced the desired effect. Carlos had maintained the physique and muscle strength of an amateur weightlifter. Close-cropped hair, good-looking square facial features, and cocky mannerisms gave him the image of a jock. That was merely the visible half of the young man. The other half was a quick-witted, well-educated engineer whose talents had (by his own frequent admission) kept Nadir running.

"Barely winded," he bragged with a satisfied grunt, addressing Garcia, who was working up a sweat on the treadmill nearby. "Six reps. Two hundred kilos. Pretty damned impressive."

"As usual, you need a reality check," Garcia responded, making a quick mental adjustment for Murkor's gravity, which was less than Earth's. "You're lifting one hundred sixty-two."

"Correct me if I've got this wrong," Carlos fired back, using a small rag to wipe the perspiration from the bar he had been holding. "Not naming names, but as a person advances in age, the tendency is to *gravitate* away from real exertion—weightlifting, just for example—to leisurely forms of aerobic exercise, which are one step up from walking, which is just heavy breathing."

"Amusing," Garcia said. "Especially when you consider that this misinformation comes from a muscle-bound fool hefting a bag of rocks like he's some Neanderthal. But let no one ever accuse you of cogitating, which is a big step up from just opening your mouth and letting foolish words pour out. And is there anything about yourself you don't wildly exaggerate?"

"Shit, yeah."

"What's that?"

"Given my obvious and considerable attributes," he said, resuming his bench presses, "just how incredibly modest I am."

Garcia enjoyed the banter with his close friend. Long ago, strict military conduct had been dispensed with, including using titles and ranks. With only five people under his command and given the exigencies of their isolated assignment, no one would construe the lack of convention with complacency. He was seasoned enough to know, or never would, what latitude to grant the people serving under him.

A planned retirement furthered the casual attitude. After thirty-three years of military service, Nadir was to be his final command. With any luck, he'd survive the next three months of active duty, followed by the six-month return trip to Earth. Home. The renewal of intimacies never to be forgotten. After three years away, he looked forward to reuniting with his father, becoming frail in his old age, and retiring from Unión politics. In some sense, it was an equal emotional exchange, for he'd be leaving behind five individuals he had come to know under circumstances most people couldn't even imagine.

"Treadmill," Garcia commanded, ignoring Carlos. *"Three-minute cooldown, then full stop."*

Tomorrow, he'd use the room's other machine, the antiquated rower obtained by convincing Central Supply that it was crucial for combating the effects of Murkor's low gravity. You may win some personal battles at sixty-one, but time always wins the war. He accepted that you must work out twice as hard as someone half your age to obtain the same results. Nevertheless, he kept physically fit despite a long career of zero and low-grav assignments.

His appearance belied his age. In some men, advancing years foster good looks. For Andrés Garcia, good looks had an early head start. It resulted in a handsome older man admired for his piercing black eyes, aquiline nose, and wavy jet-black hair, distinguishable by a touch of gray at the temples. Youth had left him behind, but the favorable impression he unconsciously made on those around him had stayed. He projected a stately demeanor with an easy, dignified deportment that could never be mistaken for excessive pride or arrogance. Garcia happened to be a very modest man.

No one could say the same about Carlos. Despite and because of their differences, he and the comandante became close friends while serving together.

"We've managed to overtax the air ventilator," a winded Garcia said, stepping down from the treadmill where he had spent the last hour of his daily workout. "Haven't you noticed it's unusually close in here? And don't bother complaining about how hopelessly inefficient the system is."

Carlos was an accomplished engineer who was kept busy maintaining Nadir's outdated mechanicals, the most important being the ESS. Everyone knew (for he told them often) that he was single-handedly keeping the base operational. It was serious work, belied by a devil-may-care attitude. "Want me to crack open a window?" he said, an obvious impossibility. "Forget the window. I've a better idea. Grant me three months leave on Varian, and I can get—" A quick read of Garcia's expression, and he left the sentence hanging in the stale air. "I'll get on it."

"Report the results to me when you're done."

"Any intel on the shuttle that buzzed us earlier?"

"Gustavo informed me that it touched down at Zenith an hour later."

"You mean *Club* Zenith," Carlos said, looking up from adjusting his jerry-rigged weights.

"The same."

"Delivering some much-needed supplies, I suppose. Like a few kilos of a delicate brie paired with a case or two of delightful and perfectly chilled chardonnay—the spoiled fuckers."

"Nothing like that," Garcia responded. "I had Gustavo tap into their ship-to-ground communications. He told me they were likely carrying one passenger and little else."

The news commanded Carlos's full attention. He stopped his workout and stood up.

"And who might that passenger be?"

"You know the answer," Garcia said. Everyone on base knew the *who*. The *when,* however, was sooner than anticipated.

"Commander Ellis—chancro bitch," Carlos said, his hatred for anyone or anything related to Coalition on full display. It was a darker shade of the feelings that most shared.

"You're reacting to a rumor," Garcia cautioned. The replacement of Zenith's present commanding officer had been the subject of much speculation.

"That's pure bullshit!" Carlos snapped back. "After what she did on Varian? Coalition sent her here for exactly one reason—to fuck with us!"

Although Garcia did not altogether disagree, it was a conversation that was best had after Carlos calmed down. "How many sets of bench presses do you have left?" he asked.

"What does that have to do with it?"

"Answer the question, sargento," Garcia commanded.

"Two," Carlos responded, surprised by the use of his rank. "But—"

"Do them," Garcia said, turning his back. Walking away, he quietly went about wiping down the treadmill, followed by his arms and shoulders. Carlos stared after him. Finding no one to argue with, he would have to redirect his anger toward fighting the force of gravity.

The arrival of Ellis was problematic, Garcia thought, though he didn't hold much stock in the disconcerting rumors preceding her. A lengthy military career taught him that inaccurate intel was often worse than none. As comandante, however, it was his duty to evaluate any sources of information, especially when the few official communiqués were a month old and of dubious value.

The intel concerning Ellis, having predicted her arrival within a few days, proved more accurate than most. The standard bio mentioned an altercation, the specifics unclear, involving her and two superior officers, which occurred shortly before her reassignment. The same communiqué repeated old news: Coalition's continuing strife with Unión was spreading to other sectors, with Murkor being mentioned as a potential flash point. It reiterated the usual warnings about remaining on high alert—an advisory rendered almost meaningless, having been repeated during the greater part of the last two years. An important question was posed, and largely left unanswered, as to why Ellis was replacing Zenith's CO before his term of service expired. More disturbing was additional information he received from another, unexpected source.

The hostile relationship between Coalition and Unión precluded any meaningful dialogue, and the same was true of their respective bases on Murkor. Each base, however, did not encrypt all routine interplanetary communications, and intercepting these messages provided a glimpse into the day-to-day operations of the opposition. Sometimes, outbound transmissions were made purposefully misleading. Garcia had to smile as one example came to mind. Aware of the opposition's water shortage, Carlos sent HQ a dispatch detailing the installation of a spa hot tub. (A subsequent encrypted message to headquarters explained the joke.) There were examples of Zenith engaging in the same chicanery.

On one recent occasion, however, the veil was reliably lifted. It occurred during the first (and last) time a merchant vessel made the long voyage to Murkor. The craft's entrepreneurial captain, trying to recoup hull damage caused while passing through the planet's orbital debris, brokered a transaction between the two bases. He hit upon the one thing each party desired most and the other could best supply. After some tough negotiations and some shuttling back and forth, five hundred liters of Nadir's water were exchanged for five liters of Zenith's premium vodka.

When the merchant extracted his commission, Garcia extracted the merchant's firsthand account of what was transpiring at Zenith. It reinforced what the transaction made evident: The opposition's thirst for water was real and becoming urgent. Garcia recalled how Carlos had been particularly delighted by this knowledge.

Playing it out—Zenith's thirst for water, the state of Coalition's internal politics, the increasing tension between hostile superpowers—Garcia concluded that the assignment of a new commanding officer, someone with a questionable reputation, spelled trouble. At a minimum, it meant that Commander Ellis, acting with tacit Coalition approval, would order forays into Nadir's EZ to pilfer water resources. Incapable of deterring the provocation, he'd be compelled to request outside assistance. Although it would take a month or more to arrive, a heavily armed T-4 Battlecruiser would be dispatched to the planet. Coalition would then answer in kind. Thinking on it and seeing the danger of an escalating conflict, any request for military assistance might be unwise. As he watched Carlos's approach, a spurious thought crept into his head. It was undeniably selfish, sure, but he couldn't exclude it: Do nothing. Three months from now, Nadir will also have a new CO. The headache could be transferred to someone else.

"I owe you an explanation," Carlos said. "As a friend. For my behavior."

"When you're ready."

"The Río Pecos Incident. Have you heard of it?"

"I have," Garcia answered, dredging his memory. "The details escape me. It occurred, correct me if I'm wrong, on Earth eight years ago?"

"Eight years and two months."

"I was on duty in the Lascor System then," Garcia replied. "I'm sure I didn't receive a full accounting."

"Not many people off-world did," Carlos said, his voice hard and cold, anger returning to his eyes. "Fewer know the real story. The government spun a version they wanted people to believe."

"I'd like to hear the truth of it," Garcia said, knowing the young man trusted him and had come to hold him in high regard.

"If you don't know the geography," Carlos began, "the Pecos headwaters and upper stretch are in the Sangre de Cristo Mountain range within Coalition control. The lower portion of the river is within Unión territory. The river is the major water source in the Pecos Valley."

"Is there no supply of desalinated water?" Garcia asked.

"Pipelines were 'economically unfeasible.' So they said. Farmers relied on flood irrigation to water their crops: Cantaloupes, cotton, alfalfa, and pecans." Carlos struggled for a moment, deciding how much to tell. "Did you ever give thought to where a pecan comes from?"

"Can't say I have," Garcia admitted. "I'm curious now that you mention it."

"A tree. And a pecan is not a nut. It's a drupe. My family owned a pecan grove in the Pecos Valley, about ten kilometers from the river. Five generations farmed that grove. I was to be the sixth." Carlos choked back his emotions before emphasizing the next word. "*Willingly.*"

"Instead, you're stuck here on Murkor," Garcia pointed out, stalling to allow Carlos time to regroup. He noticed the young man used the past tense when referring to his family's farm.

"Do you know how pecans are harvested?" Carlos continued. "A machine grabs the trunk and shakes the whole damn tree until they fall to the ground like hail. Fifty kilograms or more per tree. That's the way it should be. The way it was. Except a tree can't live without water.

"The first bad year should have been a clear warning of what was to come. You see, my parents had this stupid belief that reason would prevail. In that drought year, Coalition farmers upstream began diverting more water than the international treaty allowed. That's when some of our neighbors started calling them chancros. My parents never did.

"In response, the farmers in the Pecos Valley organized—complaints submitted through proper channels and legal briefs filed with the International Court. Nothing happened—except when a tree was shaken during that first year, forty kilograms of pecans fell to the ground.

"The second year of the drought was worse. Coalition farmers diverted more water. A lot more. And why wouldn't they? The Court's lack of response emboldened them. As their harvests flourished, ours failed, allowing them to capitalize on higher commodity prices. I was learning economics the hard way at an early age."

"Our government didn't step in?" Garcia asked.

"Low-level diplomatic overtures. No one got involved who could make a difference. As the talks dragged on, things got worse. The crop was halved. Brittle leaves covered the few pecans that fell when the trees were shaken. Trees were slowly dying.

"We tried to make both governments understand the urgency. A pecan tree needs to grow for many years before it begins producing. It isn't corn or wheat that you can replant after a year of failure. So, we organized. We marched. We hired more lawyers than we could afford. Nothing came of it. If you know anything about farming, you'll know that most small farms scrape by from year to year. My family was nearly bankrupt. I was sixteen at the time."

Carlos stared at Garcia. "Do you know what it's like watching your parents cry?"

Garcia shook his head. "Thankfully, no."

"*I do*," Carlos said, bitterness etching his voice. "You hate yourself for seeing it. You hate those who caused it much more. I would have done anything…. My father realized this. He kept a tight rein on me during those times."

"Sounds like a good man."

"Yeah, he was that," Carlos said, his eyes glassy with the recollection. "By the middle of the third drought year, I had turned seventeen. You could walk across the Pecos, the riverbed, without getting wet. They say that desperate times lead to desperate measures. Four hundred men, women, and children—many of them I knew as neighbors and close friends—crossed the international border and descended on Coalition's regional capital at Santa Fe. To the best of my knowledge, no one carried a weapon. That didn't stop things from turning bad."

"Most of this, the details, I heard nothing about," Garcia said, shaking his head. "Only the violence. You always hear about the violence. The reason behind it gets lost."

"Coalition sent in troops," Carlos continued. "'To keep the peace.' So they said. That's when it all unraveled. You'll hear versions of why. I *know* we were unarmed. Twenty-seven of us, including nine women and children, never returned home."

"Carlos, I'm sorry—"

"Yeah, well, we finally got the attention we wanted. The 'incident,' as they called it, made global news. An international crisis. Not so much because of us, of what we had endured, but because national pride was now at stake. The diplomats met. The diplomats threatened. In the end, a new water rights treaty, a bad one, was signed, and Coalition made token reparations. A fucking insult! As if money could replace what was lost.

"Six thousand of our trees had died. Trees thirty and forty meters tall. Some one hundred and fifty years old. Our family's prosperous farm was ruined. One of many.

"My parents were forced to sell the land and equipment. Want a laugh? An international corporation bought out most of the groves for a fraction of their worth. They were the only ones with enough financial capital to invest. Now, the land is plowed for cotton and cantaloupes.

"I had two younger sisters. Having three children didn't give my parents a lot of options. We relocated to a city where they could find employment. My mother found work in a genetics lab. My father mostly worked on servicing elevator motors in older buildings. He had the skills—operating a farm teaches you about heavy equipment, a rare talent nowadays. My sisters were at school. I was eighteen by then. The best thing for me, it seemed to make sense at the time, was to enroll in the military's advanced engineering program. We all made do. We still had some happy moments, but you could tell something was gone that could never be replaced. You could see it in my father's eyes, though he tried to hide it. A spark was missing—replaced by bitterness and regret."

Garcia didn't know what to say. What could he say that would make one bit of difference? Words would ring hollow.

"Damn it to hell, Carlos," he finally offered, making eye contact, then reaching out to squeeze his friend's shoulder. "I much prefer pecans to cantaloupes."

Carlos stared, saw what he needed to see in the comandante's wet eyes and expression, and then managed to laugh.

Garcia was glad the young man had shared his painful story. Little did he know how his hatred of Coalition and Zenith would ultimately affect them all.

Brrrooogghhhufff!

Until that moment, the strength of Carlos's story had relegated the bellowing sounds of the fumaroles to the background. "Somebody should teach those damn things some manners," Garcia remarked, responding to the boisterous noise.

Both men laughed, then returned to the task of finishing their workouts: Sit-ups and stretching exercises for Garcia, rock lifting, in the form of deadlifts, for Carlos.

It wasn't long before light footsteps were heard on the metal treads of the spiral staircase rising from L2. *Teniente* Amanda Cruz made her entrance, and it suited her fine when both men tried to hide their stares. The woman had a heightened appreciation of her good looks' effect on men and how physical appearance could achieve desired purposes more than intellect. Since the society of men had done little to impede this development, she learned to carry herself in ways that were alluring to the opposite sex. It can best be described as a (mostly) unconscious collection of subtleties, such as the way she positioned her long, shapely legs or threw her shoulders back to accentuate her breasts. Or how, when speaking, she shook her long hair to one side, slightly tilted her head down, and then raised a suggestive eyebrow at a captive audience.

Her comportment was precisely the opposite of Andrés Garcia's, whose attentiveness to physical detail had everything to do with staying healthy rather than being perceived as attractive. To Amanda, this easy self-assurance presented something of a challenge. In defiance of an age discrepancy of twenty-six years, she had persistently made the comandante the target of her affections.

"I can tell by the musky atmosphere in here," she said, making a deliberate point of sampling the air with her petite nose, "that you two gentlemen have just about finished your workouts."

For the briefest moment, the bluntness of the observation competed with Amanda's appearance. "Blame the ventilation system," Carlos stammered out in equal measure of defensiveness and swagger. "Just one more thing I have to fix around here."

"Not on my account," Amanda responded, throwing a suggestive glance at Garcia while gauging the younger man's reaction. "Did I say it bothered me?"

"Why would I think that?" Carlos lamely replied, watching Amanda (wearing a synthetic plum-colored one-piece, stretched skin tight to accentuate curves that needed no such assistance) slowly unroll an exercise mat on the floor. Only the clothing's color competed with the men's fantasy that she was wearing nothing. Her "warm-up" (which had a universal effect) consisted of twisting her supple body into a range of positions that, with the addition of a partner, would have made a worthy addendum to the Kama Sutra. Garcia tried to avoid taking exceptional notice. This was made difficult because he had been that partner on more than one occasion. His brief dalliance with Amanda had been inadvisable for their age, temperament, and, most importantly, rank differences.

Unfortunately, Garcia's imagination temporarily assumed command, ordering the body to go where it should not go. During two vividly memorable interludes, he had succumbed. At the time, he was twenty months into his two-year assignment on Murkor. When factoring in the long voyage to Murkor, it amounted to three years without a woman's touch.

Thinking back on it, it was soon after her arrival on base that she had begun to show interest in him. At first, she cloaked her intentions under the guise of ambiguity: An accidental touch, a suggestive word. He had excused, ignored, and then resisted these first overtures. When she made her intentions unmistakable, his resolve began to crumble. Somehow, he still held out. But the temptation was never out of sight in the base's confined space. Relenting, he had even become the aggressor.

Then he came to his senses.

Or, damn it, had he?

As CO, he was obligated to cultivate an atmosphere of objectivity and avoid any semblance of partiality. Maybe he had done so. Thankfully, no one had called attention to the transgression, even though the crew had to know its existence.

He shared his concerns with her, in return receiving assurances that she had no expectations other than continuing a physical relationship. The message "it's ended" had been transmitted but not received. There was only he to blame. He would be responsible, and deservedly so, for whatever emotional complications might ensue.

Amanda rose from the exercise mat to stand in Garcia's personal space.

"May I use your towel?" she breathed. "I seem to have forgotten mine."

Saying nothing, Garcia handed it to her. Then retreated a half step.

"It's unusually warm in here, is it not?" she said, closely observing his reaction while dabbing the perspiration collected at the hollow of her throat.

"Three people shouldn't occupy L3 at the same time," Garcia answered. "The ESS can't handle it. Perhaps you should have waited to come up."

"Exercising alone is so, so, boring," Amanda replied, drawing out the repeated word while holding Garcia's gaze. "I enjoy the company."

"It may be boring, but the results are the same," Garcia responded, observing Carlos in the background, doing his best, which wasn't very good, at acting disinterested. Who wasn't acting in this room, he asked himself. Did he see envy in the engineer's face?

Frustrated at Garcia's lack of reaction, Amanda decided to entice easier prey. Strutting over to the younger man, she grabbed his towel and began sensually patting the back of her neck and the exposed skin of her chest and arms. "Like I said, it's too damn hot in here."

"Like *I* said," Carlos chided, moving in closer. "I can fix anything that needs fixing around here."

"I've seen Red Giants smaller than your ego," Amanda responded, pressing her hands against the engineer's chest, pushing him away in mock protest.

The exchange wasn't lost on Garcia as he navigated the spiral stairs leading down to L2 and his duties as CO. He doubted Amanda intended to replace him with the younger man, but so be it. If 'youth must be served,' Carlos would receive quite a delectable portion.

Experience told him she was beyond the young man's reach.

Time would be better spent contemplating a more pressing concern—the arrival of Zenith's new commander.

AKA, the "chancro bitch."

3 ZENITH

"YOUR ARRIVAL ON MURKOR is greeted with much anticipation," said soon-to-be ex-commander Frank Trenchon as he extended his arm to indicate the direction he was leading. He could have easily inserted the word "nervousness" in his characterization of Zenith's present state of mind.

"Of that, I'm sure," Commander Ellis replied.

"Would you first like to see your quarters?" Trenchon asked. "Perhaps freshen up before our briefing?"

"I'm already quite fresh," Ellis responded, the remark earning her a sideways glance as they proceeded down the gleaming corridor. Two men approached from the opposite direction; they stared inquisitively at Ellis in passing, then acknowledged their current CO with a barely perceptible nod. Ellis noted that neither man saluted.

The spacious office Trenchon called his own was a well-appointed affair sporting tasteful furnishings and sumptuous wall-to-wall carpeting. One wall was overwhelmed by a substantial hexagonal viewport. Ellis's attention was drawn outside to a vista of sharp lava spikes, reminding her of the whipped topping of a lemon meringue pie that had been in the oven for far too long. In the distance, there was a tremendous spiraling of blackish-yellow dust, probably the kick-up of one of the dangerous 'rollers' she had heard of. Webs of lightning coursing through a rising pile of filthy clouds threw a flickering blue light back into the room.

Trenchon sat behind an oversized desk; Ellis faced him in a chair opposite. The man was unshaven, his uniform unkempt. For an awkward moment, they remained silent. The outgoing CO was the first to speak—to the mindstor in front of him:

"Mindstor. Sixty percent opacity."

The viewport noticeably darkened, and the blue highlights disappeared. Whatever lumens were lost were instantaneously replaced by the ceiling and walls brightening.

"I see you had a spat of trouble on Varian," Trenchon said.

"A bit," Ellis responded, volunteering nothing more.

"Then you were ordered here."

"And so, commander, here I am."

"You may call me Frank. May I call you Jennifer?"

"Is it customary on this base for officers to address each other so?"

"There is very little that *is* customary this far out."

Ellis nodded. "I can tolerate 'El' in private, but not within hearing of those I am to command."

"As you wish. You should be aware, however, that certain accommodations to military protocol must be made here. Zenith is mostly staffed by IMC personnel. Civilians. Nineteen men and five women, all of them hard-boiled company employees. Frankly, they are a little rough around the edges. Military personnel—six, myself included—are in the minority. I'll intro you to Captain Michele Stewart, our physician and a damn good one at that. There's Lieutenant Brian Davis, a crackerjack hydrogeologist, engineer, mindstor programmer—and just about anything else you can put your finger on, he's your man."

"Military personnel and IMC techs alike must answer to you—and soon, to me."

"They've come to accept me as their CO. May they do the same for you."

"'May' won't enter into it."

Trenchon hesitated. "I appreciate the sentiment, El, except you should keep in mind the exigencies of life here on base."

"I shall do that, Frank, once I've personally reviewed what they are. So far, I've read bullshit from headquarters and been favored with advice from a shuttle pilot. The pilot was more enlightening. From what I've seen so far," Ellis added, looking about the room, "it would appear you have a modicum of comfort here."

"In here, sure, but I'm referring to what's out there," Trenchon said, gesturing toward the viewport. "Both seen and the unseen. We've all heard versions of planet lore. Here, it's much worse. Don't discount its negative effect on those who've been here for any time. Murkor can drag a person down mentally."

"Perhaps exacerbated by people having too much time on their hands? The cessation of mining activity due to an inadequate water supply."

"The lack of water, period."

"Is it that bad?" Ellis replied.

"Nearly so. And I'm afraid you'll have to deal with it sooner than anticipated. I suspect you have wide latitude to do so. I haven't seen your orders."

"You haven't seen my orders because neither have I."

"I see," Trenchon said, stroking his stubble. "You have carte blanche dealing with the problem here."

"That being?"

"Nadir, of course."

"Is that how you would encapsulate it?"

"How else?" Trenchon said. "They have an overabundance of the one resource we need. Nadir is a rat hole of a base. Their exclusion zone is mineral-poor, but it encompasses what we believe to be the planet's largest reserve of water. Unfortunately, the beaners— Unión, I mean to say— exercises total control of those reserves as spelled out by statutes of the World Court."

"And our exclusion zone abuts Nadir's. Was that the best we could do?" Ellis said. "An entire planet and we had to breathe down their neck?"

"Murkor is very stingy with its water. A small amount of subsurface water extends beyond their zone into ours. It's found in a network of lava tubes—you'll see the extraction vehicle later."

"If hydrogeologists knew this, why not avoid the problem altogether? Establish a smaller base with a regenerative system where every drop of water is recycled."

"Anecrecium is too unstable to transport without processing. Processing uses water and generates unrecyclable wastewater. You're right, though. A recycling system would have been the way to go for drinking purposes."

"Even now, it's a good idea," Ellis said.

"Good luck finding a supporter. You're aware of the politics, the public outrage over how expensive the venture on Murkor was, and the close ties of politicians to companies awarded lucrative contracts. A profitable mining operation lent a measure of credibility to the whole affair. Earth's increasing demand for rare minerals, notably that of fusion reactors for anecrecium, led to unrealistic production quotas. Whatever water we had under our EZ was rapidly depleted." Trenchon gave Ellis a hard stare. "What's left is mostly used for personal hygiene, drinking, and cooking. Even that will soon run out. There's no way to sugarcoat it," he added. "You'll have a tough go of it."

"And you have had the extreme good fortune of being called to another assignment," Ellis responded.

"A total surprise to me, if that's what you mean," Trenchon said, chafing at the insinuation. "It seems to be more a function of getting you here to deal with the situation."

Except for the severity of the water shortage, the departing commander had encapsulated what she already knew. Hearing it again solidified her views on the matter and how she hoped to proceed.

"Given the urgency," Ellis said, "has there been any direct communication with Nadir or Unión?"

"Haven't you heard?" Trenchon asked. "No, of course not, you couldn't have. You were in transit. Coalition made a request through the face-saving auspices of a third party to allow access to, and purchase of, water reserves within Nadir's EZ. The request was resoundingly rebuffed."

"Any particular reason offered for Unión's intransigence?" Ellis asked.

"Some mention made of a prior dispute concerning water rights on Earth, I believe."

"Did that put an end to the issue?"

"Not quite. Coalition demanded that the World Court compel Unión to release its hydrogeological mapping surveys. They're adept at locating water resources, scant as they may be on this hellhole."

"We asked the Court to declare Unión Latino's hydrogeological data within the public domain?" Trenchon's expression told Ellis she had guessed wrong. "No? Then what?"

"*Mindstor*," Trenchon said into the air. "*Read Planetary Settlement Statute, Section 107.16.3. S.*"

The mindstor, choosing the voice of a human adult female, read the following:

A nation shall be entitled to settle and control an exclusion zone 100 km in diameter on any planetary body beyond the Sol System if said exclusion zone is continuously inhabited for no less than thirty Standard

Earth Days by no less than six humans. To retain title, said exclusion zone shall remain inhabited thereafter.

"Coalition," Trenchon explained, "has accused Unión of noncompliance with the statute."

Ellis had to laugh. "Nadir was established three years ago. It's a little late for making baseless accusations."

"Not according to arguments made by Coalition lawyers. They interpreted the phrase 'shall remain inhabited thereafter' quite strictly, claiming it logically refers to the constant presence of 'no less than six humans.' We're alleging that Nadir is in noncompliance with that provision of the statute."

"And Unión views the petition as a sham and an affront, refusing on principle, to submit Nadir's personnel records for review."

"It is," Trenchon volunteered, "the proverbial zero-gravity pissing match. It gives Coalition—and you—partial cover for any necessary action. If Nadir cannot, or refuses to demonstrate compliance with the statute—"

"—then their EZ does not have to be honored."

It was rare for Ellis to finish another person's sentence. It was just far too easy to follow Coalition's strained logic.

"Well, we've kicked this around enough for now," Trenchon said, standing. "We can discuss the finer points of base operation later, over dinner. We have an extensive menu here." Motioning for Ellis to follow, they crossed the room to where a door opened to the adjoining living quarters. "There is also a corridor entrance," Trenchon commented. "I had my things removed earlier this morning. I've taken the liberty of having yours brought—" Gazing about, the departing commander was surprised to see only a rolled-up mat and a duffel bag. "Sorry, El, I instructed staff to unload your personal belongings from the shuttle."

"I travel light."

"I see. Apparently, you won't need time to unpack. I shall return in an hour. We shall tour the base. You'll meet most of the crew." Trenchon paused as he turned to leave through the corridor doorway. "Oh, yes. Nearly forgot. Almost every entertainment and creature comfort metric you can think of can be activated by voice command. Feel free to change the wall colors if you like."

"It's appreciated," Ellis said.

"The least I could do," Trenchon said, leaving.

Ellis had to agree.

Standing in front of the room's viewport, looking at the wasteland that was Murkor, she had to wonder if anyone could feel lonelier: No meaningful ties back on Earth, an outcast from Varian, an isolated base full of discontented miners who she was about to make unhappier than they already were.

She spied one source of comfort: The 'sticky mat' used for yoga poses, pranayama breathing exercises, and deep meditation. Unrolling the mat, assuming the full lotus position, she stared about the room—and laughed. There was someone to talk to.

"*Wall and ceiling color. Change. Blue.*"

Not quite right, she thought, watching the transition. Too dark.

"*Change. Two shades lighter.*"

Not bad. A soft, relaxing hue.

"*Change. Orange with bright green polka dots.*"

No reaction. Nor did she expect any.

Some changes are harder to effect than others. Some are impossible.

A maxim applicable to most people. Herself included.

***

The smaller of Zenith's two domes, accessible from the main structure via a tubular passageway, housed IMC's anecrecium processing operation and three vehicles, one of them a massive excavator/extractor, also known as a harvester. With the cessation of mining operations, all three were idle in their bays.

IMC Mechanic Ed Anderson was lying on his back in one of those bays, intent on entertaining himself by modifying one of the two smaller vehicles. Lieutenant Brian Davis was equally intent on amusing himself by watching.

"This is a joke I heard back on Europa," Anderson said, his head and half his body hidden below the vehicle. "What did the munitions expert scream after eating a bowl full of habanero peppers?"

Sliding beneath the vehicle to join his friend, Davis shook his head and waited.

"Fire in the hole! Fire in the hole!"

Davis groaned. "Do you have *any* jokes that don't reference some part of the human digestive tract?"

"I most certainly do not," Anderson said, as if offended, "Is there such a thing?"

Both men were in their late twenties, attractive (Davis especially so), and physically fit. Both had expectations of life that weren't being met at the moment.

Anderson's was the sadder tale of the two. Several months prior, he had viewed the voyage to Murkor favorably, jumping at the opportunity to fill a vacant slot on the IMC team. It helped that each recruit would be entitled to a productivity bonus. In his youthful exuberance, he had downplayed the hardships of working on a hostile planet. And, if he had bothered to look, he would have discovered the Trojan Horse within the complicated language of his employment contract: *Bonuses are awarded upon the fulfillment of production quotas.* When mining operations prematurely ground to a halt, so had his dreams of riches. He was an unhappy man.

Davis's self-inflicted funk was traceable to enlisting in the military. Although he quickly rose to the rank of lieutenant, he had been given no say regarding the location of off-earth assignments. Murkor was nowhere to be found on a wish list of desirable destinations. At first, he romanticized the challenges of serving on a planet where few humans had tread. That hope was quickly squashed by Murkor's unrelenting heat, ghastly landscape, and choking atmosphere. The cessation of mining activity meant a lack of productive work.

Without a challenge, both young men confronted an unseen enemy.

Boredom.

Zenith had multiple forms of diversion: A gymnasium with the latest immersive exercise equipment, a rec room with various simulators, and a researchable library replete with artistic and intellectual pursuits. Overuse had dulled their luster. Even retro games of poker were starting to lose their appeal. A gilded cage is still a cage.

Unsurprisingly, Anderson and other like-minded IMC mining techs saw a solution to their misfortunes (and perhaps some entertainment value) in antagonizing a foe that was a mere one hundred kilometers away. Although Nadir, given its diminutive size and lack of defenses, was an unworthy and perhaps unwilling adversary, it would have to do. Those few techs who needed justification pointed out that "the greedy fucks" were hoarding far more water than they could ever use.

Water put to better use processing anecrecium.

And so, although almost everyone on base hated the departure of a CO they had grown fond of abusing, his replacement, preceded by a rumor, held forth the prospect of some excitement.

On that misassumption, Ellis would be accepted.

"Did you get a look at our new fearless leader yet?" Davis asked.

"I did," Anderson replied.

"And?"

"A bit scrawny for my taste."

"I respectfully disagree," Davis said. "I see the potential for side meat."

"Side meat?" queried Anderson. "I am unacquainted with the term."

"The glimpse of a woman's breast, viewed from the side," Davis explained in an authoritative voice. "Where have you been? That *is* the standard definition."

"I must look it up," Anderson said. "I assume this 'side meat' occurs when a reasonably endowed female isn't wearing a bra but *is* wearing a loose-fitting, open-sided dress?"

"Correct," Davis answered. "A full-frontal view wouldn't be as tantalizing, would it?"

"That depends on one variable factor," Anderson replied. "Time. I would consider a frontal view for a maximum of five hundred milliseconds tantalizing. One millisecond more would leave nothing to the imagination."

"An insightful observation."

"From me, expect nothing less," Anderson replied, satisfied. "Pass me that tool there by your head."

"What do you think Ellis will do first?" Davis asked. "She'll be forced to do something soon."

"I expect she'll give the beaners a well-deserved ball-busting. Supposedly, she has a great capacity for it, would you agree?"

"Actually, I do not," said Davis, who had a different opinion of women.

"Neither do I, gentlemen." The remark came from Ellis. She had been touring the base with Trenchon when he had been called away.

"Oh, shit," Davis mouthed, primarily for the other man's benefit. "There are six women on base, with six distinctly recognizable voices. That's definitely not one of them."

"Your math is no better than the rest of your perverted logic," Ellis replied. "There are seven women on base. Now why don't you two clowns roll your asses out from under there so you can tell me whom I'm addressing."

"You first," Anderson suggested, speaking to his friend.

"Thanks," Davis said, extricating himself from under the vehicle that had shielded him from Ellis's approach. Anderson followed.

"Lieutenant Brian Davis, Ma'am."

Ellis sized up the man. Very fit. In uniform. Good, at least she wouldn't have to 'bust his balls' about that. Another reason presented itself.

"Until I give you leave otherwise, lieutenant, you shall salute when first in my presence."

"Yes, Ma'am," Davis acknowledged.

"Commander Trenchon informs me you're a competent hydrogeologist," Ellis continued, "and a handy man to have around."

"I am good with my hands," Davis replied, not intending the sexual double entendre. Anderson, standing by his side, snickered. Ellis turned her attention to him.

"What mannerless person are you?"

"Ed Anderson, expert mechanic at your service, miss."

"You shall address me either as 'ma'am' or 'commander.'"

"I am, with due respect, not in the military," Anderson replied.

"The principle I act upon is *respect due*. Clear?"

"Clear enough."

"I assume you can describe this vehicle I'm looking at?"

"The Camel?" Anderson replied, gesturing toward the side of the vehicle where the letters CAM-L were boldly stenciled. "I am the *best* person to describe it."

"CAM-L?" Ellis questioned.

"Collect and move liquid. Credit the acronym to the manufacturer. Some a-hole in marketing must have worked overtime to come up with that one. The hump— the containment tank you're looking at—can hold three thousand liters. The cab holds six passengers. More if you want to get friendly. Four of these vehicles exist, the two you see here, the others operated by the beaners."

"Operational range?"

"The fuel cell can nonstop power the vehicle for a week. Oxygen supply to the pressurized cabin is the real limitation. Considering the difficult terrain and the time needed to locate and siphon water, we can reach the outer edge of the EZ and back. The manufacturer didn't see the need to go beyond." Anderson locked his eyes on Ellis. "But I circumvented that."

"Show me," Ellis ordered, ignoring the implication that the vehicle had been modified to intrude into Nadir's zone.

Anderson flipped open a large hatch on the vehicle's side. "I removed the tanks from the other CAM-

L and reinstalled them here. I also lowered the partial pressure of the cabin."

"Why was that necessary?" Ellis asked.

"Pure oxygen is toxic at standard pressure. Now, the tanks can be filled with pure oxy rather than air. This baby can go all day."

Anderson seemed pleased by what he had done. It was an elegant solution, Ellis admitted to herself. "Explain why you removed the tanks from a CAM-L rather than an unused harvester?"

"And put it completely out of service? Not a chance."

Just as she suspected, at any cost, IMC wanted to keep its mining operation viable. "I have a few questions for you, lieutenant," Ellis said, redirecting attention to Davis. "I've been informed that there is insufficient water supply to sustain anecrecium processing. Is that true?"

Davis took too long to consider. "Come on, lieutenant," Ellis said, annoyed. "As principal hydrogeologist, don't you have the most recent survey reports?"

"There is insufficient water," Davis answered. "Within *our* zone."

"Is there enough to sustain a base of thirty adults?"

"That is more difficult to assess, commander."

"Why is that?"

"Missions looking for water are returning nearly empty. It's just a matter of time before the resource is depleted."

"Can you determine how much time?" A lot was riding on the answer, Ellis thought to herself.

"I cannot," Davis replied. "Not exactly."

Cannot or will not, Ellis thought, wondering if the water emergency was intentionally overblown to justify incursion into Nadir's EZ. How to address the issue was better postponed until tomorrow after Trenchon had departed, when she was firmly in place as Zenith's new CO. Reflecting further, she decided to give some advance billing as to what the new order would be.

"I recognize initiative when I see it, Mr. Anderson," Ellis said. "But in the future, clear vehicle modifications with your IMC foreman and with Lieutenant Davis, who, starting tomorrow, will report such intent to me."

"Your reasoning?" Anderson asked, obviously annoyed. "Trenchon never interfered with us IMC techs."

"*Commander* Trenchon," Ellis corrected. "As for my reasons, they will be plain soon enough." Then, turning to Davis, "I want you, lieutenant, to set up a meeting of base personnel in the conference room. Tomorrow. Eight hundred hours."

As Ellis finished speaking, Trenchon approached. A brief and rigidly polite four-way conversation ensued, followed by the two commanders resuming their tour of the base.

Walking beside her fellow officer, Ellis was sure of two things:

The substance of her encounter with Davis and Anderson would reach everyone on base well before her tour with Trenchon ended.

A dromedary does not store water in its hump.

***

Early the following day, Trenchon departed on Pilot's shuttle, taking a pile of personal possessions with him and leaving a mountain of worries behind. Ellis understood she wouldn't win any popularity contests when the word 'commander' was placed before her name. Her primary concern wasn't to acquire friends but not to make enemies. Strike that. Replace with *too many enemies*. Inevitably, adversaries are made when embarking on an unpopular course of action. The goal is to limit their number, power, and duration. She had failed to accomplish the last two on Varian.

Zenith would present a greater challenge. Her hold on authority was tenuous for three identifiable reasons: There was no command structure to back her up (doubtful they would anyway); her orders would be highly unpopular with the IMC techs; there were four times as many malcontent techs as military personnel.

Taking a deep, relaxing breath, she stepped into the conference room and proceeded to a podium set up for her benefit. Twenty-nine people had gathered, eager to hear what she had to say.

"Morning," Ellis said, scanning faces to make eye contact. "In the next few days, I hope to meet everyone. If you find my door open, there's an excellent chance I'd be willing to discuss whatever's on your mind. I've been told that I'm a good listener. If that needs any qualification, it's that I hate repetition.

"It appears that my arrival has been preceded by at least one expectation, which I am now forced to debunk. In the process, some feathers may get ruffled." Ellis's next remark earned a few tentative titters. "Since you're all adults, I expect you'll be capable of doing your own preening.

"I shall address what has been described as a critical water shortage. The widely touted solution to this potential emergency entails the violation of Nadir's EZ." Ellis paused, emphasizing her following words.

"I will do everything I can to prevent such an incursion."

Ellis expected an acrimonious reaction, and she got it: A spontaneous eruption of grumbling, shouts of protest, punctuated by one singularly loud "good luck with that" that evoked peals of laughter from the raucous group she confronted. The pushback was more vocal than anticipated. So be it. Retreat was not an option. Walking from behind the podium, she took two purposeful strides closer to an angry audience. Although her physical form was slight compared to the men who opposed her, it was an unexpectedly determined presence. Together with her self-confident demeanor, it evoked a temporary fascination with whatever she might say next.

"You appear intent on provoking those ill-prepared to offer a response," Ellis resumed, taking advantage of the lull. "Contemptible as that is, you will then stand back as the real battle is fought by others above this planet."

The accusation, hitting the intended nerve, caused the shouting to double.

"Let her speak, let her speak," someone yelled—the IMC foreman, Chuck Kreechum, seated in front. "Let her dig her own hole."

Ellis took a last step forward, raising and projecting her voice to rise above the dissent. "Do you think for one moment that Unión, once alerted, will forgive the intrusion? Are you willing to risk a wider conflict between Unión and Coalition?"

"That isn't the reality of the situation, and you know it," Kreechum replied, standing. He was a sizable man, tall and broad, heavy in the shoulders and neck. He looked accustomed to getting his way. "Nadir isn't worth the trouble. You saw it. That shithole isn't maintained. From what I hear, there ain't more than a handful of damn beaners there. Not the six needed to maintain a claim to an EZ." He turned to face the group, primarily loyal IMC techs. "With no valid claim on their part, there's no violation on our part, is there?" Spurred on by murmurs of assent, Kreechum taunted: "*When* we go in and take what they don't need anyway."

"Where's the proof in what you're saying?" Ellis responded. "There is none. Only an allegation fabricated by Coalition, a flimsy pretext to justify what otherwise would be considered a reckless intrusion into foreign territory."

"And when we run out of water?" Kreechum countered. "What then? Beg the bastards?"

"In the near term, two things will be done. Now take a seat."

Ellis waited while the IMC foreman, reading her expression, reluctantly complied. One small hurdle overcome, she thought. The physical ways she could make the man sit would have been inconvenient.

"I've examined Zenith's daily water usage records," she said. "Everyone in this room knows that the amount essential for drinking and food preparation is a small fraction of the total need." Ellis scanned the group. "Is Base Manager Schulman here?"

"Oh, shit," came a tentative response, which garnered a few tension-relieving chuckles. The unwanted attention had surprised the portly man. "Sorry, I'm at your service, Ma'am—uh, commander."

"The water conservation program you designed and implemented appears well thought out. Can you do more?" Ellis asked. Although she knew the answer, it would be better accepted if it originated from someone other than herself.

"I can scan through the numbers again," Schulman responded, looking relieved. "Maybe squeeze out another ten or fifteen percent reduction. I won't be making any friends doing it."

"Do you see me acquiring any new friends?" Ellis asked.

Schulman hesitated, then, frowning, answered: "Perhaps the pilot of the shuttle that brought you to Murkor—but he's long gone."

Ellis laughed along with the group. "You probably lost a few friends a while back," she said. "When you traded away alcohol for H-Two-O."

"A few, a few," Schulman responded, shaking his head in feigned remorse.

"Damn right you did, and I'm one of them," somebody shouted to more laughter. Ellis let the noise subside before forging ahead.

"One additional measure will be necessary," Ellis continued. "The frequency of missions needs to be increased."

The pronouncement had a surprisingly chilling effect. Whatever small gains made winning the crew over quickly evaporated with moans and angry faces suddenly replacing laughter. Ellis immediately noted where military personnel, thankfully in uniform, were located. Zenith's physician, Stewart, was by herself, standing at the far edge of the group. Others were intermingled with IMC workers, including Lieutenant Davis, sitting in the last row beside his friend. Until now, service personnel had maintained an uneasy silence as she rolled out the bad news. It was unlikely they'd directly disobey her orders, but her job would become tougher if she couldn't earn their confidence.

"Permission to speak freely, commander." The request, unexpectedly, originated from Davis.

"If it's on point, of course."

"Always. The issue is going 'out and about'—being on the surface and entering the tubes. Crews are feeling increasingly uneasy. And what's the point if you're returning with a hump nearly empty of water?"

A murmur of assent greeted the remarks. "Would you rather run out?" Ellis said, leaving no room for alternatives. "I expect you and Mr. Kreechum to revise the mission schedule. Make sure no one is assigned a disproportionate share of duty. Operational decisions will no longer be made unilaterally by IMC.

"Mr. Anderson," Ellis continued, calling the man's attention. "For now, I will let your modification to CAM-L1 stand as is. But let's be clear: increasing the vehicle's operational range is solely to extend missions within Zenith's EZ. There shall be no encroachment into Nadir's territory. As for CAM-L2, you've given me reason to believe you can transfer oxygen tanks from the harvester into it."

"Effectively putting us out of business," Anderson protested, angrily looking toward the IMC foreman for support.

"You're ending any damn chance we had of a profitable mining venture," Kreechum said, his voice rising. "That's not why you were sent here, is it, commander? I suspect Coalition brass on Varian will be quite displeased when learning your intentions. Yes, yes—they'll have *a lot* to say about what you're asking us to do."

"You may be correct in that," Ellis replied, signaling the end of the meeting. "Except, to be crystal, I'm not asking."

***

Near the end of a tough first day, Ellis was summoned to a disturbance in one of Zenith's well-equipped recreation rooms. Two men had fought, inflicting only superficial damage on each other but more on the holo-sims that would have kept them entertained. Physical confrontations were to be expected on a base where morale was low. The identities of the combatants, however, were a surprise and a disappointment. One of the men, sporting an expression between amused and contrite, was Lieutenant Davis; the other, scowling and defiant, was Ed Anderson. They had been separated by what is often the most effective barrier in such a situation: a woman, Captain Stewart. No longer able to beat on each other, their belligerence was redirected toward the universe in general. Lurking in the background, several IMC men were, with bemused interest, watching how the new CO would handle the situation.

Ellis first looked to Stewart for an explanation.

"By the time I showed up," Stewart volunteered, "most of the real excitement had died. Neither one has explained his actions. I doubt a reason exists. Both are drunk as skunks."

"Thank you, captain," Ellis said, stepping in front of Davis. "Are you even worth addressing, Lieutenant?"

Davis attempted a salute. "Just a bit of roughhousin', Ma'am, capitán, kahhhmander. Can't call you Sir, no Sir. Not with a full chest—I mean a chest full of medals."

Anderson, unsteady on his feet, sneered out his version of a rejoinder.

"—but no guts—siding with a few fucking beaners..."

"Just as I suspected, both of them are useless," Ellis said, surveying the damage inflicted on the room. "Captain Stewart, since these men have no regard for civilized behavior, I am revoking their rec room privileges for a month. See that they are confined to quarters until you determine they can return to society."

Ellis turned away, having no desire to see the men's reaction.

Upon returning to her living quarters, Ellis darkened the viewport to block out blue bursts of lightning from the planet's magnetic storms. The room lighting was dimmed to coax a more relaxing ambiance. From her duffel bag, she removed and changed into loose-fitting clothing, then unrolled and placed a sticky mat near the room's center. Assuming the lotus position, she began to meditate, hoping to clear her mind.

It wasn't to be. The door to her living quarters was open. Stewart, peering in, was polite enough to knock.

"Commander? Sorry if I'm disturbing you. I'll come back. This is mostly a social call—it can wait."

It took a second or two for Ellis to reply. "No, captain, enter," she said, remaining in the lotus position. "Let's keep this informal."

"I apologize for interrupting your meditation," Stewart said, choosing to sit on the floor with her back against a couch. "May I ask how accomplished you are?"

"I can completely relax my body and mind," Ellis replied, choosing the most straightforward explanation.

Stewart was impressed. "Excellent. I'm afraid the discipline didn't work for me. Making my mind go blank tripped me up. I started thinking about *how* I couldn't clear my mind of distracting thoughts. Do you know what came next?"

"You started thinking about how you shouldn't be thinking about being unable to clear your mind?"

"Yes!" Stewart said, laughing. "How'd you know?"

"It's the usual trap. The first stage is concentrating on your breathing to help calm the mind. Meaningless distractions are first accepted, then will fade into nothingness."

"You're telling me I had it wrong?" Stewart asked.

"Seems so."

"Looks like you've given me something to think about."

"Not while you're meditating," Ellis returned, and they both smiled.

"Disciplining the mind must be of help—especially after a day like you had today," Stewart said, suggesting more was on her mind.

"Are you here about this morning's meeting or the altercation?" Ellis asked.

"Since there may be three or four of us on base who appreciate how you handled the former, I'll go with the latter—if you're willing to hear some unsolicited advice regarding Anderson and Davis."

"I had assumed the two were friends. What precipitated the fight?"

"They still are friends. What caused the fight is Murkor."

"I get it," Ellis said. She had heard similar talk from Trenchon. "Nobody, including me, particularly enjoys being here."

"It's one thing to know something intellectually," Stewart offered, "and quite another to experience it directly. You haven't been on Murkor long enough to feel it. And, unlike Davis, Anderson, and most everyone else on base, you haven't been outside. Speaking as a physician, the prospect of longer missions is more disturbing than you give credence."

"For the time being, there's no other remedy. As far as understanding, I intend to go, as they say, 'out and about.' You have?"

"Yes. The surface is a dreary, dangerous, obnoxious place. Inside the lava tubes is worse—disconcerting."

"Disconcerting is a strange word to use," Ellis said. "A bit vague coming from a physician."

"You'll hear stranger descriptions."

"What's this got to do with the two men?"

"The punishment you meted out is more severe than you may believe. Withholding privileges for a month, curtailing the social interaction that keeps them preoccupied, may accomplish the opposite of what you intend. There's something else. I see Davis as caught in the middle between you and Anderson. You may be pushing him in the wrong direction. There's no doubt he'll want to be loyal. But to whom? You, as CO, or to Anderson, a friend with whom he shared many a common experience?"

"I will consider what you said," Ellis replied, "but the punishment must stand as is. I may risk losing Davis's loyalty, but if I waver and rescind the order, I risk losing everyone else's cooperation."

"I hope you're right in that assessment," Stewart said, disappointed.

"If I appear intractable concerning the men's punishment," Ellis said, "it is because I have a particular aversion to violence."

The remark caught Stewart unawares. "Earlier today," she said, "expectations concerning you were different. A story is circulating regarding your involvement in an altercation on Varian."

Ellis waited.

"What, if anything, happened there?" Stewart prodded.

"I give you credit. You're the first person to ask me that question. Everyone else seems rather content with living with the rumor."

"Rumors are self-sustaining—especially when they coincide with what people want to believe."

"This maxim doesn't apply to you?" Ellis asked.

"No. The truth, even when unpleasant, is preferable."

"Ever hear of Major Charles Eglend?"

"*The* Major Eglend?" Stewart answered, frowning. "Better known as *Major Ego* Eglend. He has a reputation as a womanizer."

"He's a reprobate asshole if you ask the female contingent on Varian. Most of the men on base know it, too, only they prefer to label it as an overactive libido. Rank has made him immune to censure. I wanted nothing to do with him. Only he wasn't getting the message—not verbally. I added the word "no" to his vocabulary.

"I see where this is going," Stewart said, eager to hear the rest of the story.

"Major Ego was physically fit and, like most men, had about thirty kilograms on me. One late evening at the gym, he backed me against a wall. Let's say we then conversed. It went something like: 'You're in my space, major.' 'Is that a *problem*, Jennifer?' 'It's going to be *your* problem, major.'

"He grinned a sick, lascivious grin and pressed into me. I ducked under his arms. He spun around and came at me. I sent him sprawling by twisting the arm at the shoulder and using it as leverage. While this was taking place, another male officer, a friend of his, happened to walk in. They decided I 'needed to learn a lesson.' Until then, I hoped to extricate myself from this tragic-comedy without much fuss. They made it impossible. I broke the major's nose with the palm of my hand. The other officer backed off after I fractured his wrist."

"Wow! Good for you, Jennifer! Sorry, I mean commander. You filed charges, of course."

"Not exactly. Call me El when in private," she added, as she was starting to trust the base physician. "There were no witnesses, so they concocted a plausible scenario to save themselves the embarrassment of me kicking their butts while explaining away why a fifty-four-kilogram female would need to defend herself against two imposing men in an empty gym. Their story had the added benefit of putting the episode in a bad light for me."

"Tell me," Stewart entreated.

"The two bastards claimed they fought each other. Over *me*."

"What!" Stewart shouted, amazed and angry.

"And they pulled it off, formally 'apologizing' to each other, their version of the incident relegated to a mild censure entered into their military records. I protested, of course, if for no other reason than to prevent a woman less capable of defending herself from being subjected to the same treatment. There were people on base who believed me, mainly those who saw me train at the gym. That's when and why the rumors started. Anyway, there were two conflicting stories, and with nobody certain of their veracity, no formal inquiry was opened."

"I can see why they sent you packing," Stewart said. "But didn't you want to leave?"

"Yes and no. They could make life difficult for me on base, although I did relish being a thorn in Major Ego's side. When choosing my reassignment, they got a little too cute. In the warped thinking of military brass—those few who knew what happened—I was now treated as a hostile bitch. I assure you, Michele, that is the *furthest* thing from the truth. Nevertheless, when the major and Varian's two-stars were asked by Coalition politicos who might be best suited to deal with the situation on Murkor, my name catapulted to the top of the list." Ellis paused. "How do you see their recommendation working out so far?"

"Not so well."

Later, alone in the quiet, Ellis considered how her refusal to violate Nadir's EZ, while not motivated by revenge, would be perceived that way by the men who ordered her to Murkor. The thought of their discomfort gave her a moment of satisfaction, a feeling unworthy of the practice of *samatha*, the attainment of a tranquil and balanced mind. The negative thought could be suppressed; it arose from a place too deep to eradicate.

What actually motivated her actions was a tragic miscalculation she made years ago and parsecs away.

4 OUT AND ABOUT

WITH RAIDS INTO NADIR'S territory forbidden, it was imperative to undertake longer and more frequent missions to the cavernous lava tubes beneath Zenith's EZ. Acting on Ellis's explicit order from the previous day, a disgruntled Lieutenant Brian Davis and two IMC techs loaded into the extended-range CAM-L and set out across Murkor's treacherous surface.

Notwithstanding the urgency to find water, there was a deep-seated aversion to leaving the base's security. Appreciation of this mindset is impossible without mingling scientific fact with speculation, obliterating the line that generally separates the two.

Murkor's dissolution harks back millions of years to that instant a chunk of iron half the size of Ayers Rock slammed into the planet, wobbling its axial rotation and stripping away most of its life, water, and atmosphere. What was left had a gravitational mass equivalent to eighty percent of Earth's and a rotational velocity equating to a nineteen Standard Earth Hour Day.

The rotational wobble produces two interesting phenomena. The first is an erratic and subliminal waxing and waning of sunlight intensity as the sun transits through the sky. The second occurs at the start and end of each day when the sun appears to briefly defy the laws governing astronomical bodies by moving laterally along the horizon. (A handful of colonists claim they have witnessed the setting sun momentarily *rise* and a rising sun briefly *set*.) Such variations from Earth norms are proven to be the cause of physiological and psychological disorders. The finer and more debatable point is that when the mind views the sun's behavior as unpredictable and capricious, then is not everything on the planet subject to examination and suspicion?

There had been no scientific study of Murkor's climate. Nor was any planned. There was little weather to study. No warm or cold fronts. No rain. Only oppressive heat. When not blotted out by sooty clouds spewed out of fumaroles, the sun at midday (if such an event could be precisely determined) could be safely viewed with the naked eye. The pervasive atmospheric haze also acted as a tinting lens, imparting to all a ruddy look, or sepia, or some other putrid shade of brown.

The principal weather-related hazard, other than heat stroke, was from violent windstorms called 'rollers'—named for their physical appearance, a tornado flipped on its side. One or two meandering menacingly along the horizon was not unusual. Long and wide as a fifty-story building, they were short-lived, expiring from the sheer mass of accumulated pumice and lava shards. They could make quick work of a slow-moving CAM-L, and predicting the erratic storms' direction was impossible.

When the sun went down (*sideways,* some insist), crews outright refused to go out and about, the darkness so pervasive it imparted a feeling of apprehension and claustrophobia which even a CAM-L's halogen running lights failed to dispel. Murkor was bereft of an illuminating moon. The few stars struggling to poke through the murk could only flicker exhaustively before being snuffed out by the planet's debris field or particulate-laden atmosphere.

The menacing angles and sharp shapes of lava formations, the pervasive odor of noxious gases, the startling flashes of blue light from magnetic storms, and the foreboding howl that the wind makes when passing across the mouths of a thousand lava tubes all fail to convey to an outsider what it is like to exist on Murkor. Every planet has a unique environment that colonizers adapt to and accept over time. It had been impossible to do so on Murkor. Those who openly said they felt the spirits of a once-thriving planet were teased by those who kept such feelings to themselves.

Unaided, breathing was a hazard. Beyond the unpleasantness of inhaling noxious compounds in the foul-smelling air, no human could endure Murkor's low-pressure, oxygen-poor atmosphere. Personal rebreather units were essential, and the loss or malfunction of this equipment meant one or two minutes of panicky inhalation followed by hypoxia, unconsciousness, and death.

An example of this ever-present danger was provided by several IMC techs who, looking for entertainment, devised a physical trial that ignored everything science had learned about the human respiratory system. To "win," a contestant had to complete a circuit of Zenith's two domes, 'bareback,' a term coined to describe being on the surface without the aid of a rebreather. The first person to accomplish this dubious feat would claim a two-hundred-ml flask of premium twenty-year-old scotch—a rare and coveted prize.

The first (and last) contestant was Ed Anderson. He had studied the terrain, gauged the distance, weighed his self-proclaimed extraordinary athletic abilities, factored in the planet's reduced gravity, and concluded that he would be hypoxic but conscious for the last thirty meters. He was unconscious well short of an entry portal where most of Zenith's colonists had eagerly awaited his arrival. Conspicuously absent was the base's physician, Captain Stewart. She had no foreknowledge of the contest, or it might have been prevented. Once alerted, she revived her patient, then convinced Trenchon to end the madness before someone else accepted the challenge. Or, a real possibility, Anderson decided to try his luck again.

Although the contest was foolish, even dangerous, it could be seen as an unconscious early attempt by Zenith's inhabitants to rail against planetary forces both seen and unseen. In failing, they acquired an even greater appreciation of their vulnerability. They came to regard the planet itself with wariness and unreasoned suspicion.

This was equally true of the Nadir contingent, whose apprehension produced creative abstractions.

Planetary features were personified. Fumaroles were the easiest target, their bizarre and obnoxious noises earning the designation "los pedos del Diablo" (the Devil's farts). When that expression caught on, others quickly followed. Lightning was dubbed "tridente de Satanas" (Satan's pitchfork); a spikey pair of lava peaks "los cachos de Satanas" (Satan's horns); a network of lava tubes "las entrañas del Diablo" (the Devil's bowels). There was humor in these descriptions, but they also had another thing in common. They all cast Murkor in a sinister light.

Feelings of unease intensified when venturing beneath the planet's surface. Crews attempting to find water often felt shadowed. There was no accounting for the odd sensation, no tangible evidence or scientific proof to justify it, so the sentiment was usually kept to oneself or, if expressed openly, ridiculed as the product of an overactive imagination.

All of this, and more, gave birth to the notion that an unidentified life form was stalking the planet.

For now, none of this was consciously troubling the only three humans on the planet to be out and about. Instead, it was their failure to locate an adequate water supply despite having searched the portentous depths of three previously unexplored lava tubes. In their attempt, multiple rebreathers had been depleted.

For safety reasons, CAM-Ls always had a minimum crew of three; in this instance, IMC techs Lori Jensen, Bert Imholtz, and Lieutenant Davis. It was no coincidence that Davis had been included in the first extended mission. Ellis thought it was a fitting way for him to get his mind straight while setting a sober example for IMC personnel.

"We have time to enter one more tube before heading back," Jensen said, intent on deciphering a confusing holographic rendition of the path ahead.

"And when we get back," Davis, piloting the vehicle, added, "remind me to thank Anderson."

"What the hell for?" Imholtz asked.

"For modifying this goddam vehicle so we could stay out here all goddam morning and half the goddam afternoon."

"Hey, he's *your* friend," Imholtz reminded.

"Yeah, he is that," Davis replied with a hint of doubt.

"Can we get this over with?" Jensen interrupted, nerves frayed. She had spent the last several hours comparing topographical features to those that floated in front of her on the CAM-L's holo nav system. "There's a large network of tubes at bearing ninety-two degrees. See that outcropping of lava slag, the one that looks like a pile of cowshit? It's on the far side, five kilometers."

The terrain was unfamiliar, and preventing the CAM-L from falling into a crevice from which it couldn't extricate itself required a combination of intuition, quick reflexes, and luck. Considered one of the best pilots, Davis was sufficiently proficient in the first two talents to manufacture the third. Still, it had been a very long day. "Nothing closer?" he asked.

"Closer? Yeah, I'm a lot closer to losing my patience," Jensen submitted. Having gone through three rebreathers that day, she meant it.

"Yes, ma'am, on our way," Davis hastily replied, wishing to avoid an argument. Getting his ass handed to him by one woman was still fresh on his mind. Several stressful minutes later, the ponderous vehicle's wide tracks crunched to a halt in front of the yawning mouth of a lava tube.

Sonar mapping had revealed that the tube structure, like most others, resembled an ant colony—a sinuous network of tunnels opening into cavities where, on rare occasions, precious water could be found. All you had to do was get there while tugging a heavy siphoning hose as it slowly unspooled from the side of a CAM-L. Tubes with lava walls that had solidified to a smooth "ropy" texture were often large enough for a person to walk upright. Even these could be partially obstructed or made impassible by blocks of lava that had dislodged from the ceiling and crashed to the floor.

Obstacles were a concern, but more troubling was the abusive temperature, a sweltering 43° Celsius— five degrees above the planet's stifling surface. Avoiding heat stroke was difficult when outfitted with a miner's helmet and the compulsory backpack-style rebreather unit. Although safety equipment and training helped combat the effects of stress and fatigue, they did little to alleviate the claustrophobia produced by having a million metric tons of rock above one's head or taphophobia, the fear of being buried alive or a tube collapse blocking passage to the surface. A person unable to cope with the problematic conditions poses a serious risk to themselves and their team members.

Crews felt they were intruding where no human had ever been or had the good sense to be. Imagination stirred unnamed fears in dark passageways. Helmet lamps birthed monstrous shadows, and footfalls spawned strange echoes, giving life and expression to the unknown. As Stewart called it, a "disconcerting" feeling. Almost everyone else labeled it as the 'mind fuck.'

Astrobiologists had searched a tiny fraction of the tubes with sophisticated instruments. They had anticipated finding niche lifeforms but had come away disappointed: No microscopic organisms sought refuge from the harsh surface where the pathetic remnants of a once-flourishing ecosystem struggled to survive. The scientists had "felt it unnecessary" to stay in the lava tubes for any time, possibly explaining the discrepancy between their assurances that the tubes were devoid of life and the prevailing sentiment among the colonists that something skulked within. It seems science cannot be relied on to explain away the vagaries of the human imagination.

Jensen and Imholtz were within Murkor Tube Network Z784C, focused on finding life-giving water for Zenith. They were following stringent safety protocols by maintaining constant visual contact. The third team member, Davis, was required to remain with the CAM-L. Contact between all parties was enabled via belt-worn ultralow-frequency communicators. When that signal failed, and for redundancy, a wired communication link ran the length of the water-siphoning hose.

Standard team equipment included roping, mining helmet, water canisters, and a handheld instrument dubbed the "sniffer," used to detect the relative abundance of water molecules in the air. Notwithstanding a tendency to give false positives, the sniffer was indispensable for detecting water evaporating from the surface of shallow pools where it collected.

The most critical equipment was the rebreather unit, vital everywhere on the planet outside the controlled atmospheres of Zenith, Nadir, and the two bases' pressurized vehicles. Unlike scuba apparatus, a rebreather utilizes a closed system by which the wearer's exhalation, still relatively rich in oxygen, passes through a scrubber to remove toxic carbon dioxide and returns it via a hose to a mouth-covering mask for rebreathing. Microtech enhances and corrects muffled speech, facilitating conversation. A spare "backup" mask provides an additional measure of safety. Because the recycling process occurs multiple times, a small "make-up" cylinder contributes oxygen to the mix. Under normal operating conditions, a fully charged rebreather supplied two hours of oxygen.

Intentional actions and unconscious mental lapses can thwart the best equipment and procedures. Even an experienced, well-trained person can make poor decisions when under considerable physical and psychological strain. It had been an exceptionally long and trying day for Jensen. A few hundred meters into Tube Network Z784C, she and Imholtz reached an area where the ceiling dramatically arched and widened into a large dome with tunnels branching off in two separate directions.

"Fuck me," uttered a weary Jensen, pausing to look at the two choices. Her clothes had become soaked with sweat, and her skin was covered in a fine layer of irritating grit.

"Yeah, screw this," echoed Imholtz. He was in no better mood, having dragged the CAM-L's suction hose most of the way into the tunnel. Staring meaningfully at Jensen, he spoke into his personal communication link. "Hey, Davis, you comfortable back there in that nice air-conditioned vehicle?"

"It's getting a little chilly."

"You know, if I thought I could whip your ass, I would. What's in the hump?"

"Twenty-three liters."

"Twenty-three? Total?" Imholtz asked, although finding it all too believable.

"Afraid so."

"Hell, the three—excuse me—*two* of us have sweated more than that today."

"Can't say we didn't give it a good try," Davis replied.

"Maybe your new girlfriend will," Imholtz snickered.

Davis immediately understood that he was referring to Ellis. The entire base was aware of his punishment. He ignored the taunt. "Give it twenty more minutes, then head back," he ordered. "Before I get frostbite."

"Right," Imholtz confirmed, terminating the com link.

"We'll be coming back empty," Jensen said, frustrated. While her partner was speaking to Davis, she drifted over to one of the side passages leading off the main chamber. "I don't want to come back empty."

"Shit happens. We didn't get lucky."

Jensen stared back at her partner, then gestured toward the dark tunnel she was peering down. "My sniffer is up ticking a few counts per million. Shall we make our own luck?"

"Split up?" Imholtz asked. "Not one of your brighter ideas."

"I didn't hear a 'no,'" Jensen persisted. "It doubles our chances if you explore the other passageway."

Imholtz hesitated. "Violates safety regs big time. You damn well better meet me back here in less than twenty minutes."

"Or what? You can't whip my ass either."

"You got that right. I have this policy of refusing to beat up on women half my size, though I might make an exception in your case. There's to be no mention of this to Davis. He'd flip."

Separating from her partner was not Jensen's first mistake. Inattention to detail, brought about by fatigue, had caused her to leave her communicator in the CAM-L. Her mates missed the oversight because they were exhausted, and contact with Davis had consistently been through Imholtz's personal device or the hose link.

Traveling alone deep within the side passage, Jensen tried to stay calm by dimming her helmet light and staring back in the direction she had come. It was the opposite of what she hoped to see: The last vestiges of Imholtz's light had vanished, and the only sound was her labored breathing. She had never been alone in a tube before. Had anyone? The insufferable heat failed to prevent a sudden chill from overtaking her. To beat back a feeling of isolation, she began talking out loud.

No reason to turn back. Sniffer picking up a few more water molecules. Wonder how it excludes perspiration and exhalation. Probably gives false positives. Walls closing in. Won't find water if this tube doesn't open up soon. Blah, blah, blah! Thank you, Commander Ellis. Thank you. Thank you. Thank you. Wouldn't be enjoying myself so damn much if it wasn't for—

Not sure why, she halted in mid-stride. Looking ahead, she continued her soliloquy—*OK, self, stop screwing around*—then took two more half-steps and stopped once again.

Hello? Note to self: I said stop screwing—

Sure that something was hovering nearby, she violently jerked her body around, the motion slicing an arc of light through the darkness as the helmet beam matched her head's direction. Now, her back was vulnerable, exposed to the void that had been in front of her. Toward the unknown.

Fearful, she turned again. This time cautiously. Reluctantly.

Nothing, she declared aloud. *Of course, nothing.*

With a conscious effort, she managed to steady her nerves. But the underlying troubling sensation remained. Ahead, at the furthest reaches of her light's beam, the lava tube appeared to be widening—a better chance to find water.

This is foolishness. Hey! Do you hear me? I said foolishness. I'm alone. What's trying to frighten me—is me. Well, guess what—I choose not to be afraid of myself.

She continued until the tunnel terminated at the entrance to a vast cavern. Standing at the chamber's leading edge, she gazed downward, her helmet beam reflecting off a sheen of water. An amount too small to siphon. Succumbing to disappointment and exhaustion, she collapsed on the edge of one of the large wedges of crust ringing the declivity.

The day spent toiling in an abusively hot and gritty environment while carrying several kilograms of equipment had long ago lost its appeal. So, too, the irritation caused by a pinching shoulder harness and a tight-fitting facemask. It was common to seek temporary relief from the weight and adjust the fit. She unclasped a set of retaining straps and shrugged the rebreather off her shoulders. The regulator hose that supplied air to the facemask was of sufficient length to deposit the rebreather on the ledge immediately beside her while still being able to intake recycled air. A day of sweat and grime accumulation, collecting where silicone contacted skin, had begun to make her facemask chafe.

Jensen made her third mistake. Taking a deep breath, she removed the troubling mask and wiped her face with a sweaty hand.

A few labored breaths of Murkor's low-oxygen, low-pressure atmosphere are possible. On Jensen's second breath, the strange sensation that had plagued her minutes before unexpectedly returned with greater force. Impulsively reacting, she twisted her body, a leg striking the rebreather beside her, pushing it downslope to the rim of a small crevice. A frantic grab at the apparatus sent it propelling over the edge.

She had a split second to decide: Expend her last breath trying to fetch the rebreather (it appeared to be lodged just out of reach) or use her communicator to summon help.

The mind can deceive itself forever; the body, deprived of oxygen, can be deceived for only so long. Panic and lack of oxygen to the brain clouded Jensen's judgment. It would take only a few seconds to alert Imholtz, but her first impulse was to extricate the rebreather. With her upper body hanging over the edge, she reached into the crevice, her fingertips grazing one of the rebreather's retaining straps. Stretching (a centimeter more and she'd lose her balance), she seized hold of the strap and gave a tug. Several frantic pulls proved that she lacked the strength to dislodge the apparatus, the damn thing having jammed itself in place. Trembling, she stood. With any additional exertion, she would pass out.

Starved for oxygen, she began taking long, heaving gasps of air.

Seeing the cause lost, she spasmodically searched for her belt-mounted communicator. Realizing she had forgotten it in the CAM-L, an intense electric shock of panic shot through her, seizing her muscles in a vise grip. In the throes of mental and physical disintegration, her body convulsed, epileptic-like. Then, in an instinctual flight response, it staggered in the infinite directions it saw as escape until it crashed hard into the lava floor.

How odd, the hovering

Closer
A presence, directly above
Touching
How very odd, transferring life
Inseparable
"Breathe."
Vocal
"Breathe, I said. Dammit, breathe!"
A voice.
"Breathe, you crazy fool, breathe!"
A *human voice.*
"You damn crazy, crazy fool!"

Imholtz's voice. Expressed as a deep sigh of relief.

Imholtz, only Imholtz, performing the difficult task of mouth-to-mouth resuscitation while alternatively taking hits of air from his rebreather mask.

Finally, only after his partner fully returned to consciousness and could breathe unassisted, he shoved his backup mask onto her face.

Jensen's first mistake may have saved her life. After twenty minutes had elapsed and she had failed to show at the rendezvous point, a concerned Imholtz buzzed her communicator. Because it had been left and forgotten in the CAM-L, a furious Davis promptly answered. Furious not only because Jensen had left the device behind but because he made the logical assumption that both techs had willfully violated protocol by separating. To the shout of "you stupid bastards," Imholtz dropped the siphoning hose and began running. In the lower gravity, he was an excellent runner.

"Who am I?" The inquiry came from Imholtz. "And don't fuck with me." He had an imprecise idea of how long his partner had been oxygen-deprived.

"You—You're Bert," Jensen, still flat on her back, managed.

"That's a start."

"Is it gone?"

"Is *what* gone?" Imholtz asked, concerned.

"I'm not sure."

Kneeling, he shone his light around the chamber. "What the hell happened in here? And where in God's name is your rebreather?"

Jensen weakly pointed into the darkness. "There. Fell into a crevice."

"How the hell—never mind, that'll come later. Can it be retrieved?"

"I don't know—not by me-by you."

"Sit up." Watching her rise, he opened a line to Davis: "Found her. All's well."

"I expected to hear from you sooner," an irate Davis returned.

"Yeah, well, resuscitation takes some time."

After a moment's silence: "Say again? You're jerkin' me, right?"

"No time for explanation. Can't say what happened, but I think we can rule out autoerotic asphyxiation."

"You'll both have some explaining to do. Shall I run in with a second rebreather?"

"Wait on that. Be prepared to do so, pending recovery of my partner's."

Imholtz terminated the connection and then asked Jensen if she could stand. After she replied in the affirmative, they walked together to the crevice where the rebreather had lodged. With his greater strength and longer reach, the apparatus was freed.

Jensen looked furtively about the chamber. With the rebreather safely back on, she stared at her partner and mysteriously asked, "You saved me?"

"Who else? And you're welcome. Now who's gonna save us?"

"From Davis?" Jensen asked.

"Him, too. No, I'm thinking Commander Ellis."

***

Returning to the CAM-L, Jensen was forced to rest while the other two-thirds of the team stowed the safety equipment and rewound the siphon hose. During the journey back to Zenith, a much-improved Jensen offered her story.

The part of the drama that defied explanation, the strange presence felt, was attributed to mild heat stroke, exhaustion, and mental fatigue. When that failed to satisfy fully, it became one more story added to the growing lore concerning alien life in the planet's lava tubes.

Davis was still angry about the day's events. "Remind me," he asked, knowing full well the answer, "How much water did we pick up today?"

"Twenty-three liters," a disgusted Imholtz answered.

"You found nothing in your passage either?" Jensen, dismayed, asked.

"Not a drop."

"What the hell are we doing out here," Jensen spat out, "risking our collective asses? And for what? For what?!

"Not for *what*," Imholtz said with disgust. "For *whom*."

They were determined to find a scapegoat. And so, there it was, the root cause of the mission's troubles presented in a nice, tidy package:

Commander Ellis.

Davis, for the most part, kept quiet, but he did not wholly disagree.

Having his punishment fresh in mind and wishing to avoid more, a pact was reached between the three crewmates.

They would not tell the commander what transpired in Murkor Tube Network Z784C.

Not that they knew themselves.

5 NADIR'S ATMOSPHERE

TWO DREARY MURKORIAN DAYS had elapsed from that early morning when Comandante Andrés Garcia called Carlos Alvarez's attention to the stagnant atmosphere in Nadir's diminutive L3 exercise room. At the time, neither considered the problem unusual or particularly worrisome. Carlos's subsequent report on the matter, therefore, read more like a boilerplate description of Nadir's outdated Environmental Support System than a definitive cause and solution:

ESS is a hybrid, partially closed, loop-type system. The internal atmosphere is passed through a canister air scrubber to remove excess carbon dioxide, noxious compounds, and particulates. An auxiliary concentrator replenishes oxygen lost through respiration via the external intake and selective filtration of Murkor's atmosphere.

Presently, the system operates at the low end of the design parameters. Detector readings taken at the primary plenum are as follows: Particulate matter 44 μg/m³ (0-50 μg/m³ norm); Oxygen

*20.87% (20.81 - 21.36 norm); carbon dioxide 943 ppm (350 -
950 ppm norm); ambient pressure 99.08 kPa (103.00 - 99.0
kPa norm). Readings have been averaged.*

*Note: Misalignment and disrepair of exterior palladium
glass panels necessitate ESS functioning at maximum operational
capacity to maintain one atmosphere pressure and ensure gases
remain within established limits.*

During the completion of an unusually lethargic
workout, however, Garcia once again noticed that L3's
air was of objectionable quality. Intending to question
Carlos, he was sidetracked by the burden of routine
duties, including the neglected chore of evaluating the
previous week's hydrological data submitted by tenientes
Roya Allawi and Gustavo Ramírez.

Hours later, he was still at the task, sequestered at
one of the designated workstations on L2. Neither the
blue bursts intruding from an adjacent viewport (there
had been a recent spate of unusually intense magnetic
storm activity) nor the audible complaints of nearby
fumaroles were sufficient to break his concentration. A
welcome distraction from the tedium finally came from
Nadir's physician, Capitán Mariana Perez.

"Am I interrupting something important,
comandante?"

"As a matter of fact, Mariana, I could use a
break," Garcia replied, pushing aside a screen full of
numbers and hydrology charts.

Mariana had been enlisted in the military for
fifteen years, ten as a medical officer. Before her arrival
on Murkor, she had been addressed by rank—teniente,

then capitán. During medical emergencies, she expected to hear "doctora." Serving under Garcia quickly changed that. "Mariana" had become the norm, with the occasional "doctora" used in those rare instances when she was treating a crew member for some minor ailment. At first, the change took some getting used to, but there was a quiet, contagious ease to the man's manner that made the breach in military etiquette acceptable.

Conversely, it was his stately bearing (and, yes, his age—she was sixteen years his junior) that compelled her and the four others in his charge to address him almost exclusively by the title of comandante, even though he had no affinity for the appellation's formality. Over time, it had, by way of friendly intonation and repeated usage, come to have more the warmth of a first name rather than the coldness of a military title.

"Crunching numbers, I see," Mariana commented. "Not quite what you signed on for, is it?"

"Sometimes I feel more the accountant," Garcia agreed, rubbing his eyes as Mariana took an adjoining seat. "One can look at this fine detail for only so long."

"Your eyes getting tired?"

"Now that you say it, they are a little," Garcia admitted, then, seeing the satisfied expression his answer produced: "Ahh—that is what you expected to hear, is it not?"

Mariana nodded. "I doubt the cause is the columns of numbers you must stare at. No, the air quality on L2 has deteriorated. Haven't you noticed?"

Until now, he had not. "I have been remiss," Garcia said, annoyed with himself. "This morning, I noticed a similar degradation—slightly more pronounced—on L3. I intended to alert Carlos."

"Smacks of dereliction of duty," Mariana contended, exaggerating a frown. "Which leaves me little choice. I must put you on report."

"Under the circumstances," Garcia said, gesturing at the screen full of hydro data, "would you allow for a verbal reprimand?"

"Well now—" Mariana replied, as if carefully considering. "In recognition of your prior accomplishments, with.... How many days are left?"

"Seventy Standard Earth Days. Eighty-nine Murkorian days."

"With *eighty-nine* days remaining in your illustrious military career," Mariana said, "I can, in good conscience, make certain allowances."

"Appreciated."

There was a moment of silent contemplation, then Mariana softly touched Garcia's arm.

"You will be sorely missed, comandante. *I* shall miss you."

"And I, you. We have many shared memories."

"That we do." Mariana's face brightened as she fixated on one of those memories. "We *thought* that damn fumarole was dormant when we climbed in."

"Los eruptos del Diablo," Garcia said, laughing. "Sudden and loud, I recall. Scared the living hell out of us. We climbed over each other getting out of there."

"You know that's false modesty," Mariana protested. "Chivalry on this base, thanks to you, is alive. You made sure I got out first."

"I felt responsible for talking you into exploring that stinking hole."

"Was it not my crazy idea?"

"Ha! I remember the opposite," Garcia said, looking back in time, rubbing his chin with his thumb and forefinger in the near-universal sign of contemplation. "Ahh, there we have it. The wonder of many a shared experience. Memories may pale with time, but the affection they inspire shines steadily on."

"I—yes," Mariana said, reflecting on Garcia's compassionate words, doing her utmost to repress a warmer show of emotion.

Garcia stood. He lightly squeezed her shoulder and said, "I must seek out Carlos. With any luck, he's on L1, working on the ESS as we speak."

***

The enclosure housing the ESS and the associated Nexus control was large enough to warrant its own door, which was presently closed. Garcia was surprised to hear Carlos's voice within. Typically, the engineer's talent for fixing arcane equipment had him working in isolation. Stepping inside, he found this to be no exception.

"Is it that bad?" Garcia questioned. "Talking to yourself?"

"I am not."

"No?" Obligingly, for no one else could have been present, Garcia glanced beyond the confusing labyrinth of ducting, canisters, and wire chases into the compartment's deepest recesses.

"Can't see how they got past me, Carlos."

"Not they. *He*. More specifically, B.H. Hommerfel."

Garcia played along. "Someone else living on base I should know about?"

The young engineer pointed to the Nexus, the interactive screen where a colorful diorama of the entire Environmental Support System flowed. "You should become better acquainted with the deceased bastard who engineered this dinosaur," Carlos said. "He's here, in one form or another, haunting me. When you came in, I was letting him know what I thought of him."

"And what was his reaction?"

"Reaction?" Carlos said, feigning a worried look. "Seriously? You expect a reaction? You're scaring me, comandante."

"It appears you're aware of the declining atmospherics?" Garcia asked.

"Of course," Carlos replied, concentrating on the screen before him. "And I've just about ruled out the ESS being the culprit. That leaves the Nexus."

The Nexus had the complex task of regulating Nadir's internal atmosphere: Carbon dioxide, carbon monoxide, oxygen, nitrogen, water vapor, particulates, temperature, duct flow, and pressure were a few of the components for which it had oversight. Capable of limited critical thinking, it was relied upon to make and carry out informed decisions specific to its operational parameters.

"You've abandoned the idea of pressure loss?" Garcia asked.

"I've been giving that more thought. Those palladium panels have been improperly sealed for some time now. Sure, the leaks require ESS to work double-time, but I doubt they cause the malfunction. No, we're dealing with something new here."

"Which air quality parameters are the most affected?"

"Particulates and carbon dioxide."

"Carbon dioxide being the most problematic," Garcia said. "Give me a number."

"At the moment, 1484 ppm, measured on L3," Carlos answered. "Not ideal. Tolerable."

"Not if readings continue to trend higher," Garcia cautioned, knowing what he said next would inspire a swift reaction. "I'm unaccustomed to hearing equivocation from you, Carlos. Not when it concerns the most critical aspects of Nadir's environmental support."

Carlos turned from the Nexus display screen that had consumed his attention and faced Garcia. "I'll get it sorted out," he declared, renewing his customary bravado. "Have a little faith, comandante."

"I will, I will," Garcia insisted with casual assurance. "You must forgive me, Carlos, if, for the present moment only, I see your understanding of the problem as imaginary as your nemesis, the ever-present B.H. Hommerfel."

***

Garcia obtained assurances that he would receive a status report by the end of that afternoon. It troubled him how frequently equipment broke down, each occurrence reinforcing the unhealthy notion that life on base was a tenuous proposition that had to be tolerated. There wasn't much choice, with replacement parts in short supply and assistance too remote to be practical.

And so, although he was concerned about the working status of the ESS, he had confidence that his resourceful engineer would soon find a solution. In that, too, there was little choice.

Descending to L1 and his austere living quarters, he pondered a second problem: how to respond if, as expected, a threatening message came from Zenith's new CO. What he did not expect, after a tiresome bout of ineffectual contemplation, was to nod off at his desk. A quiet, insistent rap on the door woke him. Unaware of who was there (the door's "transparency" feature having long ago failed beyond even Carlos's ability to repair), he said, "Enter."

In swept Amanda Cruz with one purpose in mind.

Garcia, imagining what the purpose might be, was immediately roused.

"May I stay a moment or two?" she asked. "L2 seems a bit stuffy."

A transparent ploy, Garcia thought. At the same time, he couldn't help noticing every tiny detail of what Amanda was wearing: Tight shorts exposing long, smooth legs and a sheer, loose-fitting T-shirt that outlined the curves of her breasts. They swayed enticingly as she brushed past him to perch on the edge of the sofa opposite.

"Of course, Amanda," Garcia said, barely managing to leave himself a way out *if* he chose to take it. "Stay for a brief spell. Then I must resume my work."

"Distracted by the arrival of Zenith's new CO?"

"She's on my mind, yes."

"The witch. I'm jealous. Aren't I on your mind?"

"You are," Garcia replied, adding, a little too hastily, "so are four other people living on this base."

"Is there nothing more you can say to me?" Amanda fretted, bending forward, palms smoothing the front of her bare thighs.

Garcia hesitated. Their last sexual encounter, which he simultaneously fought to remember *and* forget, burned into his brain. It was a blazing-bright picture, indelibly etched, of her lying naked below him, panting, sweat glistening on her heaving chest as he thrust in and out.

Words of passion formed on the tip of his tongue. *Move to the bed. Let me undress you. Quiero cogerte.*

He forced his mouth shut, fiercely biting his lower lip in the hope that pain would supplant the lust he was feeling.

Amanda slowly rose off the couch. Sensing weakness in Garcia's silence, she locked eyes on his, then moved behind him, breasts lightly touching his shoulder. She pressed her moist lips to his ear and whispered, "Me haces mojada. Can you forget what *I* said to *you*? How I wanted you in my mouth? How I begged to have you inside me?"

Reaching around his waist, she lowered her hands to his lap, fingers touching him through the thin fabric of his pants to feel the hard physical confirmation he was unable to hide. It was all the proof that she needed to see.

If he moved a millimeter, he would relinquish every decision to her. A man could go mad from this torture—yet he could not fault her for what she was trying to do. Never blame her. Not if she was possessed with half the desire consuming him.

But if he failed to refuse her now, he would lose.

"Amanda, you know this—"

Both were startled by a soft rap on the door.

"No," she pleaded in his ear. "Don't answer. Please."

"I must," Garcia struggled to say, gently removing her hands from his lap. "I asked Carlos to report to me."

Face flushed from anger and frustration, Amanda backed away as the automatic door slowly slid open. "If I have to," she sneered, not particularly caring who heard, "I'll seek my entertainment elsewhere." Infuriated by Garcia's rejection, she rubbed past Carlos as he entered, saying, for both men's benefit, "And you know exactly where I'll find it."

"Find—what?" Carlos, confused, stammered out. It was a lot to process: Amanda's recent interest in him conflicting with what appeared to be her continuing intimacy with the comandante. "I thought you wanted me to report—." Turning to leave, he tossed an M-file on the comandante's desk. "There it is. Copy sent to your mindstor."

Garcia deduced much of what Carlos was thinking, visible in his sullen expression and cold demeanor, and yet he would only go so far to assuage the young man's feelings. "Not everything is as it seems," he said. "Now sit your ass down in that chair and give me a verbal report."

"As you wish," Carlos said, trying to hide his frustration.

"Just summarize the main points. I'll review the complete file later."

"Carbon dioxide is elevated on every level. You may not have noticed, your attention being otherwise diverted—"

Garcia ignored the insinuation. "You've been chasing after this problem for a couple of days. Explain why the cause has been so elusive."

"The ESS is controlled by a Nexus preconfigured on Varian. I thought it was almost impossible to tamper with and incapable of making mistakes. Only it is. It's confirming that the carbon dioxide scrubbers are online and fully functional instead of what I believe is happening."

"You're saying the scrubbers have failed?" Garcia asked, becoming alarmed.

"You see, that's the problem," Carlos answered, shaking his head in frustration. "Although the Nexus sees the scrubbers as functional, it has issued them commands to shut down."

"What you're suggesting is almost impossible," Garcia said. "The Nexus is fundamentally an orchestration of molecules in a colloidal solution. There's

97

virtually no chance for anything to go wrong. You're making it sound delusional."

"Maybe so. Beyond detailed operating instructions, it has level-one reasoning ability, a type of rudimentary behavior that can be corrupted."

"How's that possible?"

"I'm working on a vague suspicion. Nothing yet worth mentioning."

"How elevated are the carbon dioxide readings?" Garcia asked.

"As of the moment—"

"Hold off," Garcia interrupted. "I'd like to bring Mariana in on this part of the conversation."

"And Amanda?" Carlos suggested, provoking a reaction.

"Zip it," Garcia cautioned.

Two minutes later, Nadir's physician sat in Garcia's compartment. Three minutes more, and she was acutely aware of why she had been summoned.

"—It was to be expected," Carlos said in conclusion, "that air recirculation and molecular diffusion would result in carbon dioxide roughly reaching equilibrium base-wide. Last I checked, the highest reading is 1,670 parts per million and rising, registered by the detector at the primary plenum."

"Is the increase linear?" Mariana asked. "What are you projecting?"

"There are insufficient data points to determine accurately," Carlos responded. "A guesstimate? We may see 3,000 ppm in a few days. In ten days, we could be approaching ten times that."

"How can that be?" Mariana protested. "Such an increase cannot be explained solely by the carbon dioxide we exhale."

"There are contributions from the outdated and inefficient power-generating equipment, air-conditioning, and refrigeration systems," Garcia replied. "None of those, and very few others, can be placed off-line."

"I assume you want me to describe the effects of carbon dioxide poisoning," Mariana stated.

"Worst-case scenario," Garcia said, nodding.

"Just in case?" Mariana asked, looking closely at Garcia, expecting words of assurance. "*Right?*"

Garcia doubted he could deliberately mislead anyone, especially Mariana, even if he wanted to. If the atmosphere continued to deteriorate, he'd have to contemplate measures that, for the moment, were too draconian to detail. "We've been self-reliant for quite a spell," he chose to say. "Has there ever been a difficulty we couldn't overcome, individually or collectively? Do you believe this occasion will be any different?"

"I'll get back to you on that," Mariana said, the comment failing to mollify her. "As for the effects of carbon dioxide poisoning? We are already witnessing the first mild symptoms—the feeling of being abnormally tired or drowsy and unable to concentrate. At 3,000 ppm, that'll get worse, and then it will get much worse as exposure levels and duration increase. After a few *hours* of inhaling 10,000 ppm, heart rates elevate, headaches become pronounced, and fatigue sets in. After a few minutes of exposure to 30,000 ppm, you'll experience hearing loss, dizziness, and confusion. At 50,000 ppm, acute vision loss, muscle tremors, labored breathing, choking, vomiting, sweating, followed by unconsciousness as you slowly asphyxiate. Beyond that? Death as you strangle from lack of—"

Mariana caught herself at the sight of two somber expressions. "Sorry. You did ask."

It was the bleakest and unlikeliest of scenarios that she had painted, but that didn't render it any less disturbing to Carlos, who, taking it to heart, now felt the fate of the crew weighing on his shoulders. Hiding his anxiety—he viewed the emotion as a sign of weakness—he attempted humor.

"Death does provide one distinct advantage," he said. "We stop producing excess carbon dioxide."

"That would be mildly amusing," Garcia abruptly said. "*If* you knew what was going on with the ESS."

It was not the assurance Carlos was seeking.

"An answer? Ask that chancro bitch," he blurted out, no less surprised by the sudden venting of his feelings than a stunned Garcia and Mariana.

"Explain yourself," Garcia demanded.

Carlos was eager to comply. "Ellis," he asserted, the name hissed between his teeth. "Do you *really* believe her arrival on Murkor was coincidental?"

"That is precisely what I think," Garcia said. "Convince me otherwise."

"What can corrupt a Nexus? I can think of only one thing: Cloaked, function-specific nanoparticles. Coalition, violating international convention, must have found a way to render them undetectable. They can spread like a contagion once inserted into the Nexus's colloid."

"When and how was this accomplished?" Garcia asked, his impatience giving way to interest.

"Three days ago, just before Nexus misbehaved. Exactly the time when Ellis's shuttle hovered overhead. Perfect opportunity to release a nanocloud, its entry facilitated through the compromised integrity of the palladium panels or ESS's intake ports. From there, they are easily dispersed by the HVAC ductwork."

Garcia considered. Given that what the engineer alleged was not impossible, only implausible, he had to ask the next logical question.

"And the motivation behind what would be considered a serious and unprovoked attack?"

"Ellis came straight from Varian," Carlos asserted, his conviction growing as he spoke. "She was ordered here for one reason. You don't have to look hard to see Coalition's ulterior motive. They aim to sabotage Nadir to gain access to what they need most. Water."

Garcia thought back to Carlos's recounting of the Río Pecos Incident. Evidently, the suffering and sorrow inflicted on an impressionable child was a burden he carried through the years and light years to Murkor. Like an invisible nanoparticle, it had infected his thinking. What the comandante did not see was that Carlos's blinding hatred of Coalition had caused him to marshal all his considerable engineering talents into trying to prove his accusation—in the process overlooking a simple defect in ESS that would have become apparent upon further investigation. Nor could he determine with certitude that his engineer's allegation was a misdirection. On the face of it, it appeared to have some validity. Seeking advice, he turned to Mariana with a silent query.

"I don't know what to think," she said, shrugging. "Do I trust Coalition? The simple answer is 'no.'"

"Retaliation is unlikely to improve our circumstances," Garcia responded. "If your assumption is correct, Carlos, what practical remedy do you propose?"

"A temporary one," Carlos said, forging ahead with an idea that entailed a measure of risk. "I can tap into the ESS's ductwork and redirect a small, constant volume of base atmosphere to the intake port of the oxygen concentrator. Carbon dioxide is one of the gases in Murkor's atmosphere. The concentrator is programmed to remove it; it'll act as a temporary scrubber, keeping the levels in check."

A clever solution, Garcia thought to himself. "What's the downside?"

"The additional volume of air passing through the oxygen concentrator may decrease efficiency."

"That's your idea of a solution?" Marianna protested. "Shall I spell out the effects of a low-oxygen environment? Impaired judgment and coordination, fatigue, muscle weakness, convulsions, loss of consciousness. Death. That's assuming we continue to maintain standard atmospheric pressure. Symptoms begin at nineteen percent oxygen concentration. At ten percent, only a few minutes before taking your last breath."

"What I'm suggesting buys us more time," Carlos insisted. "I should be able to maintain nineteen or greater."

"And if the Nexus has been corrupted?" Garcia asked.

"What I'm proposing doesn't alter that. I'm bypassing the erroneous command the Nexus sends to the scrubber."

"Implement your plan," Garcia decided. "I'm relying on your expertise. Power off any nonessential equipment that adds to the carbon dioxide burden. Mariana, please inform the others of these developments."

"Will you be consulting Amanda?" Mariana asked.

"Yes, yes. Of course."

When Mariana and Carlos got up to leave, Garcia remembered something else.

"One more thing. Pass the word. We shall convene to discuss possibilities over dinner."

***

Sitting in the solitude of his cabin, Garcia evaluated what had transpired in the last few hours. None of it was good: ESS malfunction; the possibility, however remote, of sabotage by Zenith; the distraction of Amanda.

In retrospect, he was dissatisfied with how he handled all of it: Forgetting to consult Carlos about the air quality on L3; inability to find a suitable response to a possible incursion by Zenith (shit, falling asleep thinking on it); the irresolute manner he dealt with Amanda.

His concentration was slipping. A symptom of the carbon dioxide?

More likely a symptom of Amanda Cruz.

He couldn't get his mind off her. *Me haces mojada.* She said that to him. Right now, he could take three steps down the hall and, well, damn it, no good, no good. What in hell would he do if she came on to him again? With no way to avoid her, *could* he resist her? What harm if he didn't?

He knew better. He had already jeopardized his authority by having a sexual relationship that led to emotional and unpredictable behavior in two of his crew. Amanda's and Carlos's attitudes toward him and each other could ultimately affect how they discharge their duties. Not good considering the problems we're facing.

As for the harm inflicted on himself? He didn't have to look far. Mariana was right when she suggested that Amanda, an accomplished chemist, should be consulted. Had she been temporarily excluded to avoid the sexual distraction?

He asked himself for the hundredth time: What would he do if she pursued him?

The question would never be asked if he were younger, say, Carlos's age.

No way in hell.

Or on the closest thing to it, Murkor.

***

Six humans who had much in common sat at the L2 dining table. Nearly identical DNA. Born on Earth. Citizens of Unión de Naciónes de la América Latina.

On the other side of the ledger, they were separated by six distinctive personalities and equally divided between two genders.

Carlos came straight from working on the ESS, arriving just after Amanda discreetly informed her colleagues that she had conducted her own spectral analysis of Nadir's tainted atmosphere. Unaware of her actions and confident that his colleagues were anxious to hear the results of his repair efforts, the engineer took a seat. "I can fix anything," he proudly proclaimed.

The engineer's claim was an overstatement. Although he had managed to avert a more immediate crisis by curtailing the rise of carbon dioxide, oxygen values were now beginning to sink below the crucial nineteen percent safety threshold. When prodded, he protested that this was merely a temporary setback he would soon rectify. "Have I ever failed you?" he said with an eye toward Amanda's approval.

"No," Gustavo interjected before anyone could respond, "but your first time might be your last."

"There's a first time for everything. But not that."

"You boast too much," Gustavo responded. "'The true genius 'prefers silence to saying something which is not everything it should be.'"

Somewhere in his forty-three years, Teniente Gustavo Ramírez had found time between earning advanced degrees in hydrogeology and communications to become versed in the works of Poe. It was an

105

inclination he cultivated on Murkor. It suited the planet perfectly.

"I like that first part," Carlos responded, "about being a genius."

"Didn't take you long to break the silence," Gustavo answered back.

The retort was too subtle to divert the young man's attention away from Amanda, hands clasped in front of her mouth, lips slightly parted to nibble the edge of her forefinger. "I, for one, feel we're in good hands," she chirped, patting the young man's muscled forearm. "If it weren't for the arrival of Zenith's new CO, we wouldn't be concerned about any of this."

"Is conjecture now being accepted as fact?" Garcia protested, looking around the table.

"There does seem to be compelling circumstantial evidence," Gustavo said. "And Zenith does have a great need for our water."

"And what do you think, Roya?" Garcia asked.

Roya Allawi was the only non-Latino crew member. Of Arab ancestry, she was born in what had once been Morocco and benefited from a childhood immersed in the region's rich cultural diversity. As a young adult, she relocated with her family to the Iberian Peninsula to escape climatic changes and the relentless encroachment of the Sahara Desert. Water, or the lack of it, played a large part in her career choice. An M.S. in hydrology, fluency in Spanish, and wanderlust taken to the extreme all contributed to how she wound up on Murkor.

"Before offering an opinion," she said, "I'd like to pose a question. We're assuming Zenith's thirst for water is the motivating factor behind an attack. Okay, I can buy the premise. So why not just come and take it? Isn't jeopardizing the lives of six people rather extreme?"

"You're not giving Coalition credit for being devious," Carlos replied. "A blatant incursion would trigger an immediate Unión response that Coalition may wish to avoid. Everyone knows Nadir was poorly designed and constructed. Without proof, who'd believe that the insertion of an elusive nanoparticle incapacitated us? Can't you people see what's happening?" Carlos added, his voice rising. "Coalition is forcing us to abdicate our claim here."

Roya remained unconvinced. "I believe you have strong feelings about this. Except that too much of your supposition is predicated on the idea that nanoparticles have infected the Nexus." She turned to Garcia, "I reserve judgment in the matter."

"Fair enough. And what about you, Mariana? Care to wade in?"

"If I were a jury member, I'd probably vote guilty. Except the accused does have a right to face their accuser. Have you considered confronting Ellis with the 'evidence?' She might tip her hand."

"I've given it thought," Garcia responded. "If she is behind this alleged sabotage, she has no assurance of its success. For the moment, I prefer to keep her in the dark to see if she gives away her intentions by making an obvious move against us."

"Have you sent a message to our liaison in the Varian System to apprise them of what she's done?" Carlos asked.

"To what aim?" Garcia inquired.

"For them to respond on our behalf," Amanda said, joining ranks with Carlos.

"It's premature," Garcia replied. "And it would only strain the damaged relationship between Unión and Coalition."

"Is that how you characterize it? Only damaged, not broken?" Amanda asked, stroking the top of her bare foot against his calf beneath the table.

"That remains to be seen," Garcia replied, swallowing hard. Somehow, he managed to shift his leg. "Does anyone else have additional comments or suggestions? Gustavo? We haven't heard much from you this evening."

"With good reason," he replied.

"Here it comes," Roya said, winking at Mariana.

Gustavo was undeterred. "'In one case out of a hundred, a point is excessively discussed because it is obscure; in the ninety-nine remaining, it is obscure because it is excessively discussed.'"

"And you prefer not to be accused of tipping the balance?" Garcia asked, smiling.

"Exactly."

"Poe?"

"Who else?"

"Well, if there's nothing more—" Garcia said, signaling the end of the meeting. As he stood, one more detail belatedly came to mind. "Sorry, almost forgot. Roya, how much water is in the storage vaults?"

"Almost two thousand liters."

Too low, Garcia thought to himself—his fault. The storage vaults located below the base needed replenishment. The ease of finding water and a growing reluctance to enter the lava tubes had led to complacency and fewer missions.

"Carlos, can the ESS still be used to refill the CAM-L's air tank?"

"Yes. Remember that the vehicle's air chemistry and the rebreathers will be identical to the base's air."

Garcia pondered this momentarily, then said, "Roya, we must anticipate the interruption of water recovery missions. One last quick excursion early tomorrow should bring the storage tanks up to half capacity. Assemble the team: You, Gustavo, and Amanda."

6 THAT WHICH HAS VALUE

HEY HAD LEFT NADIR BEFORE the sun might decide to appear. A mercurial hot breeze had managed to scrub half the murk out of the atmosphere, leaving the air a somber tincture of iodine brown. The eye eagerly welcomed the slight hint of color. On Murkor, it never got any clearer or more appealing.

"Look there! Do you see it?" Gustavo pleaded, pointing, his face seemingly intent on embedding itself in the front windshield of the CAM-L he was piloting.

"No," insisted Roya, "I don't see it. I rarely see it, so why do you pester me?"

Gustavo, incredulous at the curt answer, ignored the question. Fortunately, he had a second crewmate to annoy. "Amanda?" he petitioned, in return receiving a blank look. "Not you, too? Tell me you can't see it."

Amanda peered up from her navigation duties to concentrate on the sun's aberrant movement relative to a promontory on the horizon.

"Okay," she relented, "I see it."

"I knew *you* would," Gustavo said, gloating until he caught Roya and Amanda exchanging smiles. "Uh, huh. I get it. Cute. So why don't you tell me, Amanda, in which direction do you think the sun is moving?"

"Down?"

Sunrise. The reply made no sense. Except, that is, on Murkor.

"No, it's *left*," Garcia exclaimed, exasperated. "The sun moved to the *left*. What's the matter with you two? Are you blind?"

They had this discussion before, and on a few occasions, they actually agreed on the direction of the sun's lateral movement relative to the horizon.

"Any objection to scouting an outlying sector?" Amanda asked. She had taken command of the vehicle's navigation holo. *Outlying* meant lava fields beyond an imaginary ten-kilometer circle, with Nadir as its center. Water recovery missions undertaken within Nadir's EZ were much shorter and less arduous than those conducted by neighboring Zenith. Typically, filling a CAM-L's water tank requires the exploration of only one or two close-in lava tube networks.

Roya tended to be more prudent. "The comandante's intention," she reminded, "was for us to make this a short trip."

"We're halfway there already," Amanda replied, which was a distortion of the facts. She had discounted Garcia's requirement for a shorter mission solely out of pique. The distance to the proposed destination would be longer due to the intervening crevices that needed bypassing.

"OK, then," Roya conceded, unaware of the excess travel time. "Plot the safest course."

"Head for that low, jagged ridge," Amanda directed.

"You mean los dientes demonios?" commented Gustavo, who assigned most of the descriptive names to the planet's hideous topography.

"I like it," Amanda said. "It shall forever be identified as such by the holo-mapping program. What I have in mind lies a few kilometers beyond."

The lavascape on the opposite side of the ridge was more treacherous than Amanda anticipated, requiring Gustavo to firmly grip the throttles that sent power to the CAM-L's rotating tracks. Several teeth-rattling jolts tested the vehicle's heavy-duty suspension. "Gus," Roya admonished, "one of these days, you're going to send us hurtling headfirst into a crevice…hey, there's a sight you don't often see!"

On the CAM-L's port side were three rollers ominously barreling across a wide-open mesa. Witnessing more than two at the same time was rare. Seeing three this close was unheard of.

"I think the sensible thing is to observe which direction they take," Gustavo advised, bringing the vehicle to a halt, even though stopping did little to increase their safety—a roller's movement was too fast and unreliable to predict. They watched nervously as the storm repeatedly altered directions, in the process approaching, receding, and crisscrossing each other's paths. Within moments, the CAM-L was in the center of all three, forcing an anxious crew to repeatedly shift in their seats to keep sight of the storms' varying locations. "One appears to be heading right for us!" Amanda warned, singling out the closest, a kilometer away and closing fast. "Gustavo, get us the hell out of here!"

"Not a great idea," Roya declared. "It won't stay on a straight vector for long." But as she spoke, the roller had moved closer, its outer turbulence sending lava projectiles pinging against the vehicle's metal plating.

"Damn you, Gustavo!" Amanda screamed, competing to be heard above the storm's deafening noise. The *hissing* sound of a wave receding on a pebble-covered shore amplified a hundred-fold. "Move us!"

Hands bleached white from clenching the acceleration throttles, Gustavo remained steadfast. He breathed a sigh of relief when the oncoming roller veered off at the last possible second, leaving behind two, each laden with 100,000 metric tons of tumbling pumice, shards, and lava chunks.

Nothing on the face of Murkor could halt the forward motion of a roller. Rotating at 800 kilometers per hour and a forward velocity of 200 kilometers per hour, it attains sufficient mass and momentum to exhibit some of the physical properties of a non-compressible solid.

And solids can collide.

The probability of a roller collision was thought to be statistically insignificant. The phenomenon had never been observed.

"I have a bad feeling about this," Amanda warned.

"Can you gauge their distance?" Roya asked.

"Not precisely. Their movement is too erratic. Perhaps *now* we should turn around?"

"I say we stay put a little longer," Gustavo said. "Eventually, they'll alter course or collapse under their own mass."

"They're heading straight for each other," Amanda cautioned, her eyes widening in disbelief.

"Better hold on!" Roya yelled as the two monsters met head-on.

What happened in sequence seemed instantaneous:

A blinding flash of white light—the brilliance of a billion sparks of electrically super-charged pumice particles—followed by a shock wave radiating through solid rock.

Microseconds later, a supersonic blast hit the seven-metric-ton CAM-L, violently propelling it backward.

An earsplitting krrhhump!—the sound wave radiating outward from the cataclysmic collision—even in Murkor's thin atmosphere, to be heard and felt ten kilometers away by the startled occupants of Nadir!

Upright and undamaged, the CAM-L had come to a jarring halt fifty meters from where it had previously rested.

Stunned, Roya looked to her crewmates for signs of injury. "Is anyone hurt?"

"I'm ok," Gustavo tentatively answered.

"Amanda?" Roya had to ask again. "Amanda?"

"Uh, no. Don't think so. A little hard of hearing at the moment."

All three had been violently jostled but kept firmly in place by their safety harnesses.

"They're gone," Gustavo said, mouth agape, staring at where the explosion had been. "Completely and utterly gone."

"We should report—" Roya began before being interrupted by the vehicle's audible com.

"What the hell happened out there?" the comandante demanded. "Is everyone alright?"

"Shaken, that's all," Gustavo replied. "You won't believe it. That was two rollers facing off. Neither gave."

Silence, then Garcia: "That's not supposed to happen."

"You heard it?" Roya asked.

"Felt it first. For a second, we thought it might be an earthquake. Registered mag eight here."

"I wouldn't believe it myself if I didn't see it," Gustavo said. "Not sure if it was an explosion or an implosion. Maybe both. Total annihilation. If we had the resources and a couple of hot-shot physicists—"

"If anybody's interested, I'm okay," Amanda pronounced, unintentionally raising her voice to compensate for her temporary hearing loss.

"Of course," Garcia replied. "If it shook us here, it must have scared you."

"At first, did you think Zenith was to blame?"

"Carlos's first thought," Garcia said. "The epicenter was in proximity to your last known position."

"A third roller headed off in your direction," Roya advised. "Did you see it?"

"No," Garcia answered, pausing to add, "You're telling me *three* rollers were in the same vicinity?"

"Affirmative," Roya replied, looking out where two had been a few moments ago. "None now, though. Do we have permission to continue on?"

After a silent second or two of uncharacteristic hesitation, Garcia spoke up. "Check for vehicle damage. Run a systems diagnostic."

"That's performed automatically, comandante," Gustavo reminded.

"Right… right. Proceed, then. Report every ten minutes. Out."

Before traveling to the targeted tube network, a curious Gustavo decided that taking a short detour to ground zero was worthwhile. Donning a rebreather and grabbing a communicator, he left the safety of the CAM-L. He walked to the outer fringe of the blast site, a mounded wasteland of pumice that had fused into shiny fragments of lava glass smaller than a grain of sand. Interspersed in the ruin were lava chunks greater than a meter across. Squatting down, scanning the hot rubble at his feet, he wondered aloud into his communicator if Zenith had detected the blast. Neither Amanda nor Roya ventured an answer. Both encouraged his immediate return to the safety of the vehicle.

Before returning, the desolation unexpectedly prompted a disturbing reflection, a comparison to human behavior.

How two similar but opposing forces, failing to coexist in the same space and time, could extinguish each other in their fury.

***

Arriving at their final destination, the crew wondered why they ventured so far. There were closer, productive tube networks that they had visited multiple times. Little was known about outlying Lava Tube N119 other than it was located in an area with a high probability of a successful mission.

Nadir's equipment, manufactured by the same multinational corporation, was nearly identical to Zenith's. Standard safety protocols were followed: Gustavo was to remain in the vehicle while Amanda and Roya, trailing the siphoning hose behind them, entered the convoluted passageways of the tube. All three exhibited mild aftereffects from the violent roller explosion and fatigue from breathing air in which the carbon dioxide content exceeded norms. (The CAM-L and rebreathers had been replenished from the malfunctioning ESS.)

Gustavo, sensing a potential problem, put his own words to it. "No screwing around in there," he cautioned through the communications link. "I don't want to come in after you ladies."

"Roya, did he just call us *ladies*?" Amanda inquired.

"He means nothing by it," Roya said. "It's just his way." Both women understood they were being teased. "Isn't that right, Gus? Being a condescending ass is just your way?"

"I certainly meant no disrespect, ladies. Now get it done and get your little fannies out of there ASAP."

"I love a man who speaks his mind," Roya replied. "And since you have nothing to talk about..." Smiling, she abruptly terminated the com link.

"This tube looks accessible," Amanda suggested, bringing her headlamp to bear onto the passageway's striated walls, sparkling in the first light they had ever seen.

The tube's geology was unremarkable. There was nothing to distinguish it from several of the others explored. "Only diamonds," Roya commented. "They were once measured in carats, mere milligrams, before that discovery in the Epsilon system. That's when they started weighing them by the metric ton. It's funny how some things, once considered precious, can become almost worthless. To me, they're still pretty, though. Amanda? Don't you think so?"

"Meter's acting strange," she replied, trying to decipher the fluctuating readings displayed on the recently calibrated sniffer she held. "Diamonds? Cheap costume jewelry."

The passageway began to widen and decline. Smaller side branches, appearing too challenging to navigate, opened in multiple directions. At one intersection, Amanda stopped. "Picking up water molecules. Meter's gone off-scale. Don't see that often. Should be water to waste up ahead."

"Waste?" Roya objected. "I watched a once-thriving region abandoned by its people because of a *lack* of water. Shallow wells choked with sand. Even those drilled deep running dry. It's hard to raise livestock when dunes replace grassland."

"No water? Let that be Ellis's headache," Amanda said.

"When a resource becomes precious, there are those who will go to great lengths to obtain it," Roya said. "Let's hope that's not true of Zenith's commander. Anyway, who would have imagined? Diamonds worthless, fresh water, precious."

"That's interesting," Amanda said, obviously uninterested.

Getting little response, Roya changed topics. "Maybe I shouldn't be so serious. Ever get pumice in your bra? I have. It can be a bit chaffing."

"There's an easy solution to that," Amanda volunteered, laughing.

"Like the other afternoon?"

"You saw?" Amanda answered, surprised.

"You were coming from the comandante's cabin." She omitted that Amanda had appeared agitated while hastily leaving Garcia's cabin. Roya had guessed why her crewmate was upset, even without hearing her last irate words, those thrown into the air meant for Carlos. Later in the day, she sensed the change in her crewmates' behavior and the undercurrent of tension. Most disturbing was watching the usually imperturbable Garcia wrestle with his inner demons, the palpable battle taking place in the man, evident by the distracted look in his eyes. Even Mariana expressed concern for the comandante's well-being, wondering aloud if elevated carbon dioxide affected his concentration.

Amanda, smirking behind her mask, faced the other woman. "I had hoped to stay longer."

Roya had acquired a pretty good understanding of her attractive crewmate's personality, including the inordinate emphasis placed on the physical side of self-image. Although they had become friends, confiding intimacies with each other was rare. Getting her to share now would be tricky. There were no signs of how it might go due to the partial darkness and facemask obscuring part of Amanda's face.

"When I saw you," Roya said, choosing her words carefully, "I was in a hurry myself, or I would have chatted you up. You seemed flustered. I assumed the comandante did nothing improper. I can't imagine he ever would…"

"Shall we continue on?" Amanda said, redirecting her helmet light into the darkness of the lava tube. The conversation appeared over, but after a minute of walking together, she volunteered more: "It's what he didn't do."

"What should I make of that?" Roya replied, continuing down into the tube. She knew *exactly* what to make of it. Having it explained without coaxing would be better.

"He can be very stubborn," Amanda maintained, sounding indignant. "But I can be stubborn, too. We'll see what happens next time."

"I can't see how he'll be able to turn you away," Roya said. "After all, you're a damn attractive woman."

"Do you think so?"

"You're irresistible!" Roya protested, continuing the ego stroking. "It won't be a fair contest."

Amanda basked in the compliment before saying, "Does everyone know what went on between us?"

"Everyone suspected."

"Figures."

"Nothing disparaging has been said. We know how lonely it gets out here on the edge. And Garcia is a handsome man."

"He's an extremely passionate man."

"Why, then, did he choose to be alone?"

"Oh, who knows—something about wanting nothing to influence his command."

"Is that what he told you?" Roya asked, noting from the sound of Amanda's voice that she did not accept Garcia's reasoning.

"Why the question?" Amanda replied, turning defensive.

"I mean, do you believe there's another reason? Something he's refusing to tell you?"

"Why, no—"

"So, *he* believes what he is saying?"

"Apparently so."

It was the admission Roya wanted to hear. "Then it must be important to him. Do you have any idea just how difficult it is for a man like him to give up what you have to offer? It's damn near impossible."

"I hope so," Amanda declared, laughing, trying to back away from the serious tone the conversation was taking.

"Wait a minute," Roya said, trying to rein her back in. "You don't love him, do you?"

"It's not like that. What's the difference if I did?"

"Hell, I don't know," Roya said. "Speaking for myself, being physically attracted to a man is as commonplace as diamonds. Love's different—love is precious and always will be. I guess you can say it has infinite value."

In the silence that followed, Roya could not tell if the message she tried to deliver had been received. She had cautiously avoided giving specific advice. Experience told her that when shown the wisdom of walking a different path, a person is often inclined to start running down the one they're already on. Perhaps she had gone too far by meddling in a private affair. If so, it was because she had been with the comandante on the planet from the start, and a special closeness had developed. In her understanding of the man, she knew that losing his internal struggle meant losing self-respect—and everyone would be the worst for it, including Amanda.

"Bzzzzzz! Time's up. What's going on in there?" complained an impatient Gustavo, speaking through the com link running the length of the siphon hose.

"Hey, Gus," Roya said, "we thought you left by now. I mean you are a little absent-minded and all."

"I contemplated leaving. That was *after* I remembered you two were in there screwing around. The comandante asked why we were operating in an outlying area. Then questioned me as to why we were in an unexplored tube network. Last but not least, he demanded to know why we were exploring a network in proximity to the epicenter of a shock wave. Admittedly, three real good questions."

"He's worried about the tube's structural integrity?" Roya asked.

"Bingo! The possibility of collapse. Should he be?"

"I hadn't considered it. Very low risk, in my estimation. Are we being ordered out?"

"No," Gustavo said. "You're advised to proceed at your own discretion."

"There's no sense leaving now," Amanda said, trying to hide her growing unease. The selection of N119 had been entirely her idea. She didn't want it to be a bad one. "Sniffer's maxed out. Water, lots of it, just up ahead."

"Are we agreed then?" Gustavo urged, "If water isn't found in the next few minutes, you're out?"

"I'm fine with that," Roya said. "Besides, this place is starting to creep me out."

"The usual?" Gustavo asked, referring to the feeling that Amanda was trying to hide and, to varying degrees, troubled anyone who spent a long time in Murkor's lava tubes.

"A little more so."

"How about you, Amanda?" Gustavo asked, knowing she was more impressionable. "Bogeyman coming to get you, too?"

"Sure, joke about it," Amanda snapped back, "while we're in here and you're safely out there."

"I'll be quiet now," Gustavo said.

Five minutes later, the beams emanating from two helmet lights reflected off the surface of a placid pool of water in the dead center of an enormous chamber.

Amanda uttered, "Excellent," then rushed to the water's edge. With a head tilt, she directed the powerful arc of light from her helmet into the crystalline depths. "Roya, come take a look," she insisted. "I can't see the bottom. The light disappears first."

"This is the deepest pool I've ever seen," Roya said, adjusting her beam to point downward.

"You're welcome," Amanda replied, taking credit for the discovery.

"Hey, Gus, you're about to get wet," Roya said, using the customary phrasing to denote that the waterproof com link on the siphon hose was about to be submerged, rendering it temporarily out of service.

"That's good news," a relieved Gustavo replied, activating the CAM-L's suction pump. "The comandante will be mollified that we didn't come this far only to return with an empty hump."

After feeding the hose deep into the pool, Roya rested on a nearby ledge. She noted with great interest that the water level did not lower as siphoning progressed. Three thousand liters were safely stored in the CAM-L's tank within minutes.

Below ground, the comlink on the hose was much more reliable than a personal communicator. Team members followed it out of the tube to prevent damage as it was retracted. Except during an emergency, the rule was deemed inviolate. On this occasion, Amanda thought otherwise. Although she had done her best to submerge her anxiety, the strange atmosphere in the tube was becoming unbearable. "Why must we wait for the hose?" she said, then offered an excuse for leaving. "The heat in here is getting to me."

"Come, sit down beside me," Roya urged,

sensing the real reason behind her crewmate's anxiety while coping with a milder version of her own.

"No, I can't sit," Amanda protested. "I won't sit."

"You *know* it's nothing," Roya contended. "Just our minds playing tricks on us."

"We have to leave," Amanda demanded, retreating from the pool of water, nearly knocking herself senseless by backing up hard against the nearest wall.

A wall which she hoped would be a defensible position against an invisible assailant.

"We can't let this place get to us," Roya repeated, seeing Amanda's desperation and rising to her feet.

"What the heck is going on in there!" Gustavo chimed in. Out of caution, he had kept the com link open. "You two are freaking me the hell out."

The familiar voice, only a momentary distraction to Roya, became an irresistible beacon summoning Amanda to the outside. Unable to withstand the feeling overtaking her, she bolted toward the chamber's exit, screaming, "Get the hell out of my way," to Roya, who had firmly planted herself in the way.

The forward momentum that propelled Amanda careening down the long, dark tunnel toward freedom sent Roya sprawling. Facemask dislodged, gasping in the thin Murkorian atmosphere, she struggled to stand. Frantically reattaching her mask, she embraced what her desperate crewmate felt.

She was not alone.

"Talk to me, somebody," the comlink squawked again. "If you two ladies are pranking me…"

"Yellow One alert!" Roya shouted through labored breaths.

"Type?" Gustavo asked.

"Panic attack. Amanda's headed your way. So am I."

"Understood," Gustavo replied.

Retaining enough of her sanity, Amanda traced the length of the siphon hose back to the CAM-L, where Gustavo was waiting with a mild tranquilizer.

Not long after, all three crewmates were reunited. The safety equipment was stored away, and the siphon hose retracted without incident.

Gustavo was informed of what happened and had a question.

"Amanda, what *the fuck* were you thinking?"

Before she could offer a reply, Roya came to her defense.

"You weren't in there."

"And what's that supposed to mean?" Gustavo asked.

"Want to go in alone and find out?"

"Sure—"

"No—don't!" Amanda interrupted. Surprised by the strength of her reaction, she repeated the word in a barely audible whisper. "*Don't.*"

"You got spooked," Gustavo said, shaking his head in sympathy. "It happens. But you, too, Roya?" He had been listening in on the com when she came running out of the tube, trying to bolster her idea of a sensible universe. "What was that you kept saying? 'I *am* a scientist!?' Shouted several times if I recall—"

"I repeat," Roya said, responding to the teasing, "you weren't in there."

"Okay, okay, I get it," Gustavo professed as he piloted toward what they assumed would be the base's security.

No one spoke. Halfway home, having dredged his memory for the most apropos Poe quote, Gustavo said what they were thinking:

"Want to know the truth? Maybe I *don't* get it. None of us does. 'There are some secrets which do not permit themselves to be told.'"

7 SORELY TESTED

ELLIS HAD HOPED FOR BETTER.

Six arduous water recovery missions over two consecutive days had yielded a scant thirty-eight liters of the precious resource, and the prevailing mood inside Zenith had gone from bad to worse. Anxiety would find its outlet in anger, the easiest target being herself. Reflecting on the alternatives open to her, there were two choices: Run from the storm or meet it head-on. Reading the facial expressions and body language of the twenty-nine assembled, she estimated there were only four reliable allies and perhaps a handful of uncommitted.

"As you are well aware," she began, "we have reached a tipping point where water demand outpaces supply. This development has come upon us sooner than anyone anticipated and will require additional actions on our part. I have asked Mr. Schulman to explain exactly what must be done. Share your conclusion with us, Mr. Schulman."

"Uh, certainly, commander. In brief?"

"Preferably."

"There are currently 11,233 liters of fresh, filtered water in storage. At our current rate of use, that gives us a fifteen-day reserve. For that to last forty-five days, as you directed me to calculate, consumption must be reduced by two-thirds. That means restricting each person to 8.6 liters per day."

"Doable, Mr. Schulman?"

"Oh, it can with a concerted effort and, how to say this politely, toleration for the affront to one's olfactory sense."

"Explain," Ellis requested.

"Well, you see, each person requires a bare minimum of three liters of water for hydration. That doesn't leave much for food preparation, waste processing, and personal hygiene. You know, washing up and the like."

"Hey, Schulman," somebody shouted to general laughter. "Did you count on extra savings from Johnson in those numbers? He never bathes."

Not everyone was amused. "Why forty-five days?" asked Chuck Kreechum, the IMC foreman. "You have something specific in mind?"

"I do," Ellis said. "It is the time necessary for a transmission, if I choose to send it, to arrive at Varian, added to the time it takes a transport ship to travel here."

"And the purpose of that vessel?" Kreechum asked, his temper rising along with his voice. He damn well knew the answer.

"The transport will stay in orbit and be used for emergency evacuation, if and when it becomes necessary, of all non-service personnel."

"You mean to abandon Zenith!" Kreechum declared over several shouts of protest.

"As I said, if it becomes necessary," Ellis replied. "For the present, I'm hoping the developing situation allows leaving behind six personnel, the minimum needed to comply with the provisions of Section 107.16.3."

"What you're suggesting," Kreechum spat out, barely maintaining self-control, "is the permanent shutdown of mining operations on this planet! That's bullshit when all we need to prevent that is so close that, well, shit, I can spit further."

"You've voiced that opinion before, Mr. Kreechum," Ellis said. "Forty-five days from now, would you rather have a Coalition transport ship in orbit or a Unión T4 Battlecruiser?"

While Kreechum was thinking of a suitable reply, Mechanic Ed Anderson joined in: "Water *and* testosterone seem to be in short supply around here," he said, whispering loudly enough so everyone, especially a weakly smiling Davis, could hear.

Ellis's retort, half-premeditated and half-gut reaction, was swift. "I can barely tolerate ignorance, Mr. Anderson, but not disrespect to me or the other women in this room. Interrupt again, and I'll have Lieutenant Davis escort you to your quarters. Is that clear?"

The warning aimed to accomplish two goals: shutting down Anderson and, more importantly, forcing Davis's active cooperation, which was vital if she was to keep a firm hold on command. The lieutenant now had to choose between supporting her or a friend, openly demonstrating his allegiance in front of the base.

It took three long seconds of silence for her gambit to play out.

Sitting rock-still, both men stared hard at her— Anderson full of repressed resentment, Davis uncertain, sizing her up. Anderson seemed willing to escalate the confrontation when Davis, saying nothing, reached across and firmly grasped his friend's forearm. There was no misinterpreting what he meant.

"Clear…commander," Anderson reluctantly said, and the crisis was temporarily averted.

There was an unexpected added benefit to her warning to Anderson. Four women, including three of the five female IMC techs, were now smiling at her. Divide and conquer, Ellis thought with some regret. The fourth woman was Captain Stewart.

"Let's get back on point," Ellis said. "First, missions must continue unabated. I won't concede that water sufficient to maintain the minimum base population of six can't be found. Second, I believe that cooperation with our Unión neighbors is possible. In the next few days, I shall attempt to open a direct line of communication with Nadir's CO."

Ellis weathered another round of scornful looks and barely suppressed derisive laughter. More disturbing was the silent look of hatred emanating from Anderson.

"Permission to speak candidly, commander." The request wasn't from an IMC tech but from military personnel.

"That's why we're here, Sergeant Cooper."

"Ma'am, I remind you of what took place on Phenos. And, more recently, the skirmish within the Laster System. Can any good come from dealing with the bastards?"

"It can. Recall the recent exchange of water for alcohol."

"There's a difference," Cooper said. "They presently have us at a disadvantage, and they damn well know it."

"They may have an accurate assessment of our thirst for water, but I have seen the poor condition of their base." Ellis directed her following remark at the IMC foreman. "From the reports I have studied, correct me if I am wrong, Mr. Kreechum, upwards of 1,000 liters of water per day is required to process unrefined anecrecium ore."

"One thousand liters to reduce a metric ton of ore to ten kilograms of refined material, stored on-site, then transported off-world on bimonthly supply ships. The last shipment was several months ago. No water, no anecrecium. Period."

"And no fuckin' production bonuses, exclamation point!" someone shouted, then thought better of the outburst. "Sorry, commander."

"What's your name, mister?" Ellis asked.

"IMC tech Bert Imholtz, ma'am."

"When was the last occasion you were out and about?"

"Just yesterday," Imholtz replied. "When Lori had her accident..." his last words trailed away as he belatedly tried to cover his slip-up. Embarrassed, he stared at his feet. He had agreed to keep the incident shielded from the commander. A few chuckles came from several IMC workers who had been let in on the secret.

"I am unaware of any accident," Ellis replied. Her first thought was that she may have been remiss in reviewing a medical report sent to her mindstor. A quick read of the base physician's expression went a long way in dispelling the notion.

"Captain Stewart?" Ellis inquired. "Were *you* apprised of this incident?"

Stewart shook her head in disgust. "I can assure you I was not."

"And the subject of this accident is Lori Jensen," Ellis said, looking her way. "You appear to be in good health, Ms. Jensen?"

"I am, commander."

"And exactly what was the nature of your accident?"

"I had to be revived after losing my rebreather," Jensen replied.

"Dumb ass!" someone shouted to almost everyone's amusement. When the laughter subsided, the tech provided an abbreviated and defensively worded summary of the incident. The accounting, sterilized of essential details, ended with a thinly veiled accusation. "It was one of the longer missions you ordered us on. The whole thing probably wouldn't have happened otherwise."

"Your duty," Ellis said, "was to report what happened and why."

"Duty?" Jensen answered with a scowl. "That I did. I provided a summary to my foreman."

Ellis knew that reporting the incident solely to Kreechum was a willful attempt at undermining her authority. Had the IMC foreman deliberately kept his silence? Watching him sneer provided the unwelcome answer. There were, it appeared, forces lining up against her. Might as well complete the ugly picture, then deal with the mess.

"And who was the third member of your team?" she asked, aware that the critical detail had been one of the Jensen's glaring omissions. When the tech hesitated, Ellis threatened. "There's a roster for every mission," she continued. "I won't ask again. I assure you it's in your best interest to reply."

Before Jensen could respond, and there was no indication she would, a clear and determined voice rang out.

"*I* was in charge of that mission, commander."

Ellis showed no outward reaction, disappointing techs gleefully expecting an emotional display. If she felt anything, it was betrayal, despite knowing Davis for only a short time.

"You felt no obligation to report the incident to me or Captain Stewart?" Ellis demanded.

"With due respect," Davis said to a backdrop of grumbled assent, "I'm obligated to protect the crew I serve with,"

"And exactly what were you protecting them from, lieutenant?"

"Mistakes were made on that mission. Human mistakes. Lapses in judgment due to exhaustion and the unsettling environment of the tubes themselves. I considered it inappropriate for discipline to be meted out by someone who lacks proper appreciation for these factors."

"Let me get this straight. Although your involvement renders your objectivity suspect, you prejudged my reaction as too severe."

"By prior example, commander," Davis asserted, calling to mind the punishment assigned to himself and Anderson.

"And what of Captain Stewart?" Ellis continued. "Is her medical counsel to be ignored?"

"She would, in turn, be duty-bound to inform you."

"Exactly, lieutenant. It's referred to as 'chain of command.' Seeing that you can still recall certain aspects of your military discipline is refreshing. I'll expect you in my office after this meeting."

As the meeting ended, Ellis received a look of sympathy from Stewart, but she regretted seeing it, for nothing could make the tenuous nature of her new command any clearer. It was time, she reluctantly decided, to take the "conversation" to a different level.

***

"At ease. Have a seat, lieutenant," Ellis said when Davis appeared in her office.

He complied without saying a word, waiting for her to fire the opening salvo. No sense being predictable, Ellis thought. "You know, you're turning out to be one big pain in my ass."

"Not my intent, commander," Davis replied, trying to act indifferent.

"And just what is your intent? Proving that you're as great a fool as your friend?"

"'My friend,' you say. You tried to drive a wedge between us. I'd appreciate not being put in that position again."

"Something I'll bear in mind—when you assume command. In the meantime, you'll comply with my orders, as will everyone else on this base. Understood?"

"Understood," Davis said, adding, "but you risk pushing too hard. I'll say one thing for Trenchon, he knew how to relate to the men on this base."

"That's crap, and you know it. He was good at managing the status quo. And where has it got any of you?"

"I know where we've been; the question is, where are you taking us? Off the planet, it would seem."

"Are you as anxious as Kreechum to push Coalition and Unión into a confrontation?"

"No. Except I keep asking myself why in hell Brass ordered you here if you're unwilling to take *any* risks."

"Because I was misjudged," Ellis said. "Exactly like you're doing now."

"Is that the way you see it?"

"Exactly the way I see it. You've avoided an outright insult but think I'm ineffectual and weak. I can relieve you of your misconceptions. Later today, in the gym where I'm going to kick your sorry ass."

"You can't be serious," Davis said, laughing, yet uncertain whether to dismiss the challenge as a joke.

"Dead serious. A mixed martial arts contest. I've heard that you're an accomplished kickboxer."

"You've heard correctly, which is why—"

"If you are worried about my safety," Ellis interrupted, "think again. I have a black belt in judo. If I were you, I'd be more concerned about your welfare. We'll follow the usual rules to prevent serious injury. A 'tap out' ends the match."

"Respectfully, commander, other than the satisfaction I'd get from kicking your...well, what do I gain by this match?"

"You said I was too severe (as did Captain Stewart, Ellis distinctly remembered) in setting punishment for your drunken brawl. Perhaps a month without rec privileges is an excruciatingly long time on Murkor. You can tack on another month for failing to report Ms. Jensen's accident. Or you can wipe the slate clean. If I 'tap out' first, you decide the punishment. For both you *and* your friend."

Davis weighed the proposal. Both he and Ellis had years of military service. It was commonplace for men and women to spar together. "And on the off-chance you win?" he asked. "What do you get out of this?"

"Bragging rights. Can your ego handle it?"

"You meant to say my 'male ego?'"

"If you prefer to think of it in those terms. I don't."

"The aim of this contest," Davis asked, "is to make the other person tap out?"

"You have a better idea?"

"Something in addition. The general fitness room has one door. The first person to exit through that door is declared the winner."

"The room with the viewing gallery?"

"Yes."

"Perfect." An audience was precisely what she wanted.

"I shall make sure the room is kept free," Davis said, rising to leave.

"Sit down," Ellis ordered. "You're not dismissed. I want to hear exactly what went on during your last mission."

"I wasn't in the tube. Much of my knowledge of the incident was acquired secondhand. You'd do better interrogating Imholtz and Jensen."

"I intend to. Now let's get on with it."

Alone in her office, Ellis took time to reflect. Ignoring Davis's arrogance, she couldn't help but take a liking to the man. Smart. Attractive. A little fucked in the head, but she hoped that was temporary.

He was known to be the toughest man on base, Anderson a close second. Except for the unmarked face, the lieutenant looked the part: A shy two meters, one hundred perfectly proportioned kilograms, Earth weight.

Like herself, no stranger to the gym. She doubted his body fat was above ten percent. Given half a chance, a female anatomist would be more than pleased to examine his well-defined muscle groups.

It would be a worthy physical contest for the first time in a long time.

Too bad she had to find an inconspicuous way to lose.

***

The first shout originating from the fitness room's viewing gallery was broadcasted for general consumption: "Isn't this the same room that Davis put Anderson on his ass?"

On the heels of that comment came another, louder, primarily for Ellis's benefit: "Hey, Davis, I know you're tired of beating on the rest of us, but isn't this a little ridiculous?"

Finally, and most specifically: "Commander, any last words?"

Each remark was followed by boisterous laughter.

Sense of humor intact, Ellis addressed the crowd peering down at her. "Not smart, trying to make me angry. Isn't Lieutenant Davis in enough trouble here?"

"Not if he manages to stay awake," someone replied to more laughter.

With little in the way of live entertainment on base, word of the match had spread at light speed. Ellis noted with satisfaction that the viewing balcony, designed to hold ten people, was crowded with twice that. All were hoping and expecting for her to get a thorough ass-whipping. And, of course, there was the betting, with Davis being the heavy favorite. One objective accomplished: For a few welcome moments, colonists would be preoccupied with thoughts of something other than the water shortage.

Noticeably absent was Stewart, busily prepping the treatment room. Although assured that the combatants would be protected, she knew better: The risk of bodily injury was mitigated, not alleviated, by the padded headgear, open-finger boxing gloves, and the groin and breast protectors customarily required in mixed martial arts matches.

The garb worn for the match befitted each contestant's training and personal preference. Ellis wore her *judogi*—a loose-fitting pair of white short pants and a short robe cinched at the waist with the black sash emblematic of her judo rank. Davis filled out a sleeveless tee and boxing shorts. Both were barefoot. Besides what went on between the ears, feet would be their most potent weapons.

Ellis sized up the room, an organo-formed chamber measuring ten square meters and five square meters high. Exercise equipment had been removed, leaving only a durable mat covering the floor and the bottom half of all four walls. A meter-wide sliding door directly opposite the viewing gallery could be activated by proximity motion or verbal command. Reaching that opening and passing through it first made winning this contest much more difficult. Davis, superior in size and strength, could force his way to it, conceivably dragging her along with him. The possibility of her doing the same was slim to none. He probably realized that when he suggested the idea. Clever bastard.

Ellis had learned never to underestimate an opponent. Not a problem, she thought, sizing up the formidable-looking Davis as they faced off in the center of the room. A lesser-known addendum to the same rule was never to assume an intelligent opponent, and her opponent was undoubtedly that, would underestimate you. "The odds are four to one," he advised. "I would say no more than two to one is appropriate."

"Favoring me or you?" Ellis asked, causing Davis to grin.

Her best opportunity was to take him down before he reached the exit, then immobilize him with a joint lock or stranglehold. Either technique could inflict permanent injury, but unbearable pain came first. Invariably, a subdued opponent signals defeat by using a free hand to tap their opponent's body or the floor before they pass out. Often, the great equalizer was combatants' tolerance for pain, which had nothing to do with gender, size, or physical strength.

The first steps Davis took, predictably, were toward the exit. He had no intention of going there. Turning back, he lifted his right knee high in front of his body, pivoted off his left leg, and sent his right instep snapping straight at Ellis: A roundhouse kick, blurringly fast, but she was faster, ducking barely in time as his foot passed a centimeter over her head. If the blow had connected, it would have been lights out. Instead, she had learned something important about her opponent, accurately measuring his kick's reach and speed.

Her next lesson wouldn't be as painless.

He unleashed a left jab/right cross combination at Ellis's head, followed by a left jab, left hook, and right cross to the body. The punches were narrowly evaded by stepping backward or parrying to the side. Except one.

Davis's hand speed was even faster than his legs. A sweeping hook, although partially deflected, rocked her backward, sending a bolt of pain shooting up her side.

A satisfied hoot erupted from the spectator gallery. "You'll have to do better," Davis prodded. "The bleacher seats are getting restless."

"And I had thought them so patient," Ellis responded. She had yet to attempt overtly aggressive judo techniques, passing on several opportunities to use her skill at *atemi*, the focused body blows that would blunt Davis's attack. Instead, she would follow a fundamental tenet of her discipline by maintaining a defensive posture, exploiting the moment when her opponent was off-balance.

There were physical and psychological ways of inducing that moment. She had determined the range of Davis's dangerous roundhouse kicks by repeatedly positioning herself just out of reach. Now, she intentionally moved a few centimeters closer, too small an adjustment to be perceived as deliberate, yet sufficient to be detected by Davis and invite his attack. She would have to be quick, anticipating and moving with the brute force of his leg. It would be his right leg, but she was prepared for a diversion, prudently keeping her hands up to protect her face until the last possible moment.

Davis took the bait. Crouching, then turning and taking a half step *forward*, she met his kick, slapping her right hand onto the front of his rising knee and using her left arm to wrap behind and secure the lower part of the same leg. The top of Davis's foot, aimed at her head, was now wedged against her shoulder. Bending forward at the waist and twisting, she torqued the leg at the knee, redirecting his momentum, sending him off-balance and crashing down hard onto his stomach.

"Holy shit," someone shouted, "when's the last time you've seen Davis taken down!"

Followed by, "Hey, Davis, you need some help in there?!"

Only now, there weren't as many in the audience laughing.

A second fundamental martial arts tenet is understanding that your opponent is only as strong as his weakest point. It was the principle behind *kansetsu-waza*—the joint locking techniques of which Ellis had become a master. A minor repositioning of her hands on Davis's leg would instantly put him in an *ashi-hishigi*, the ankle lock. An appropriate application of pressure (it was surprising how little was needed) would compel him to tap out.

Win this battle, Ellis thought to herself, lose the war.

She deliberately released her hold.

No one noticed the missed opportunity. Even Davis couldn't be sure if Ellis's failure to act was intentional. As they separated, he rolled onto his side and defensively delivered a straight–leg kick up and into her shoulder. The kick was more of a reflex, but Ellis, crouching and leaning in, took the full force of the blow. Only the combatants heard the popping noise as her shoulder dislocated, an excruciating injury, but everyone could see Ellis's arm dangling horribly at her side. It took every gram of her self-discipline to sublimate the pain.

A hush came over the viewing gallery. "Let's get you to Treatment Bay," Davis, visibly disturbed, was heard to say. He had no intention of causing harm.

"Can't disagree," Ellis managed to utter through clenched teeth.

She had the presence of mind to ensure the man was first to exit through the fitness room door.

***

Davis and Anderson had agreed that a poker game using an actual physical deck of playing cards was a good way to bypass Ellis's month-long suspension of rec room privileges. Four accomplices had joined them in one of the tech's living quarters.

The game was not entertaining without some form of betting. On commerce-forsaken Murkor, where currency was absent, a suitable substitute had been found: Shot-sized, consumable spheres of alcohol dubbed *Nanos*. Lightweight and convenient (no bulky packaging to transport and discard, no serving container to wash), the item could be found in every mining colony beyond Earth's Moon.

"One more time, let me get this straight," Schulman, new to the game, said. "Browns are 151 proof rum, reds are ten-year-old scotch, and clears are vodka. Browns are worth two reds, and reds are two of the clear; therefore, one brown is worth four clear."

"Hate for there to be any doubt as to which of these little beauties is which," Anderson joked, popping a brown sphere in his mouth for the fifth time that evening. "Yup, brownies are rum," he happily commented as the outer coating dissolved. "You got it right, Shule. Glad to provide confirmation."

"In that case, I'll wager two browns," Schulman submitted, pushing them into the center of the table.

"A good bet. A mighty good bet," commented Imholtz. "I'm perceiving a high level of confidence in you. Totally counterfeit, of course. I raise you one red."

Anderson, who was dealing, watched as two players, Kreechum and Davis, folded by throwing their cards into the center of the table. "What about you, Coop?" he said, talking to Jess Cooper, the sergeant who had spoken up at the morning meeting.

"I'm out."

"I call," Anderson stated. "Leaves just the three of us, Shule. What do you have? Or do you know?"

"Two pair. Tens and fours."

"No good," Imholtz replied. "Queens and threes."

"Sorry, gentlemen," Anderson said, flipping over his cards. "Three sixes. Read 'em and weep."

"Speaking of weeping," Kreechum said, "how *is* Ellis?"

"Hey, give her credit," Cooper objected. "Weeping is the one thing she did *not* do. Davis'll tell you. I was with him in the treatment room. Doc said her humerus was knocked clear out of the ball joint. You could see the head of the bone bulging beneath the skin."

"Okay, okay, we get the picture," Imholtz, flinching, remarked.

"Thinking back on it," Cooper continued, "wasn't it the same injury, worse, that Maxwell suffered when the stupid bastard fell off the harvester? Max's a tough fucker, but *he* whimpered like a baby until Stewart dosed him up, but good. But there wasn't a peep out of the commander, even when Doc popped the bone back into place. Doc says she's expected to make a rapid recovery."

"Yeah, thanks for the fuckin' medical update," Anderson sneered as he swallowed another Nano. "And you can cut out the *commander* bullshit—she ain't listening in."

"No, but I am," Davis advised in a low, firm voice. He had remained relatively quiet since the match.

"Do I detect a change of attitude since Ellis put him on his ass?" Kreechum interjected before Anderson could manufacture his own insult.

"Just for the record, it was on his stomach," Schulman observed, trying to lighten the conversation.

Davis ignored Schulman. "That goes for you, too, Kreechum," he said. "It's *Commander* Ellis from now on."

"Yeah, whatever you say," the IMC foreman responded. A furtive glance sideways at Cooper had made it clear that he had one less ally: The sergeant would take his cues from his superior officer.

Anderson wasn't buying any of it. "So, what's this? She calls all the shots? We abandon the mining? Turn tail and run?"

"Don't push it, Ed," Davis warned. "You're in no condition to."

"What the fuck?" Anderson slurred. "You give up drinking, too?"

"I won't be tearing up any more rec rooms. Neither will you."

"Meaning what? Privileges are restored starting tomorrow, ain't they?"

"I didn't win," Davis stated matter-of-factly.

"What the hell are you talking about?" Anderson said, slamming his fist on the table.

"She should have won that match," Davis said.

"What?! Is that what she's claiming?"

"Just the opposite. Only I know otherwise."

"You're confusing the shit out of me," Anderson said.

"Me, too—and I'm sober," Imholtz added. "Twenty people saw you walk out that door first."

"Don't you get it?" Davis said, staring at Anderson. "I can't prove it, but she wanted to lose so I would be responsible for our punishment. In the process, she had her arm torn out of the socket by making an evasive move she would never do. I'm not repaying her confidence in me by shirking my duty. We busted up the damn rec room. Privileges stayed denied. That's for both of us until further notice."

Anderson, far along to being drunk, sat sullen and silent. Reaction came from a different quarter.

"Hell, Ed," Kreechum snickered, aiming to drive a wedge between Anderson and Davis, "with a friend like that, who needs an enemy?"

"Don't be a dick, Kreechum," Schulman said, his anger surprising everyone, including himself.

"Just saying—"

"I know what you're saying, Kreech."

"Yeah, well, none of this bullshit matters," the foreman said. "Ore production has come to a fucking halt, *and* we are almost out of water. Tell me, what the hell is being done about that?"

"I'd cut her some slack," Schulman said. "There's more to our new CO than we've given credit."

"Blah, blah, blah, are we here to play cards, or what?" Imholtz complained. "Davis, you've got the deal."

***

It came as something of a revelation to Ellis just how modern, almost state-of-the-art, Zenith's medical facilities were. That said, advancements such as auto-surgery, bio-replacement, gene-matched drugs, and others were still unable to replace a skilled physician, and Stewart was undoubtedly that. Now, hours after her traumatic injury, Ellis was experiencing no discomfort and had regained mobility in her arm and shoulder. In a couple of days, she would be completely healed, the last vestiges of her physical injury to be temporarily outlived by the memory of the pain she experienced.

She would, however, never forget the look of confusion, dismay, and amazement displayed on Davis's face. In some respects, it was almost comical how much emotion he showed while she was busily masking hers. Admittedly, he did have a lot to process in a very short time: Why she hadn't taken advantage of her superior position. Dismay at having unintentionally caused her injury. How, despite the pain, she had remained totally composed.

Later, while immobilized and receiving treatment, Ellis overheard two techs talking. "It took *cojones* (ironic, them using the Spanish word) to square off against that big bastard."

Not really, she had answered to herself, especially when you're a *Hachidan*, an eight-degree black belt.

The techs were fooled, but not Davis. After processing what happened (to his credit, it didn't take him long), he began questioning whether he had won the match. Of course, he won, she informed him. Wasn't it his rule that whoever passed through the door first was declared the victor? Had he ever specified that victory was predicated upon one person exerting *physical* superiority over the other? No. If they chose, one person could have pushed the other through the open fitness room door.

Succumbing to the logic and spirit of her argument, he had responded in kind. If he were to be acknowledged as the winner, if it was up to him to determine his and Anderson's punishment for their drunken behavior, then he was not obligated to reduce that punishment. For the present, he was disinclined to do so.

It was hard to imagine a better outcome. Walking back Davis's and Anderson's punishment would have made her appear weak and indecisive to those already forming such an opinion. By having the "*cojones*" to face a physically intimidating man, then finding a subtle and suitable way to lose to him, she had shown flexibility from a position of strength. She had won him over, perhaps some of the others too, by refusing to use superior force. It was a general principle that had wider application to Nadir's relationship with Zenith and, expanding the thought, to their respective governments back on Varian and Earth.

She was playing with abstractions. Time could be better spent finding out who she could rely on in a crisis besides the five military personnel under her command. Maybe Schulman and a few of the female IMC techs? Certainly not Kreechum or Anderson or most of the other IMC workers. They had come to Murkor seeking fortune and would refuse to leave here empty-handed. Kreechum and Company had deduced how weak her support was back on Varian. They might risk the penalty for violating the orders of a base CO by secretly initiating a move against Nadir.

Eliminating their reasons for making such a move was paramount. To that end, she had hopes of a rapprochement with her counterpart, Andrés Garcia, at Nadir. It was hard to imagine what he was contemplating at this moment. Was he approachable or afflicted with the same intractable mindset as those who had ordered her to Murkor?

Almost forgotten, for it seemed unrelated to more pressing concerns, was the mishap in Tube Z784C. Jensen had been reticent to discuss the incident, worried she would be deemed unfit. A hardened IMC tech would do anything to prevent their work assignment from being curtailed. It meant giving up the chance of production bonuses, no matter how remote earning them now seemed.

Examination of several disparate pieces of information, including mission time logs and a partial tube network diagram, had made Jensen's story even more intriguing. The tech spent an exceedingly long time unconscious in Murkor's low-oxygen atmosphere with no lasting ill effects. Very strange. Having no desire to increase the trepidation crews felt when entering the tubes, she decided, for the time being, to keep this to herself.

Given time and opportunity, she would directly acquaint herself with what Jensen and others felt here. Until then, she refused to doubt their personal experience. Not when her own transcendental meditations took her mind to a place few would appreciate. What she had told the tech, and it had thrown the headstrong woman off-stride, was that there was little the imagination could conjure that didn't have the possibility of becoming a reality.

It could also be said that people have competing realities.

8 WORSE THAN BAD

UHHMMMFAHH-PHANNGAHFAA!

Damned distracting, Comandante Garcia remarked to no one but himself. The sounds erupting from the nearby fumaroles, now clearly discernible on all three of Nadir's levels, were louder and more frequent than ever. Sitting alone in his confining cabin, he wondered why, with so few days left in a long career, everything was conspiring to turn to shit. Even the damn coffee he was drinking tasted insipid.

Following her harrowing (and largely inexplicable) experience in Tube N119, Amanda insisted that the surest way for her frayed nerves to be soothed could best be found later that evening in the security of his private cabin. The suggestion, he well knew, was another shallow pretense, but his reply had been awkward and hesitant. He regretted not forcefully saying 'no.' There was also a strong possibility that Marianna had overheard the exchange, as brief as it was. Nadir's physician would have seen his lack of resolve and, being perceptive almost to a fault, would have comprehended the reason behind it. Self-doubt, and now he was wallowing in it, is particularly ill-suited to a person with leadership responsibilities.

Bigger problems loomed, threatening to overwhelm. A harried and dejected-looking Carlos now approached him. Before a word was spoken, his senses told him that the engineer's efforts to improve their breathing air had failed.

"My report won't make your day," Carlos said, crestfallen, the confidence he displayed a mere day ago having vanished.

"Then best be out with it," Garcia responded, trying and failing to keep irritability out of his voice.

"Air quality…the oxygen concentrator is not doing a good job of removing excess carbon dioxide…"

"Is that why you're so glum? Can it be so bad?"

"It's worse than bad," Carlos answered. "Oxygen levels are falling."

"*Slowly*," Garcia stated, as if saying so would make it fact. He received a despairing shake of the head. "No, what then? What has changed since your last report?"

"The Nexus is behaving like we aren't here at all, almost as if six humans aren't occupying the base."

If Carlos hadn't looked so fatigued and worried, Garcia would have thought he was joking. "My good friend," he said, "you have worked too hard to solve this. Have you slept?"

"Why else would the Nexus shut down the carbon dioxide scrubber?" Carlos continued, talking as if to convince himself. "And now it's starting to do the same with the oxygen concentrator, powering *it* down, reducing the amount of oxygen it extracts from the planet's atmosphere. There's no other explanation possible. It's all traceable back to the invasive nanoparticles—"

"And not rising carbon dioxide levels?" Garcia asked, attempting to channel Carlos away from an unproven accusation to more actionable information.

"No," Carlos insisted, put on the defensive. "Both the oxygen concentrator and the scrubber receive instructions from the Nexus. I tell you, the Nexus has been subverted."

"Have you tried reversing the scrubber bypass?"

"Done. No effect."

Garcia searched for suggestions but found none. "Time-wise, what's the bottom line?"

"Say again?" Carlos asked.

Garcia impatiently repeated the question in a louder voice. "The bottom line, time-wise, what's the bottom line?"

"I wish I knew. We're headed below the nineteen percent oxygen level Mariana warned us about. I can extrapolate the rate oxygen is consumed and, and...what was I saying? That's it... oxygen used, and carbon dioxide produced. And, oh yes, there's the small losses caused by the misaligned exterior panels. How can I predict what the damned Nexus will do next?"

"I need a better answer."

"Maybe we have a few days before stabilizing at Murkor's nine percent oxygen."

"And the synergistic effect of carbon dioxide levels rising simultaneously?" Garcia asked, alarmed at the time constraint.

"Shouldn't you ask Mariana, comandante?" Carlos said. "You know, her being the physician and all?"

Garcia considered responding with a rebuke, but, no… perhaps it was a reasonable question. "You're right, you're right. It's best put to Mariana. I intend to consult her. I guess we aren't thinking straight. Get some rest. When you resume work, start over. Go through everything again, every cubic centimeter. Overlook nothing, no matter how trivial. Tell me of any new developments." He held back from agreeing that a corrupted Nexus was the root cause of the ESS problems. Despite Carlos's protestation, some other explanation must be found.

"I *will* solve this," Carlos promised, feeling accountable for the worry and doubt so plainly visible on the comandante's face. Turning to leave, he stopped to scowl at the drinking vessel he had been sipping from. "You'd think Unión could provide us with good Manizales coffee. I bet the damned chancros at Zenith drink better than this."

"Perhaps they lack water to make coffee," Garcia said, trying to smile.

"We can only hope."

"Get out of here. Get rest. That's an order."

After Carlos departed, Garcia chastised himself for failing to offer more words of encouragement.

He then contemplated how and when to evacuate Nadir safely.

***

Carlos had convinced himself that Ellis, at the behest of the Coalition, was responsible for Nadir's emergency. The inability to counter that threat meant he was failing Garcia just as he had helplessly stood by while his father lost everything at the hands of the same enemy. This subconscious association greatly influenced his approach to solving the simple technical problem causing the ESS/Nexus malfunction. Although he had correctly surmised that the Nexus was responsible for shutting down the carbon dioxide scrubber, he was blinded as to why it would issue what only appeared to be an illogical command.

The Nexus made decisions based on real-time information supplied by scores of detectors, historical operational data, and a cache of previously infused technical knowledge. Its programming specific to carbon dioxide levels was to assure that both upper *and* lower thresholds, those amounts determined to be deleterious to human health, were never exceeded.

It is commonly known that breathing in too much carbon dioxide is detrimental. Outside those in the medical field, it is less known that *too little* carbon dioxide (hypocapnia) can be fatal. This condition rarely results from poor ambient air quality rather than some underlying physiological cause. That distinction wasn't the Nexus's concern.

The carbon dioxide detector in the ESS's main air plenum had passed multiple inspections.

(Independent air samples had confirmed the readings it was actively displaying.) The detector's defect was more insidious. It was erroneously signaling Nexus that carbon dioxide levels were far *below* the threshold required for respiration. At first, the Nexus reacted cautiously, ramping down the scrubber to *increase* the amount of carbon dioxide in the air. Unaffected, the faulty detector continued transmitting erroneous readings. In response, the Nexus took the scrubber off-line even as carbon dioxide levels increased.

Carlos's clever attempt to fix the problem only worsened matters. Redirecting plenum air to the oxygen concentrator to remove carbon dioxide was an action the Nexus was unfamiliar with and, therefore, confusing. Unable to reconcile several streams of conflicting data ("low" carbon dioxide, reduction in oxygen produced by the concentrator, reduced volume of air passing through the ESS's plenum), Nexus concluded that Nadir was unoccupied. Overcompensating, it curtailed oxygen intake from Murkor's atmosphere by deactivating the oxygen concentrator.

Another pair of experienced eyes, those not looking through a fog of hatred, would have discovered the original defect and swapped out the faulty carbon dioxide detector. Problem solved.

No one else on base had the expertise to diagnose the defect, and all Garcia could do (which did nothing to bolster his flagging confidence) was to coax Carlos into looking at the ESS/Nexus problem in a different light. Given the engineer's current state of mind, the prospects of that happening were exceedingly unlikely.

***

Shortly after maneuvering Amanda Cruz into discussing her failed sexual overtures toward Garcia, Roya Allawi sought a second opinion on the matter. An opportunity presented itself when she and Marianna Perez met over lunch in the L2 area designated for such purposes.

"Yesterday, I had an enlightening chat with Amanda," Roya began.

"You won't be violating any confidences?" Mariana replied, not particularly caring if the answer was "yes." She'd insist on hearing it anyway.

"A confidence on this base?" Roya responded. "Is there such a thing?"

"Very few," Mariana agreed. "Not with you and me around."

"This isn't one either. If it were, I'd still be disinclined to keep what I learned to myself. It concerns Amanda's dealings with the comandante."

"You have my attention," Mariana remarked. "Maybe it'll shed some light on his recent behavior. I'm worried about him."

"You and I both. What Amanda volunteered to tell me explains some of it. Putting it bluntly, she has her claws in him and won't let go."

"Did you ask her to?" Mariana knew that Roya's affinity for Garcia made her capable of defending him in any way she thought necessary.

"Not in so many words. She appeared blissfully unaware of my hints."

"And he can't extricate himself?"

Roya shrugged. "There's more. Earlier, I overheard them talking. She seems intent on cornering him."

"Can you blame her?" Mariana said, looking carefully at her friend.

"What do you mean?"

"You never get lonely for a man's company?"

"Of course. It'll wait. Has to."

"It has to," Mariana repeated. The reply was perfunctory, as if disappointed. "I've been here as long as anyone. Sometimes, I feel that I'm only one look, innuendo, or casual touch away from doing exactly what Amanda is trying."

"But you don't," Roya replied. "And if you did find yourself in a similar circumstance, you'd know when to back away. Amanda hasn't a clue. Maybe she never will."

"Okay," Mariana said, "but I'm not sure what we could do about it. Should we be meddling—"

"Meddling in what?" Gustavo interjected, slumping into an empty seat as two purposely blank stares greeted him. "I see…I had no intention of interrupting." On the table, the topic for a safer conversation was two unfinished plates of food. "Not hungry, ladies?"

"You know, Gustavo," Mariana said, "you have a talent for pointing out the obvious."

"Just one of my many. Or is that obvious, too?"

"Be careful," Roya replied, "you're starting to sound like Carlos."

"He'll be flattered by the comparison." Gustavo turned to Mariana. "Would you mind dispensing a little doctorly advice? I hesitate to ask, seeing you got up on the wrong side of the bedside manner."

"She's not a psychiatrist," Roya commented.

"Seriously."

"What's troubling you?" Mariana asked. "Don't say lack of energy. That's the air we're breathing."

"Not that. I do a lot of reading. Until two days ago, I had no difficulty seeing number ten font. Now I'm having trouble making out eleven."

Mariana immediately became more attentive. "Is there a difference in acuity between eyes? Any headaches? Do you see halos around lights?"

"No difference between eyes. No halos. Sorry, what was the other question?"

"I forgot it myself," Mariana said. "Oh, yes, headaches. Any headaches?"

"Minor—"

"Likely from eyestrain, maybe the air we've been breathing. Stop by later for an optical exam. Lacking proper instruments, I can do little more than rule in or out the obvious."

"Understood," Gustavo said. "But I don't recall you saying that low oxygen causes headaches."

"Didn't I? It does. That's not our problem, though."

"Sure is," Gustavo insisted.

Mariana looked to Roya for help.

"Gustavo apparently knows something we don't," Roya said.

"That would be a first."

"Neither of you has been informed?" Gustavo asked. Upon receiving two shakes of the head, he explained the latest troubles with Nadir's atmospherics. The moment's urgency had yet to sink in when Garcia and Amanda stepped off the staircase that spiraled up from the crews' private quarters on L1. The fact that the two were together indicated nothing, but Mariana and Roya exchanged speculative glances—noticed and outwardly ignored by Amanda.

"Good, we're assembled," Garcia said as he and Amanda took places at the table. "Carlos is preoccupied at the moment. For now, I think it best that he not be distracted by what we're about to discuss."

"Gustavo just filled us in," Roya said.

"My apologies," Gustavo said. "I should have told them sooner."

"No, it is I who have been remiss in communicating the gravity of our situation," Garcia insisted. "I am no longer persuaded that whatever has affected the ESS can be rectified. I'm contemplating some very unpalatable choices—"

"We've never seen an engineering problem stump Carlos," Gustavo said.

"True enough," Garcia agreed. "Except if it traces to a subverted Nexus, there may be no remedy at his disposal."

"Zenith conspiracy or not, do you doubt that's where the defect lies?"

Garcia pondered this for a long moment. "Yes. To the extent that I asked Amanda to perform a separate air sample analysis—"

"And it confirms precisely what Carlos has previously reported," Nadir's chemist interrupted, her irritable manner suggesting to the other two women that Garcia continued resisting her advances.

"Can the oxygen loss be attributed to the misaligned exterior panels?" Roya asked. "We know that pressure loss is taxing the system."

"You're joking, I hope," Amanda said. "Selectively purging more oxygen than nitrogen?"

As an accomplished scientist, Roya knew this was not a reasonable possibility. She did not try to cover up her mistake. "Pretty dumb of me," she said.

"None of us are thinking clearly," Garcia observed. "Mariana? What's ahead for us?"

"We're already feeling the first effects of hypoxia and carbon dioxide poisoning. As conditions worsen, there will be impairments to our physical and mental abilities. Below fifteen percent oxy, we'll have difficulty putting on our shoes. That is if we can even remember where to find them."

"When I pressed Carlos," Garcia said, "he projected oxygen loss at somewhere between one-half and one percent per day. Under the circumstances, it would be wise to make important decisions now."

Mariana nodded in agreement, thought a moment, and then said: "I have a few stimulants that can alleviate symptoms. A short-term solution at best."

Garcia turned to Gustavo. "Are there any Unión vessels within six days of Murkor?"

"None known. Our resupply ship is at least ten days out."

"Oxygen is just below eighteen percent now," Garcia said, struggling to remember the exact number. Having difficulty projecting outcomes in his head, he fixated on Mariana. As usual, she grasped what he was thinking.

"Is that survivable?" Mariana said. "With great difficulty, comandante. But what if Carlos is wrong? There's no margin of error. What if the oxygen loss accelerates? And there's the debris field to consider. The supply ship could arrive a day or two too late. Or never. Even with no delay, we will be in bad shape waiting."

"Then I see no other reasonable alternative," a resigned Garcia responded. "I am forced to request assistance from Zenith."

"And if Carlos is correct," Amanda protested, "we played right into Ellis's hands."

"And what in hell would you have us do!?" asked Roya.

"You heard. We have sufficient time. We wait Ellis out."

"I see that hypoxia is affecting some of us more than others," Gustavo observed.

"How can you jest?" Amanda demanded.

"How can you not?" Gustavo replied. "And who's jesting?"

"That's enough!" Garcia insisted. "I can—I will defer contacting Zenith for a few more hours. I should give Carlos at least that much time. Let's listen to what he has to report later this evening. After dinner."

"Sure," Gustavo said, once more focusing, or trying to, on the two barely touched plates of food resting on the table in front of him. "If anyone has an appetite to hear it."

Conversation turned to more mundane matters.

No one, including Garcia, fully apprehended what would befall them.

That would come soon enough.

***

"Where's Gustavo?" Garcia asked hours later, everyone else having collected at the dining table, the only furnishing that could accommodate six people comfortably.

"He asked that we start without him, Roya answered. "Mumbled something important came up."

"More important than us asphyxiating?" Mariana said.

"That's not going to happen," Garcia protested, grimacing at the remark.

A look around the table belied his optimism. They were starting to look as tired as he felt. In comparing experiences, the typical complaint was lethargy and reduced appetite. Loss of mental acuity, which they all marginally labored under, was more challenging to quantify. Gustavo and Amanda complained of blurry vision and Roya of impaired hearing.

Earlier in the day, Mariana ordered physical exams for the crew. The limited tests she could perform revealed ailments typical of mild hypoxia/elevated carbon dioxide, although there was some unexpected variation in symptom severity and onset time among the crew. She attributed discrepancies to the human body's ability to respond differently to the same affliction.

Five hours had elapsed since the previous meeting. Carlos had nothing favorable to report except a slight, unaccountable decrease in the rise of carbon dioxide. That only made him more adamant in assigning blame.

"I did exactly as you asked, comandante," Carlos contended. "I went through every subsystem and detector again. There is no defect in ESS. The answer lies with the Nexus."

"Then we must request assistance," Garcia said. "What's to be gained by delay?"

"Because I'll find an end-run around the damn thing," Carlos replied, refusing to relent. Seeing no response to his optimism, except, perhaps, in Amanda's face, he exclaimed: "Wait a second! Is this meeting about begging Zenith for help?!"

Garcia was about to respond when Gustavo's arrival was preceded by the rattling sound of his footfalls on the spiral staircase leading from the lower level. He seldom looked angry. He did now.

"Those Coalition bastards tunneled into our mindstor!"

"What?!" Carlos shouted. "I told you—"

"How did they find their way in?" Garcia asked, cutting Carlos off.

"By latching onto our CAM-L's com signal the last time we were out and about. I'm afraid they acquired the data residing on its memory."

"That gives them," Roya said, "the location of every water resource in our exclusion zone!"

Gustavo nodded in agreement. "And that breach is the one I'm sure of. I suspect they used our internal transmissions to access the base's primary mindstor. It's anybody's guess what they obtained once there."

"You see what's happening?" Carlos implored. "They expected us to come crawling. We didn't, so now they're getting desperate. It's just a matter of time before they'll use the information they stole to make an incursion."

"One problem at a time," Garcia cautioned, gesturing for Carlos to be silent. "Was an attempt made to compromise any of our operating systems?"

"None that I could determine," Gustavo replied. "Perhaps they didn't have time. The intrusion could have only been during transmissions back to base. They also have to decipher what they obtained."

"So, what put you on to this?" Garcia asked.

"Zenith did."

"What?" Garcia said, wondering if he was hearing right.

"I was performing a routine check of our security protocols when a solitary word unexpectedly appeared on the view screen and faded away—like it never existed. I traced the source backward—"

"Are you going to make us ask?" Amanda protested.

Gustavo hesitated, glancing in Carlos's direction, then Garcia's.

"Venimos."

The word hung in the still air like a cloud of sarin gas.

"Fucking chancro bastards!" Carlos screamed, rising out of his chair. "Well, let them come! Let them come!"

"Quiet yourself," Garcia ordered. Except there was no heart in the command and no remonstration in his voice as he watched the young engineer, shaking in anger, kick back his chair and storm to the room's viewport, where he silently stood looking out.

Searching for the enemy he despised and finding only a lifeless, forlorn landscape.

"What do you see, Carlos?" Garcia said knowingly, coming behind him to place a reassuring hand on his shoulder. "Are you seeing our future somewhere out there or your past?"

"I see—I see both..."

"Come back to the table," Garcia urged, leading him away. "We have the present to deal with and can only do so when we're all together."

After they were seated, after their pent-up anger toward Zenith and Coalition had been vented, an exhausted silence set in. Five expectant faces stared intently at Garcia, hoping he could make sense of what was happening to them. Waiting for direction.

His crew, Garcia thought. Was Gustavo breathing heavily? Probably the effect of running up from the L1 com hub in the poor air… and Carlos, eyes glazed, sublimating his anger… Amanda, massaging and flexing the fingers of her right hand…

"Comandante," Mariana whispered into the silence.

"Gazing through the wrong end of a telescope," Garcia mouthed, half to himself yet expecting to be understood.

"Comandante?" Mariana repeated, trying to focus his attention.

"The message," Garcia finally explained, shaking his head in doubt. "I'm thinking about the message. Is it really from Ellis? We know nothing of her—"

"But why would anyone taunt us this way?" Roya inquired.

"Simple," Amanda responded. "To goad us into retaliating."

Roya suppressed a laugh. "Retaliate? Us? How?"

"They're provoking us in ways we can't prove. Why? So that when they request access to our water, we refuse them. They use that as justification to steal what they want for their mining operation."

"Let me get this straight," Roya said, her suppressed laugh becoming a scowl. "You're really saying we should just avoid the complication and give them the water now? By the way, that's fine by me."

"Don't twist my words; that's not what I'm saying," Amanda insisted, reaching for and accidentally spilling the last traces of her coffee. "Comandante, wasn't it you who suggested we wait for Ellis to reveal her intentions before we alert Unión? What more do we need?"

"What we need," Garcia declared, watching a tiny rivulet of coffee meander its way across the table's surface, "is to find an acceptable way off this base."

"Carlos may yet find a solution," Amanda said, patting the engineer's arm. "Besides, if forced to leave, let's do it on our terms. We can hold out for the return of our resupply ship."

"We've been over that," Garcia countered. "The wait's too risky."

"I have a slightly less distasteful alternative," Roya volunteered.

"Let's hear it," Garcia said.

"A C5 shuttle can accommodate—what? Five people?"

"Yes, five, pilot included," Garcia answered. "Seven would be exceedingly uncomfortable. Why ask? There are no—oh, I see. You're recommending we contact the same vessel that conveyed Ellis here?"

"I am. The vessel may still be within hailing distance."

"There's little chance of that," Gustavo observed. "She may have jump-drived. If not, figure three days for the ship to decelerate and return, depending on whatever g-force the pilot chooses to withstand. And if our message arrives during the pilot's sleep cycle—"

"She's a vessel operating under Coalition contract," Amanda interrupted. "The same one that may have dumped a nanocloud on our head. Do you believe the pilot would accede to our request for aid? Why would he take on the risk when help from Zenith is just one hundred kilometers away?"

"Because the overland trek between bases is at the top end of our CAM-L's operating range," Roya said. "The shuttle pilot would realize it's a perilous undertaking. As for the other arguments? I'll concede the odds don't favor us. Still, it's better than being houseguests of that bitch—damn it, Carlos, now you've got me saying it—I mean, Commander Ellis."

Staring into the thinning air, Carlos contributed little to the discussion. "I'd like the additional time," he said in a subdued voice. "I can solve it. I know I can solve it."

Garcia had a tough choice to make. The most prudent course of action—contacting Ellis and requesting immediate assistance—was also the most repugnant. Even if she weren't the mastermind behind recent events, her superiors on Varian, learning that Nadir was to be unoccupied, would order her to seize control of their EZ. In short order, Unión would respond in force.

Garcia, meeting Carlos's hopeful stare, committed to a decision. "One thing at a time. Gustavo, I shall compose a message for you to transmit to the Coalition vessel."

***

An active imagination can be a blessing or a curse, a weary Garcia thought, staring at the faded brown stain directly over his bed. Carlos had repaired the plumbing leak months ago, but the stain could not be painted over. Amanda had seen the mark first. Lying naked on her back.

He had decided to welcome her when she came to him later that night. Why should he treat her differently from any other crew member, male or female, by excluding her from his console? He would use the opportunity to defuse the tension between them. No harm would be done if they were together one last time.

A damnable lie, he confessed to himself. It was a decision made in a moment of weakness, knowing full well that he'd be at a distinct disadvantage once they were alone. It is easier and far more commonplace to lie to oneself than others.

There she was, early, softly knocking. Struggling off the bed, he went to the door, hoping to have the willpower to send her away. He was surprised to discover that it was not Amanda standing in the opening.

For a second, neither party spoke until Mariana mysteriously said, "Congratulations. I think you just set a record."

"It's infrequent," Garcia managed to say, "that I don't comprehend your meaning—"

"A record for the sheer number of expressions that could pass over a man's face in one second. Let's see. Surprise. Confusion. Curiosity. And, maybe, disappointment?"

"Ahh, then," Garcia said, recovering and smiling. "You omitted one: Relief—to see you."

"I see it now," Marianna professed, making a point of looking directly into his eyes. "It was there all along, hiding behind a wall of worry. Maybe this will take your mind off things?"

Mariana held up a small box. Garcia recognized it immediately as *Dendrite*, an enjoyable, low-tech mind game. "We haven't played in weeks," he said.

"I can't think of a better time than now," Mariana said, reciting the excuse rehearsed to justify her late-night presence. "How well we play shall tell me the current state of our cognitive abilities. I shall leave now if you're tired or—"

"No, you must stay," Garcia insisted, vaguely aware of the motive underlying Marianna's visit. Mutual respect and affection alleviated the need for an apparent declaration between them.

Moments later, hunched over a game board placed on a cleared table, two close crewmates found a respite from their cares. Only once did the conversation turn serious.

"What's to become of us?" Mariana asked, looking up.

"Are you frightened?" Garcia asked softly.

"A little. Shall I tell you of a dream?"

"Do you hold faith in them as portents?"

"No. But this felt so real. I dreamt I was watching myself dreaming. That's weird enough. Then my *awake* dreaming self tried to awaken my *dreaming*, dreaming self, and couldn't."

172

"Not sure I understood that. A dream within a dream? I don't know what it means, but you certainly must be well rested."

They were both laughing when a rap was heard at the door.

"It would be impolite to ignore it," Mariana said, knowing who was on the other side.

"My sentiments exactly," Garcia acknowledged, projecting his voice to say, "Enter."

The door slid open. Amanda stood in the hallway, transfixed and speechless, trying hard to process the scene in front of her.

"Would you care to join us?" Garcia entreated.

"I can still think clearly, you know," Amanda, finding her voice, said. She had made her mind up about what the scene meant and, to her credit, was not too far wrong.

"Of course you can," Mariana said. "That's why we're inviting you to come in and play."

"It's late."

"Late? Perhaps so," Mariana responded. "You know how it is when you play a game."

"I'll get Carlos's opinion on the latest air chemistry values," Amanda responded, implying more. "Then call it a night."

When Amanda departed, Garcia glanced at Mariana, trying hard to keep from smiling.

"How many emotions did you see on *her* face?" he inquired.

9 REMEMBERING THE PAST x2

WHAT AN ADRENALINE RUSH!

Lieutenant Brian Davis watched the black-headed gulls gently tip their pointed wings as they floated the updrafts rising from the bluff that plunged perilously close to his side. An invigorating tang from the ocean hissing far below mingled with the scent of balsam firs clinging to the ridge he was ascending. It was all good.

And all an illusion promptly dispelled by a biometric panel suddenly and obtrusively coming to life:

BIOBIKE 2340/Program 241A/Davis
Elapsed time: 55 minutes
Distance: 33.21 km
Heart rate: 178 bpm
Blood Oxygen Saturation: 92.2%
Current Heart rate 51 bpm
Body Fat 5.8%
Cardiovascular Report: No pathology detected

Five minutes later, thirsty as all hell, he was gulping down precisely one-third of his three-liter allotment of drinking water, the precise amount calculated by Base Manager Schulman and ordered by Commander Ellis. To adhere to the restriction, he would have to reduce sweating by eliminating the cardio workout and sticking to a regimen of stretching exercises.

Head tilted back, he let the last few drops of liquid splash on his tongue. For sure, he would never again take water for granted. The recent rationing wasn't nearly half of it. No, it was being confined to live on a planet so parched that not even one damn solitary puddle collected anywhere on its surface. Where the few remaining life forms lived and died in the smelly shadows of the fumaroles. What was the point of a world without water?

He thought of the rec room's scuba diving sim, detailed down to the sound, sight, and sensation of water on skin. It was an artificial divertissement that suffered in comparison to the real thing. What was absent, what could not be quantified or duplicated, was the vibrancy of Earth's sea life that radiated around you. None of Zenith's environmental bio-sims could imitate that indescribable energy. He enjoyed them anyway.

Past tense. They were off-limits, a punishment self-inflicted from being stupid drunk. Ha! Ellis cleverly put the matter in his own hands! He would restore the rec room privileges only when the month assigned had elapsed or Anderson demonstrated an attitude adjustment, whichever came first. He expected it to go full term. His friend was a stubborn fucker. He met his match in the new CO, though.

He had yet to embrace the course of action she seemed intent on. He was, however, finding it easy to like her personally. He'd even use a word he didn't parcel out often: *Respect*. She certainly was different from the prior commanding officer. You rarely had to question Trenchon's orders. There was nothing to question. At least Ellis was making things interesting. Shit, it would be a cold day on Murkor before Trenchon thought of fighting him in front of the entire base. Only Anderson had the guts to do that on equal terms. And her confronting that arrogant a-hole Kreechum was one of the more amusing encounters in recent memory. At the rate she was going, maybe he wouldn't miss rec privileges after all. She'd be dishing out all the real excitement they'd ever need.

Maybe not *all* the excitement he needed. Damn, if only they had met under slightly different circumstances. Like on an entirely different planet, unencumbered by fraternizing rules that officers must follow. It was hard to explain why he found her so damn attractive. Alluring might be a better fit. She was thinner than most. Maybe forty Murkor-kilos soaking wet—he could imagine the wet part—yet the proportions were pleasing. There was an intangible quality to her beingness that was hard to pin down. It was not overtly physical. Perhaps the embodiment of intriguing contradictions? She parsed her words but didn't hold back; she was thin but had a forceful presence; she seemed unassailable, but her eyes didn't look away when conversing.

No, they locked on as if searching for an answer.

If she could read his thoughts, he'd never see the rec room again.

He toweled dry, then cleaned using a waterless compound manufactured by the chem lab. Dressed in uniform, he reflected on how he hadn't seen much of Anderson or half the IMC techs. They were trying to avoid him, especially Anderson, who was still jacked off at having his rec privileges withheld.

There was more to Anderson's absence than Davis knew. The tech had found another way of entertaining himself by attempting to hack into and decipher Nadir's mindstor. Proud of his accomplishment, he nevertheless was forced to conclude that the intelligence gained was not actionable unless shared with the CO. Because she had not sanctioned his efforts, the best way to bridge the gap, or so he believed, was through speaking first with Davis. That involved a fair degree of uncertainty. The relationship between the two men had been built less on similarities in personality and temperament and more on the trying circumstances they found themselves in. They had different worldviews. Both men joked about women, but only Anderson was a misogynist. It followed that the arrival on the base of a strong-willed woman would adversely influence their friendship.

Hoping to work and eat undisturbed, Davis grabbed lunch from the main cafeteria and took it to his quarters. His current assignment was to formulate contingency plans for base evacuation. The least radical scenario left six people behind, the bare minimum needed to ensure Coalition's control of Zenith's EZ. Military personnel would be ordered to stay. Thanks to the absurd dictates of Earth politics, the base would subsist as a remote and useless outpost. The hardest part of it was being unproductive. He'd be just going through the motions, not really living. Gazing out the room's hexagonal viewport, he saw a static panorama devoid of life and promise. The only movement was a barely visible ash plume from a roller that disappeared into the haze.

Nothing out there to dispel feelings of futility and loneliness. If there's someplace south of hell, this is it.

The entry to his quarters softly shimmered. A spoken command, "*clear*," allowed him a one-way view of Anderson sporting an evil grin and flashing an obscene gesture.

"*Enter, ass wipe*," Davis announced, knowing Anderson would hear the words as the portal slid open. His friend, appearing nervously excited, clutched a purple crystal, a CLT, commonly used to copy information to or from any mindstor.

"To what do I owe the displeasure of your company?" Davis asked in greeting.

"To *this,* my part-time friend," Anderson answered, holding the faceted crystal up to shine in the light. "And you shall rue your insults, for I hold the future of Zenith in my hand."

Davis sat back as Anderson pulled up a chair. This can't be good, he thought to himself. He nodded toward the CTL. "I take it *that* is the reason for your recent disappearance?"

"You noticed. I'm touched. It is."

"What type of file?" Davis asked.

"Symbolic. Mostly words, characters, and numbers. A few graphs. It took time to decipher."

"Give me," Davis insisted, extending his hand. The deciphering comment had confirmed his unease. He inserted the CTL into an open slot and wore a pair of view glasses. Leaning back, he let the info stream to the pace of his eye movement on the lens's interior. In five minutes, he had the gist: The location of Nadir's water resources. More problematically, ESS operational data suggested that the base was occupied by fewer than the six mandatory occupants.

"How did you get this?" Davis asked, removing the view glasses and doing his utmost to stay impassive.

"It took considerable patience," Anderson replied. "The hydrological data is from their CAM-L's mindstor, taken from right under their noses during vehicle-to-base transmissions. The rest is from an instantaneous peek into their primary mindstor's memory." Anderson's evil grin returned. "Stupid beaner bastards."

"Very clever," Davis commented, committing himself to volunteering little else. "You found a backdoor in."

"You don't seem too excited by what this could mean," Anderson said, trying to read his friend.

Before Davis could respond, the portal signaled someone's presence: Kreechum, the IMC foreman. He entered, deliberately avoiding eye contact with Anderson.

"Didn't know you had company," Kreechum lied.

"Gentlemen, let's cut the bullshit," Davis said, removing the crystal from the mindstor and holding it up for the IMC foreman to see. "You know."

"Never said I didn't," Kreechum insisted.

Of course, he knew, Davis thought to himself. Anderson had sought out the IMC foreman first. They had conspired to ambush him at the same time.

"Who else has seen this?" Davis asked, although he already had a pretty good idea. They were attempting to undermine Ellis from the bottom up. He was last on their list. "Wait. Let *me* provide the answer. Everyone knows. Everyone, that is, except Commander Ellis, Captain Stewart, and perhaps a handful of others."

Anderson said nothing.

Kreechum, with a scowl on his face, shrugged. "Well, shit, maybe she knows, maybe she don't. Good news travels fast. I tell you what we *do* know. We know the bastards have enough fucking water to run our mining operation for ten years."

"And we know exactly where to find it," Anderson added. "So, are you with us on this?"

Both men looked to Davis.

"I think the CO needs to be informed of this immediately," Davis answered.

"You'll come with us?" Anderson asked.

"I wouldn't miss it," Davis replied. "In fact—"

Davis, motioning for the men to be silent, spoke into the air. "*Connect. Commander Ellis.*"

"Yes, lieutenant?"

"I have Misters Kreechum and Anderson listening in. They're eager to see you about a matter of some importance."

"Namely?" Ellis asked.

"I believe the matter is best handled in person."

"Come now. You with them."

"That was my intention."

Davis entered Ellis's quarters first. Handing her the CTL, which he had retained in his possession, he whispered for only her to hear, "Whatever it takes," quickly followed, louder, by: "Commander, this was just brought to my attention."

Ellis noted that Davis was vigilant. His first remark to her had been cryptic, though it seemed to indicate what she wanted to hear. If she were wrong, the odds against her would be insurmountable. Still, this drama would need to be played out.

She turned her attention to the body language of the other two men opposite her. Kreechum had his jaw set and fists clenched; Anderson, muscles tensed, had his arms tightly folded across his chest. Both were prepared for a confrontation. In canine behavior, Anderson would be the dominant aggressor, Kreechum more likely a fear-biter.

There were three plush chairs in Ellis's office. "Gentlemen, grab seats," she said. Two men complied. Davis did not budge. Another favorable sign, she thought. She concentrated her attention on Anderson.

"I suspect this CLT," she said, casually tossing it on the desk before her, "contains data obtained from Nadir without my prior authorization. I can save us some time. I have already seen it."

"You *what?*" Anderson declared, stunned.

It was precisely the response Ellis expected. On the other hand, Davis's slight hint of a wry grin was not. The man was quick. He had studied her and, in doing so, had caught on that she knew what Anderson and Kreechum were scheming and would face them head-on.

What Davis did next surprised her even more.

Taking two purposeful strides, he placed himself directly behind Kreechum, who had just deposited his considerable bulk in a chair. "Son of a bitch—" the IMC foreman began, attempting to rise in anger.

"Sit your ass back down and listen to what the commander has to say," Davis warned, placing two strong hands on Kreechum's shoulders and enforcing the order with a hard shove downward.

Caught unawares, the IMC foreman grunted an expletive, followed by, "What the hell's going on here?" But he stayed put.

Anderson glared at his one-time friend. "You lying bastard," he said, spitting out words like they were poison. "You lying fucking bastard."

"Not true," Davis replied. "I did exactly what I said—accompany you here. Later, if you think long and hard about it, you might find my presence kept you out of worse trouble."

"You have much to answer for, Mr. Anderson," Ellis stated.

"And you'll answer to Coalition," he scoffed.

"That prospect isn't my concern," Ellis said, grabbing and holding up the CTL. "My concern is what mischief you caused in obtaining this data."

"A great deal, I hope," Anderson replied. "Absent a crew of six, the beaner claim on Nadir is worthless. You may ignore that fact, but I doubt those pulling your strings will—*ma'am*."

"You have a hatred of all things Unión," Ellis said, undeterred. "Why is that, Mr. Anderson?"

In reply, the young tech stiffened, blanking all expression from his face.

"Nothing to say?" Ellis remarked. She would not ask again. Her next words were to the com link: "*Connect—Cooper.*"

A moment later, the sergeant's voice was heard.

"Yes, commander?"

"My office. Immediately."

"Straight away."

Cooper arrived, wary as to why he had been summoned. Ellis promptly clarified the matter:

"Until I decide exactly what to do with you, Mr. Anderson, you're confined to quarters. Sergeant, escort him there directly."

Cooper was in charge of base security but had little to do under Trenchon's permissive command. After a second of hesitation, for it took a moment to see that his new CO was dead serious, he took Anderson behind the elbow and began to lead him away.

"One more thing, sergeant," Ellis said, judging Anderson's submission too easy. "Remove the personal mindstor from his quarters and reprogram the entry so it can be operated only from the exterior."

With Anderson now gone, Kreechum, realizing it was in his best self-interest to fight another day, made a motion to turn tail and leave. "Not so fast," Ellis said. "I want a word with you." If the foreman had any thought of resisting, it was erased when Davis put his body in the doorway.

"You've done your best to undermine me," Ellis said. "If you continue to do so, I will restrict you to quarters."

"I can't always control my people," Kreechum warned. "You're ordering them to risk their ass looking for water that ain't there. A few more days, you'll have half the damned base confined."

"Then I shall turn the gymnasium into a brig, and you shall enjoy internment together."

Ellis nodded, and Davis stepped aside from the doorway. As the foreman passed by, he grabbed him by the arm. "Make no mistake, Kreechum, if any tech steps out of line, I'll slap them down hard."

"I see you've taken a liking to Kreechum," Ellis commented after she and Davis were alone.

"Just following your lead. You don't give any quarter."

"Does that surprise you?"

"Not anymore. How did you find out about the data on that CTL? Was it Captain Stewart?"

"No, Schulman—keep that to yourself. I wish to avoid putting a bullseye on the man's back."

Davis considered for a moment. "And when were you going to let me in on this?"

The expression on Ellis's face suggested no time soon.

"I see," Davis said. It was another test of his resolve.

"I don't apologize often," Ellis said, seeing the lieutenant's disappointment. "You've earned one. I won't doubt you again. Not after the way you just handled yourself."

"It's not over, you know. The temptation's too great," Davis replied, referring to what every person on Zenith had suspected but now knew in tantalizing detail: Nadir's exclusion zone was awash in water.

"They could have a dozen underground Lake Baikals," Ellis countered. "Not one drop is ours."

"I had hoped to water ski," Davis said with a grin.

"I am puzzled by one item on this CLT," Ellis continued, placing the object in the palm of her hand. "Why is Nadir's environmental support functioning at reduced capacity? Any ideas?"

"Not enough information was copied from their primary to make an accurate assessment. For all we know, their ESS was powered down for maintenance or repair."

"Then I see no need to trouble brass at Varian with this," Ellis said.

"No need at all," Davis echoed, comprehending the implications while at the same time wondering just how far ahead his CO had thought this through. "If they haven't already, Varian will learn about this from Kreechum. They'll spin the data and—" A look from Ellis stopped Davis mid-sentence.

"Our transmissions are auto-encrypted," she said. "I instructed the mindstor to render all outgoing references concerning Nadir's operational status indecipherable."

"And the sender doesn't have a clue," Davis said in appreciation. "You were able to do this in time?"

"Maybe."

"What do you intend to do with Anderson?"

"Suggestion?"

"That's tough," Davis admitted, hesitating as he decided what confidences to share. "What Anderson keeps to himself may help explain his behavior."

"Let's hear it."

"The way he tells it, his mother died when he was young. Shortly afterward, his father became addicted to heroin produced from poppies genetically engineered to thwart treatment protocols. He became incapable of properly raising his son. When Anderson was four, an uncle stepped into his brother's shoes and never took them off." Davis paused. "When you think about it, Anderson's love for his uncle became stronger than many father-son relationships."

"Why so?" Ellis asked.

"Because of the prior emptiness it had to replace."

"That's a sensitive insight," Ellis said, impressed. "I continue to misjudge you."

"Do it a few more times, it'll even the score," Davis replied. "Anderson's story didn't end there. Many years later, it took a bad turn when the uncle, a captain in the reserves, activated his unit in response to an incursion along the border with Unión. He was murdered in the line of duty."

"Murdered, not killed?" Ellis asked. "There is an unhappy distinction."

"It's the word Anderson chose to use. A young man at the time, he was given a firsthand account of the incident by an officer who had served with his uncle. The reservists, an armed company of eighty, were separating local civilians from a hostile Latino mob that had fashioned weapons from dismantling a temporary barricade. It was an untenable situation. The reservists were outnumbered ten to one, and the close quarters negated using aggression-nullifying psychchems as a counter-measure. There were warnings of bloodshed if the barricades were breached. It's unclear exactly how it escalated, but several hundred people crossed the line in an attempt to confront unarmed civilians the reservists were protecting. In the mayhem, Anderson's uncle was beaten to death. He was one of eight who died that day. Several others were hospitalized with severe injuries."

"I remember hearing about this," Ellis said. "Can you put a name on it?"

"I believe Anderson called it the Rio Pecos Incident. "His version of it. It closely matches what Coalition reported, for whatever that's worth."

Ellis nodded. "That area is a flash point. I learned of the conflict while living in the unaligned colony of *Hestia*. "I suggest you research the account from the Unión viewpoint."

"I expect it to be different," Davis acknowledged. "But what good does that do Anderson? From his perspective, he lost an uncle at the hands of the Latinos. An uncle whom he loved like a father. For him, arguing specifics is meaningless. Can any of us be sure we would not harbor a similar hatred?"

"No," Ellis said upon reflection. "That's reason enough to prevent these conflicts from occurring. We must break the cycle."

"Any way you can?" Davis asked, wondering how far Ellis would go to impede Coalition purposes on Murkor. "You're going against powerful forces. You'll wind up losing more than your command."

Ellis was unfazed. "Much can happen until then," she said, motioning that she had to attend to other duties. "Besides, I have a reputation as a bitch to live up to."

"Some might say you're doing a damn good job," Davis said, heading for the safety of the corridor, but stopped when partway there.

"Lieutenant."

"Yes, commander?" a wary Davis replied.

"You can drop the rank when we're in private."

Davis flashed the wry grin Ellis was coming to appreciate. "And risk losing another month's rec privileges?"

"That much? You'd be way too hard on yourself," Ellis replied, almost smiling.

Ellis devoted time to her daily routine of deep meditation. When finished, a glimmer of an idea compelled her to stand and gaze out the viewport. It was now midday, a term that had no real significance on Murkor, partially due to the sun-blocking haze.

The lavascape was a depressingly empty palette, making it hard to envision what it was like eons ago when the planet was teeming with life. There were hints: Fossilized imprints of strange and wondrous creatures of great size and remarkable structural complexity. All gone, the eradication of larger organisms similar to what happened on Earth sixty-four million years ago when a lesser meteor heralded the Cretaceous extinction.

The species that had survived the cataclysm could fit on the palm, yet the *smallest* surviving life form on Murkor could be seen with the naked eye. Where were the microorganisms similar to the bacteria, protozoa, fungi, and viruses that populated virtually every square centimeter of Earth? It was inconceivable that similitudes never existed on Murkor. Why had none endured?

She flexed her right shoulder. Almost completely healed. Captain Stewart had scheduled one more treatment—a good opportunity to make her intentions known. Conceivably, what she had in mind would require more of the doctor's services.

The lavender corridors leading to Stewart's medical suite remained blank. Entering her personal preferences for mindstor-generated murals was the last thing on Ellis's mind. This was not so for Base Manager Schulman, who approached from the opposite direction. Absorbed in his thoughts, he was only vaguely aware of the images progressively displayed on the walls beside and in front of him and just as soon disappearing behind: Colorful renditions of classical paintings, many depicting zaftig, semi-nude women.

"Mr. Schulman," Ellis said, smiling inwardly as they converged.

"Commander—I was just—ohh. *Images off!*"

"Was that *Leda and the Swan?*" Ellis asked, catching a glimpse of the erotic painting and others of similar description before they faded from view.

"A Correggio," Schulman acknowledged, recovering.

"Renaissance period. Are you familiar with *Leda Atomica?*" Ellis asked, referring to the surrealistic painting by Salvador Dali depicting a nude woman, a swan, and several objects suspended in space. "Dali's treatment introduced a precept of twentieth-century physics into his work—that objects do not actually touch. In his painting, nothing touches. Nothing. Leda, the swan, and not even the ocean touches the shore. A conversation for another time. You were coming to see me?"

"With a suggestion, respectfully, commander. I thought it better communicated in person."

"You may do so now."

"Missions are contributing nothing to our water reserves. Protecting what we have left is critical."

"You're recommending further rationing?" Ellis asked.

"Heavens, no," Schulman replied, his expression turning grave. "And please don't ask me to, or you'd have to assign me a bodyguard. No, what I had in mind was the storage tanks. I don't know of any specific threat—except, well, if *I* could think of it—"

It took Ellis a few seconds to grasp the base manager's meaning. If Zenith's water supply were sabotaged, there would be little choice except to seek water in the one place on Murkor where it could best be found.

"I like how you think, Mr. Schulman."

"Yeah, it's a curse," the base manager said, acknowledging the compliment.

"Can the tanks be secured from tampering?" Ellis asked.

"I believe it is possible."

"I'll have Lieutenant Davis consult you on the matter," Ellis said. "It is regrettable that we must protect ourselves from ourselves. Satisfy my curiosity, Mr. Schulman. Regarding the transitory images displayed on these walls. What transpires when two people with radically different views of art converge? Does one party predominate over the other?"

"The mindstor searches for images compatible with both persons' tastes," the base manager replied. "That's the norm. On occasion, when there are no suitable matches, or when several people converge, the walls revert to a neutral color."

"Seems to me that the mindstor has it right, then, does it not?"

It took Schulman a few seconds to grasp Ellis's meaning.

"I like how you think, commander," he said.

***

"You, of all people, should be more receptive to the idea," Ellis remarked, continuing her chiding to no apparent effect. "What were your exact words? 'It's one thing to know something intellectually, another to experience it.'"

"Hold still," Stewart ordered.

Ellis was lying prone on a well-padded exam table. She had breathed in a specially formulated nano-laden medicinal vapor. Now, a beam focused on her exposed shoulder was activating the nanite healing agents within the area of trauma. Neither officer spoke until the cessation of a slight hum indicated the procedure had terminated.

"You can sit up," Stewart advised. To assess the range of motion, she placed two hands on Ellis's arm and carefully rotated the shoulder into different positions. "Any discomfort?"

"No."

"Without a doubt," Stewart said, "you're the most flexible person I've ever treated."

"If only you were."

"So, I should stand by why you deliberately risk injury to yourself—again, I should add."

"I'm only doing what you have done," Ellis said, knowing the comparison was absurd.

"I seem to remember wearing a rebreather," Stewart replied. "They come in handy, you know."

"Funny."

"You could join a mission."

"Given the present circumstances," Ellis said, "I'd prefer not to leave the base for that length of time."

Stewart shook her head in disapproval. "You know I should stop you," she said, alluding to her responsibility as Zenith's physician. "Just remember that the only other person to try it was Anderson. That says a lot."

"Fair point," Ellis admitted, though no argument would deter her from becoming the second person to attempt circumnavigating Zenith without a rebreather. Asking Stewart to be ready with a resuscitator only meant she was half as crazy as Anderson, who was motivated by boredom, braggadocio, and booze.

Her reasoning was more substantive. Newly aware of the precise coordinates of Nadir's water resources, there was now little to prevent a crew from testing her and the border. Except, perhaps, another distraction. Added to her bout with Davis, the stunt might also accrue to her persona. Having the techs think of her as crazy, reckless, gutsy, or even as a bitch might be acceptable. Anything was better than ordinary.

Davis nearly got it right. She would risk anything to avert a confrontation between Coalition and Unión. Her compulsion was the equal and opposite of Anderson's. Everyone has abiding life experiences that influence their behavior for good or ill. For Anderson, undoubtedly, the violent loss of a father figure.

She would never forget what happened on *Diverna*, a peaceful farming colony that, finding themselves preyed upon by a rogue band of armed mercenaries, had been unable to protect itself—isolation being their only defense.

Responding to the colony's urgent appeal for assistance, she had ordered the deployment of a sonic shock weapon, a low-risk, nonlethal deterrent. Tragically, the concussive wave generated by the device, unexpectedly amplified by the planet's dense atmosphere, destabilized and collapsed several old brick structures. Occupied houses. *Homes.*

Scores were injured. A Divernian and his two young sons were found dead in the rubble. Learning of the tragedy, she had reached out to the mother, inconsolable in her grief.

Later today, she would take a small step in fulfilling a silent commitment made to that mother and countless others like her by reaching out to Garcia.

She would go on telling herself that there were times a person could circumvent the evil other people create. In no other way could she continue to command.

***

Most of Zenith's population, having enjoyed watching Anderson's failed attempt at rounding Zenith's two domes, were hoping Ellis had similar results. Accordingly, they had strategically positioned themselves at viewports along the last section of her travel. Stewart, Davis, Cooper, and Schulman stationed themselves at the portal where she would exit and, hopefully, reenter.

At Stewart's insistence, Davis had donned a rebreather and held another. "We can monitor your progress on the perimeter cameras," he advised. "Run into trouble, I'll be at the ready. If you're unable to use the rebreather, I'll bring you inside."

"That won't happen, lieutenant," Ellis said. "This is one portal I intend to pass through *before* you. Now, please give me a moment. I want to calm myself before stepping outside." Positioning herself directly in front of the portal, she closed her eyes.

"What's she doing, captain?" Cooper asked, expecting the CO to hyperventilate to boost the amount of dissolved oxygen in her bloodstream.

"Meditating," Stewart answered, "to lower heart rate and slow breathing. It'll improve her chances. Did you think I'd allow this otherwise?"

"Why didn't you tell us this before?" Schulman complained. "I would have doubled my bet."

"*Portal open.*" Ellis suddenly commanded. There was a brief expulsion of pressurized air as an opening formed, then, sensing passage, rapidly sealed behind her.

The oppressive heat and foul odor of Murkor was like a slap to the face; a first, shallow breath almost panicked her. There was no time to waste. Running the three hundred meters over loose and uneven footing would take forty-five, maybe fifty seconds. Doing so would be a mistake, dramatically increasing her body's demand for oxygen. Maintaining firm control of respiratory and heart rates was the only real chance of accomplishing this insanity.

Fighting the unbearable urge to sprint, she began jogging slowly and steadily.

The effects of breathing in the thin Murkorian air started taking their toll, each hollow breath sending a spasm of pain shooting into her chest. Her legs began to ache, and she felt heavy despite the low gravity. Beyond the pain, there was an undeniable fascination for being out and about on an alien world. Bareback, unencumbered by the clever artifices of humanity, the contact was more intimate, more visceral: The glorious blue webbing of a magnetic storm coursing through a dirt-brown cloud; a crimson sun winking in and out of view as it fought to break through the shimmering haze; the sting of windblown particles on her exposed skin.

In the distance, fumaroles lined up like sentinels, watching her progress.

Krezakgrfel! Merfalger! Levishnuplef!

She had not realized that they could be so expressive!

And there, further out, a roller kicking up a tumbling spiral of glistening lava shards!

Losing focus—running too fast.

To prevent her mind from wandering, she tried concentrating on the rhythmic sound of footfalls on granulated pumice.

Crunch Crunch Crunch, Crunch, Crunch Crunch, Crunch Crunch Crunch.

A cadence to mesmerize a mind starved of oxygen or the muted conversation of an almost dead planet?

And, nearly indiscernible through the pain, the vague sensation of being watched, experienced by Jensen and others.

At last! To her immediate left, a faintly visible indent on the luminous monstrosity of Zenith's central dome: The personnel portal she had exited, now tantalizingly within reach.

Seconds or an eternity away.

She was in trouble. Her lungs were turning to ash, her legs into stone pillars.

To end the pain, to be saved, she considered allowing herself to pass out, then reluctantly discarded the idea. Not out of fear. Out of fairness. Fairness to Davis and Stewart and the image she must maintain and project.

Stewart. Stalwart Stewart, Stewart Stalwart. Stewart...

An idea floated to her in the blurry line between delirium and selflessness:

Stop moving. Calm the mind.

The way to gain control is to lose control. To become encompassed by whatever out here wishes to pass into and through her, too elusive and transitory to be frightening.

Inside Zenith, four crewmates stared at a split-screen image that showed Ellis framed by a list of her biometrics, ominously showing red.

"What the hell are you waiting for?!" Stewart shouted at Davis. "Get out there!"

"No. She's still standing," Davis responded, staring intently at her image. "We can't let her fail. You've seen what she's capable of."

"Get out there, lieutenant!" Stewart repeated. "That's an order!"

Davis was contemplating disobeying when several of Ellis's biometrics suddenly flashed green. A moment later, she took a surprised look around and began to move. Incredibly, she began to jog.

"She's going to make it!" Schulman shouted.

"*Portal full open!*" Cooper commanded, having the presence of mind to realize the commander would lack sufficient breath to utter the words.

A second later, desperate for air, she stumbled inside, prevented from falling by Davis's firm grip.

"There's a flask of premium scotch with your name on it, commander," she heard Schulman say.

Ellis nodded, looking up from an oxygen mask shoved on her face.

"Say something," Zenith's physician requested, concerned that Ellis had not spoken.

"Oxygen," she gasped, "precious as water."

Whatever small benefit the stunt accrued to her was about to be short-lived, Ellis realized, when later that same day, Sergeant Cooper informed her that Nadir had disabled their planetwide com link. Until the link was restored, contact between the two bases and any hope of rapprochement and cooperation would be impossible. Left with no alternative, she would have to set in motion orders to evacuate Zenith.

10 REACHING OUT

JAHHHKATKERPOOOF-BERJING!

Garcia watched as scores of boisterous fumaroles sent a noxious smoky pollution into the blazing late-day air. Trapped by a temperature inversion, the wispy black threads collected and flattened into a low-hanging blanket that effectively blotted out what remained of a retreating sun.

In the distance, a parched patchwork of blacks, pale yellows, and grays: The salt and mineral deposits of an ocean that had evaporated into space. To the south, a flat section of lava was riddled with an intricate network of cracks and crevices. From a distance, the expanse bore a striking similarity to the drought-plagued regions of Earth. It was said, and he knew it to be false, that it was impossible to cry on Murkor's surface—that when tears formed, they were immediately lost, evaporated in the hot, arid air.

Darkness came on rapidly, snuffing out whatever details could be seen through three years' accumulation of dust and ash on a window that would never know the touch of cleansing rain. A remote seismometer recorded what he could barely feel: a series of temblors, the constant creaks and groans of a massively injured planet. The disconcerting motion and apocalyptic landscape reminded Garcia of what scientists claimed as fact: that Murkor was too damaged to heal itself, that it would forever be a forlorn and fractured world.

One hundred years ago, Earth narrowly escaped a similar fate when (in a rare instance of global cooperation) a planet-killing asteroid was deflected. Biomystic's seeking proof of Earth as Gaia had to look no further: Our species had been nurtured for this saving purpose. Their optimism was challenged by skeptics insisting it merely evened the score for the innumerable wounds humanity inflicted on the planet. That Earth was given a reprieve from the insanity to come, the folly of meganations having the ability to obliterate all.

Unión and Coalition had acquired this damnable power—apocalyptic weaponry created by the same human intellect that had devised a way to deflect an asteroid. Are these aspects of our nature the complimentary yin-yang of Chinese philosophy or nothing more than contradictions? Philosophical musings are like the unending reflections of two facing mirrors. He took one last look out the viewport. All he could see was his image in the glass. Night, as it always does on Murkor, had come apace with the absoluteness of death.

Feeling the effects of hypoxia, exhausted from sleep deprivation and stress, his bed made a tempting destination. Garcia chose to sit at his desk. He needed to stay awake. If Gustavo's calculations were correct, a message from the Coalition shuttle would be received within the hour. There was little to do except wait for a response.

The decision to solicit help from an adversary had been a necessary evil. It had the bitter taste of surrender for Carlos while Amanda's vocal opposition to seeking any reproachment with Zenith had waned. She gave no explanation, and none was needed: The debilitating and frightening effects of breathing in a low-oxygen environment were manifesting themselves.

By every metric, physical and mental, they labored. Despite Garcia's age, or maybe because of it, he appeared to be the least affected. Nevertheless, there were signs of a steady decline: Loss of appetite, lethargy, impairments to the senses, and changes to long-term memory and cognitive abilities. Curiously enough, he saw his libido affected, lessening what had become an injurious sexual distraction.

The symptoms they were experiencing were not exactly like what Mariana anticipated. More precisely, not every crew member was affected in the same way. Even the ability to think clearly seemed to vary, Roya and Gustavo chiding each other as to who was affected more. It was harder to laugh about other differences, such as loss of vision and hearing. Concerning these variations, Mariana confessed bewilderment, wondering aloud if her powers of observation were also compromised.

"We have an incoming message from the Coalition vessel," Gustavo said, speaking on the internal link Garcia had asked his communications officer to keep open.

"Thank you. Accessing now. I'd like you to listen in, of course. I'll need your opinion."

They waited anxiously as the automated eight-second delay timed out, replaced by a tired, placid face: Pilot, and he got right to the point:

Comandante Garcia. Received your urgent request. Returning with due haste. ETA forty-one Standard Hours. I concur that an overland trek to Zenith is inadvisable. If possible, hang tight till my arrival. Regarding your other concern, Commander Ellis and I shared no special confidence during our transit to Murkor. My strongest impression can be distilled down to one word: Stubborn. I should append that. Based on her stoic response when we took the short way in, I'd say she's tough to rattle. If you have to deal with her, which seems unlikely, I suggest these qualities may just as easily work for you as against you. Although not stated outright in your communique, I venture to guess this inquiry is driven by the fact that your emergency seems to have occurred shortly after our arrival on Murkor. I assure you, there is no connection, though as a citizen of Coalition, my words are suspect—we do bear the burden of our provincial prejudices. Ha! Upon entering the Varian System, I expect we'll have some explaining to do to those in our respective governing councils. Screw them. My only regret is that I will be several weeks delayed in seeing my wife and children. For that inconvenience, comandante, you will owe me. No worries there. The barriers our respective governments place between us mean it is a debt you'll never have to repay. Anyway, I hope you people get along well together. We will have a cramped, uncomfortable voyage ahead of us. Advise your crew that all but the most essential personal effects must remain on the planet. Bring sufficient food and water to sustain each of you for our return to Varian. Can't think of anything else. When I have reached the outer edge of Murkor's debris field, I shall communicate my imminent arrival. Out.

The pilot's image faded and was replaced by Gustavo's.

"Everyone shall be relieved," Garcia said, reacting to the positive news.

"Everyone?" Gustavo asked doubtfully. "I can think of one person who may react differently."

"Right, Carlos is beating himself up pretty bad about this. I shall break the news gently to him. What do you think of the message?"

"I think there's a shitstorm coming, and we've been handed an umbrella."

"That doesn't sound like Poe," Garcia commented.

"Problem is, I'm having trouble remembering any of my Poe."

"What the hell, Andrés, is that true?" a worried Garcia asked. But it was too late for Gustavo to hear. Believing the conversation was concluded, the communications officer terminated the internal link.

Garcia's apprehension was understandable. Gustavo was known to have committed to memory dozens of quotes from the works of his favorite author. Could he have forgotten them all? Maybe he was overtired. He would consult Mariana about the crew once again. Later. If *he* remembered. One issue at a time. For now—the message. He'd seek a second opinion regarding the sender's credibility from a source he had scrupulously avoided using.

"Mindstor. Analyze the last incoming message for speaker's veracity."

Veracity is eighty-one percent. Analysis uncertainty thirty-one percent. Optimal criteria: Speech pattern, intonation, facial expressions, eye movement. Sub-optimal criteria: Coalition citizen; unable to evaluate body language; unable to evaluate biosigns; insufficiency in duration and quality of transmission.

That was useless, Garcia thought. Subtracting the analysis uncertainty from veracity left an accuracy probability of fifty percent. As always, he'd have to rely on his judgment and instincts. They told him that the shuttle pilot (he never did give his name) was a truthful man.

***

Marian had ordered the cessation of strenuous workouts to conserve Nadir's dwindling supply of oxygen. Carlos was holding to the spirit of that command, using the exercise room for one specific purpose: To test his muscle strength. During the last few hours, he had begun to sense a change, an alarming feeling of becoming progressively weaker. Maybe it was his imagination. The bench press was the easiest way to find out without unnecessarily worrying the comandante or inviting another round of medical tests.

Lying flat on his back, he gripped the metal bar resting on the stanchions above him. Pushing hard, neck veins bulging under the strain, he could not move the combination of laden mesh bags used as free weights.

He tried to reassure himself. Anyone can have a lousy day of powerlifting. Rising, he removed one mesh bag from each end of the bar. Feeling drained, he made a few nervous circuits of the room, then returned to the exercise bench to rest. Staring up at the apex of Nadir's pyramid, his mind wandered to events of the previous evening.

Amanda had come to his cabin to discuss air chemistry, or so she had claimed. The lateness of the hour made him immediately wary of her intentions. He got that right. They exchanged a few cursory words, then, matter-of-factly, she reached beneath the neckline of her loose-fitting T-shirt and slipped it slowly over one exquisite shoulder and down the side of her arm, exposing one breast. Her stare became a challenge. No, it was more than that. It was arrogant.

"You better leave," he had said. Those were the words he could remember. "You better leave."

At first, she didn't believe him until he reached out, gripped the fabric of her T-shirt, and carefully pulled it back over her shoulder.

She became angry. Up-in-his-face angry. The last thing she hissed was, "When you regret this, and you will, there'll be no second chance."

In an apparent physical way, he already regretted it. Badly. But would have regretted it more if he had acted on the urge.

He had finally figured it out. Should have sooner. Amanda was using him to get at the comandante. What had he once warned? *Keep far away; she sucks up emotions like a black hole.* Her behavior last night made that seem like pretty good advice. If she and the comandante had problems to work out, fine. Why be drawn in? He owed his friend at least that much, especially when he might be forced to prematurely abandon the last command of a long and distinguished military career.

All because *he* had let him down.

In frustration and anger, he grabbed the weighted bar and pushed, expecting to lift it handily.

The bar barely moved.

A bolt of fear shot straight through him.

The weight was half the amount he had benched five days ago.

What in hell had that Coalition bitch done to him? Descending the stairs leading to L2, he lost his balance. For a brief moment, he teetered, trying desperately to save himself. There was nothing to prevent or obstruct a fall: The spiral staircases had been designed, like much of Nadir, with the crews' safety subordinated to the speed and cost of construction.

Clutching the air where a safety handrail should have been, he pitched forward, tumbling head over heels, gaining momentum until he spilled over the stair's open side. Falling three meters, he landed with a bone-jarring thud on the unforgiving floor, where he lay, unmoving, on his back.

Garcia, searching for Carlos to relay the news of their impending rescue, saw the accident unfold in slow motion. Although close enough to break the engineer's fall, he had lost the alacrity of body and mind to do so.

Mariana arrived moments later, the mishap causing the poorly built staircase to shudder violently, creating an ominous vibration felt throughout the base. Not far behind, distress registering on their faces, were Gustavo and Roya, followed by Amanda.

"Did you see what happened?" Mariana asked, pushing Garcia aside. Crouching, she pressed her middle and forefinger against the back of Carlos's jaw, feeling for a pulse.

"He fell off the stairs," Garcia replied, stating the obvious.

"I mean, did you see *how* he landed?" she asked, examining the bleeding gash on the engineer's forehead. "How did he strike his head?"

"On the treads. While falling. His back and right side absorbed the brunt of it when striking the floor."

"His pulse is faint but steady," Mariana said, standing. Medical supplies were steps away. "I need a few items. Make sure he doesn't move."

"Poor Carlos," Roya said, the sight of the vital young man brought low arousing her sympathy. "Do you know why he fell?"

Garcia shook his head. "I should have done something." Responding to the voice, Carlos moaned and opened his eyes. "My friend," a worried Garcia said, leaning in. "How are you?"

"Been... better," he replied, attempting to move. The comandante's firm hand prevented him from rising.

"Apply this compress against the wound," Mariana directed, having returned with her medical kit. She handed Garcia a moist pad impregnated with synthetic platelets. "It'll help stem the bleeding. Gustavo, bring a chair from the conference table. Now, please."

"Sorry. Straightaway, doctora," Gustavo replied, moving slowly.

"Where do you hurt?" Mariana asked her patient.

Carlos touched his head.

"Anywhere else?"

"Everywhere else," Carlos replied, trying to joke.

"I see you can flex your fingers," Mariana observed. "How about your toes?"

"I'm okay," Carlos insisted, complying with the directive, noticing for the first time that one shoe had come off.

"You're okay when I say you're okay," Mariana said, continuing her cursory exam. You have a mild concussion. She wondered silently if the fall was the result of oxygen deprivation. "Let's get you into that chair."

"You gave us quite a scare," Roya said, fumbling Carlos's shoe before slipping it onto his foot. "What happened?"

"I missed a step. An accident."

"Next time, try missing the bottom step, not the first," Gustavo said.

"What were you doing on L3?" Amanda asked. "The area is off-limits."

"I wasn't exercising, if that's what you mean," Carlos said, not mentioning his waning strength.

"Except there's no other reason to be up there."

"Give it a rest, teniente," Garcia said in a firm voice. He had his back to her but kept his body still and waited. An unmistakable warning for her to desist.

"Just pointing out—now that we have to abandon this shithole."

Angered, Garcia rose to face her. "So there's no misunderstanding," he said, standing so close he could feel the heat from Amanda's face, "I'm giving you an order. Keep still."

"I won't breathe another word. If I can breathe at all, that is." And in so saying, she made a hasty retreat.

Roya and Mariana exchanged glances. It had been a long time since they heard the comandante give a direct order. *Who* he gave it to made it satisfying.

"Is it true?" a dispirited Carlos asked.

"Yes, Carlos. We've received assurances from the shuttle pilot. In two days, we'll be out of here."

"And if his message is only a delay tactic?"

"I fail to get your reasoning."

"Two days. No shuttle. What then?"

"I think you know the answer," Garcia responded. "You see what's happening to us. Waiting for our supply ship is not an option."

"Never really was," Mariana added.

"Better than the alternative," Carlos persisted.

"Ask yourself, by leaving, what do we relinquish?" Garcia asked.

"If we are forced out? Our pride."

"Is that worth risking our lives?"

"If it deprives the enemy of the water they need."

Garcia kept his patience, for he had great affection for his tormented friend. "The shuttle pilot's message is in your mindstor. I suggest you replay it."

"And don't forget to repair the dent," Gustavo said, earning himself a blank stare. Pointing up at the stairs, he smiled. "Where your fucking head contacted the metal tread—*cabeza dura*!"

Even Carlos had to laugh.

It was a commodity, like oxygen, that would soon be in short supply.

***

It had been perfectly natural for Doctora Mariana Perez to feel a surge of nervous excitement when she first heard of her two-year commission to a distant world. Discounting brief excursions to Unión's massive armada of orbiting "monitoring" stations, she had never left the confines of Earth. Only the nervousness remained upon learning of her new assignment's terrible location and unwise constraints.

Foremost, she had virtually no say in equipping Nadir's medical facilities. Those decisions were made by others during the base's planning stage. Despite her protests, only the most rudimentary diagnostic equipment was transported to Murkor. Treatment options were also limited, little more than the primitive medicine of a prior century when physicians relied heavily on pills and cocktails made from crude chemical compounds.

The justification for the mission planner's disregard for safety was that each crew member had undergone screening for genetically inherited disorders and, like so much processed meat, been certified to be disease-free for a minimum of three years—their maximum term of service at Nadir. During training, they were scanned, probed, and poked to safeguard against the introduction of outside pathogens. The crew transporting them to Murkor were similarly screened. Lastly, Murkor's biota had been declared safe for humans, and, in the unlikely event that the astrobiologists were wrong, Nadir would be equipped with an advanced foreign-body detector/sterilizer unit.

In theory, all that remained as a viable health threat was an accident or a deliberate act of violence. Both possibilities, Mariana was assured, were statistically remote. Nevertheless, yielding to her vocal insistence, she was allotted a small quantity of bio-engineered cellular repair nanobots. The irony of their use was lost on an aching Carlos when she had injected, post-accident, a bolus containing ten to the ninth power of these industrious agents directly into a vein of his muscular arm.

With coaxing, Mariana learned that a temporary loss of balance had precipitated the engineer's fall. There was more. Thanks to her dogged persistence, he admitted to a growing lethargy and hearing impairment. The young man, whose pride in physical conditioning was arguably excessive, foolishly tried to hide his loss of muscle strength and, one day later, the blurry vision that he attributed to the knock on his head. Despite his young age and peak conditioning, he was worse off than the five older crew members. Mariana had baseline medical data for all of them, though much of the information was useless without the diagnostic equipment necessary to make real-time comparisons. Delving into Carlos's medical history, she confirmed that his auditory faculty had been exceptional. Viewed through a crudely effective otoscope, his outer and middle ears were normal. From this and a few other rudimentary tests, she was able to rule out possibilities and deduce nothing regarding the cause of his loss of hearing and balance.

She anticipated more of the same obstacles in diagnosing her current patient.

"What *did* you do?" Roya asked, being her usual inquisitive self.

"About what?" Mariana replied.

"You know what," Roya said. "The comandante was right in Amanda's face."

"And you think I had something to do with that?"

"C'mon. Share."

"Really, there's nothing to it," Mariana said. "A late-night game of *Dendrite* in the comandante's quarters. Amanda walks in. Sees me. Amanda walks out. Credit him with anything else."

"Uh huh," Roya said, coming to her own conclusion. "And her nuclear winter attitude toward Carlos?"

"That has me stumped," Mariana replied.

"Not me," Roya said. "Especially after what you just told me. As incredulous as this sounds, I'm betting she's finally run out of options."

Mariana considered her crewmate's statement. "Why not go after Gustavo?"

"Say again."

"Yeah, I know," Marian said. "That was ridiculous of me."

"No. I didn't hear you." Roya's face was somber. Her hearing had worsened. "I had to listen carefully to distinguish every word you said."

"And your appetite?" Mariana asked.

"Like yours. Nonexistent. How are the others faring?"

"Not well, I'm afraid," Mariana said. "Tell me the level again—"

"Sixteen point four," Roya responded, having to repeat the ambient oxygen level she mentioned in a previous conversation.

Mariana had begun to question why some of the symptoms of hypoxia had demonstrated early, diligently plumbing the mindstor for an explanation, concentrating efforts on the combined effect, if any, from Murkor's reduced gravity and sunlight and elevated carbon dioxide levels. The mindstor offered nothing revelatory about the subject, and she was forced to entertain the notion that *all* the symptoms they were experiencing were within the realm of the possible.

Her confidence in this assessment was severely shaken after administering two simple tests on Roya and comparing the results to historical norms. Mariana knew, or thought she knew, one physiological principle to be invariably true: In a low-oxygen environment, heart and respiratory rates increase as the human body struggles to acquire and assimilate more of the life-sustaining element.

Inexplicably, Roya's heart and respiratory rates had *decreased*.

"You look confused," Roya said, observing Mariana's puzzled reaction to the results.

"Confused and frustrated," Mariana replied, believing that if the modern tools of medicine were at her disposal, or those available a mere one hundred kilometers away at Zenith, she would have a clearer picture of what was happening to them.

In this, she was wrong.

***

The same day the shuttle was due to arrive, Carlos had to be awakened from a deep sleep. Later, when he approached the table where the crew had gathered for a breakfast that none would eat, he absently kicked into a chair leg and briefly stumbled.

"Easy, my friend," Garcia said, reaching out to steady him with a hand under the elbow. The comandante looked inquiringly at Mariana, confirming that she took note of the incident.

"Let's start with what we know for certain," Garcia urged. "Carlos?"

"Yes, comandante?"

"Bring us up to speed."

"Oxygen 16.1. Falling. As predicted."

"Anything else?" Garcia prodded.

"Anything—?" Carlos repeated. Dismayed that the engineer was hopelessly confused by a simple question, Roya leaned in and sympathetically whispered loudly in his ear. "Oh, yeah," Carlos continued. "Carbon dioxide 1245. Steady. Maybe falling. Don't know why. No progress to report on ESS or Nexus."

"I know you won't give up," Garcia said reassuringly, having decided that his struggling crew, Carlos especially, were not to be admonished for sub-par performance of their duties. "Roya, what news do you have for us? Do you have the results of the water analysis?" He had ordered testing of Nadir's water, air, and food supply when Mariana expressed confusion about what was affecting the crew.

"Ultrafiltration and the UV sterilizer both functioning at specs," Roya responded. "Our water is pure."

"As expected," Garcia said, attempting to remain positive. "Amanda—how is the air we can't get enough of and the food we have no desire to eat?"

"There's nothing to report," Amanda replied, her tone suggesting that the testing was a waste of time. "No toxic chemicals. No foreign substances. No pathogens. Sorry to disappoint you, Mariana. You'd probably be grateful if I had found *something* to entertain you."

"Damned right, I would," Mariana replied. "Wouldn't you, if it would help us understand what's afflicting us?"

Amanda eyed Garcia, then self-censored a nasty reply. A warning line had formed that she was reluctant to cross.

"Look at us," Mariana continued, gesturing. "Loss of appetite, headaches, lethargy, changes to vision and hearing—the effects of hypoxia. So why aren't we struggling to breathe? Why have our heart rates decreased?" Reaching into a pocket of her lab coat, she pulled out a pen-sized instrument and pointed it directly at Amanda's exposed throat. "And if that isn't bizarre enough, I took my temperature this morning. It's nearly two points *below* my norm." Squinting, she read the instrument's small digitized display. "Exactly like yours, Amanda. Oh, and one more thing—I entered everything on my mindstor so I wouldn't forget—there may be an inverse correlation between advancing age and onset of the worse symptoms." She forced a smile. "You're going to outlast us after all, comandante."

With a puzzled expression, Garcia looked at Carlos, who was repeatedly clenching his hands into tight fists, then opening and spreading his fingers wide in what appeared to be a test of dexterity and strength. "Does anyone wish to advance a theory to explain what the hell is going on?" the comandante asked.

Roya risked a response. "What happened in that tube a few days ago coincides with our decline. Did Amanda and I bring something inside with us?"

It was the first time such a connection was proposed, and it marshaled everyone's attention.

"And what exactly happened?" Garcia asked.

"Nothing," Amanda blurted out, surprising everyone. "I got spooked, that's all."

"El respiro del Diablo," Gustavo declared, his face gloomy and gray. *The devil's breath.*

Amanda paled. It had been four days since the incident in Tube N119. She had used the intervening time to convince herself that nothing inexplicable had transpired. Contemplating the alternative was far less comforting.

"Was I 'spooked' too?" Roya demanded.

"Am I supposed to know what you feel?" Amanda said. "What any of you feel?" Seeing that her temperamental outburst would not suffice, she added: "If there were microbial life on Murkor, the astrobiologists would have found it. If *they* were wrong, our detection and decontamination procedures would have identified and sterilized it. And if that counts for nothing, my testing would have discovered it. There is absolutely no life form or agent infecting us."

"Be that as it may," Mariana said, "as Nadir's physician, I'm duty-bound to order a quarantine of the Coalition shuttle and everyone aboard until we are examined and cleared by Varian's medical board."

"Agreed," Garcia replied, circumventing Amanda's protest. "With apologies to the shuttle pilot who was anxious to reunite with his family, that is the most prudent course of action."

"You're wrong," Carlos interjected in a weakened voice.

"How so?" Garcia asked though he knew what the engineer was compelled to say. Let him say it. Had anyone presented a plausible explanation as to what was going on?

"Ellis," Carlos pronounced, the name revealing everything he thought and felt.

The opinion went uncontested. No one had the energy or the heart.

"It would seem," Garcia said equitably, "that we shall leave Murkor having more questions than answers."

At the last, it fell to Gustavo to have the final say. "The Coalition shuttle is approximately eight hours out. Arrival expected in the dead of night."

With the meeting concluded, the crew slowly went their separate ways, silently reflecting on the communication officer's poor choice of words.

***

By nightfall, preparations for departure were finalized, and the base secured for abandonment. The cessation of useful activity and Murkor's enveloping darkness conspired to remind the restive crew how abject and alone they were. Ushered back into L2's central area, they huddled together, impatiently awaiting a transmission, now overdue, from the pilot of the Coalition shuttle. A second outgoing message had gone unacknowledged.

An apprehensive Garcia approached Gustavo. The communications officer shook his head. "Still no word."

Nearby, Carlos, glassy-eyed, slumped lower in his chair. He could no longer disguise the loss of muscle strength that they all were beginning to experience. Sitting alongside, Mariana took his pulse, then looked to Garcia, her eyes asking for help she knew he was unable to give.

"Gus, amplify and scan the "S" band in the prior incoming transmissions," Garcia requested, hoping his hunch was wrong. "Go back two hours before the shuttle's ETA, then have the mindstor filter the result for a human voice imbedded in the static."

"We've been misled," Amanda said, fear in her eyes. "A cruel deception."

Roya, who appeared to have given way to sleep, opened her eyes, looked despairingly at Amanda, and said in a voice that practically pleaded, "Can't you see what happened?"

Before she could answer, Gustavo raised his hand for silence. His expression froze. "It's faint." His face bleached to white. "An hour ago. I'll filter out the static."

"Make it loud," Garcia demanded, his worst fear realized. "We need to hear it."

There was no image, only fragments of audio, widely spaced and broken by static:

"...close-in...child's play...switching to..."

Unmistakably, Pilot's strained voice.

"...shields...reaching you..."

After an unbearably long stretch, a resumption:

"...apologies...worse than I...oh, God!"

Then, jarringly, an ear-piercing metallic sound followed by deathly silence.

"No—" Mariana gasped into the thin air. "No."

219

"Nothing more?" Garcia implored.

"Sorry, comandante," Gustavo said, crestfallen. "The signal vanished."

"I understand."

They all did. The debris field had claimed a life, to which they quietly mourned.

None more so than Garcia, who had decided to recall the shuttle. He grieved not for himself or his crew, for they were still breathing, nor for the shuttle pilot who had breathed his last. He grieved for the pilot's family, who would have to endure the suffocating pain of a loved one lost.

"Re-establish the planetwide com portal!" Garcia declared, shattering the troubled silence. "Connect me to Zenith."

They were fitting words, offered in response and homage.

As the meaning of Pilot's death overcame the crew of Nadir, the fear they felt, no longer tempered by the hope of leaving Murkor behind, came on in full force.

11 GHOSTS TO GOD

HOW BEAUTIFUL!

Floating, gazing up. Witness to a trillion splintering sparkles of liquid light splashing down on her. Beyond a million shades of blue, water can accept any color.

Brehhp Brehhp Brehhp

Inevitably, she must leave this glorious place.

A place her mind created.

For the present, she refused to relinquish control.

Submerging, diving under. Suspended in the depths beneath the cascade.

How long could she evade the world above?

Dreams are reality without the bother of physicality.

The physicality of matter exploded by quantum theory and the proofs that followed.

But even in dreams, one needs to breathe.

Brehhp! Brehhp! Brehhp!

From somewhere, a grating noise intruded into her half-consciousness, summoning her.

It was time to surface.

"Commander, I must disturb you."

It took a second for Ellis to recognize the sound of the door alert and respond to the voice of Sergeant Cooper.

"Proceed."

Cooper, standing in the darkened corridor, inwardly smiled. He was becoming accustomed to Ellis's abbreviated utterances. "There's an IM from Nadir. Someone representing themselves as a Comandante Garcia."

Ellis immediately recognized the name. "When did they reopen the link?" The com link's closure had been a source of supreme frustration, preventing her from initiating contact of her own.

"Apparently, just now. When I referenced the early hour, this Garcia person said it was urgent—if you didn't know that already."

"'If I didn't know?' Those were his exact words?"

"Pretty much exact," Cooper replied. "One more thing. It's bloody early, but he looks like shit missed Christmas. Pardon the expression, commander."

"I'll access it here, sergeant," Ellis said, moving quickly to her desk and opening the link. An image appeared. Cooper was right. Garcia was a handsome man. And he looked like hell.

"Commander Ellis, I presume?" he said directly.
"Yes."

"Can I trust you, Commander Ellis? How can I trust you?"

Good, Ellis thought. He wastes no time. "Unfortunately, comandante, I know one reason you should not."

"An admission?" Garcia said, leaving it open for her to specify as to precisely what.

"Intrusion into your mindstor. The unauthorized and regrettable action of someone in my charge."

"You admit to nothing more?"

What the hell else could there be, Ellis thought, noting that Nadir's CO was putting great effort into conversing, straining to hear and enunciate. Still, he was doing a competent job of sizing her up.

"No offense I'm aware of," she answered. Then, alluding to Zenith's potential use of the stolen hydrological data: "And none whatsoever contemplated."

"I must proceed on that basis, asking you to accept similar good-faith assurances from me." Garcia paused, his countenance becoming graver. "Together, we are saddened. I never learned his name. Doubtless, he was a brave and good man. Did you know him well? His family?"

"You have me at a loss—" Ellis said, a horrible suspicion forming in the back of her mind.

"You do not know?" Garcia said, stunned. "No communication sent?"

Ellis remained silent, refusing to believe. Nadir's CO would have to say it plainly for her to accept.

"Then I have heavy news," Garcia continued. "The pilot of the shuttle that conveyed you to Murkor lost his life risking the debris field. I bear responsibility. If only I had considered the consequences—it was at my request that he came urgently to our aid."

Ellis suppressed the urge to cry out. "From what I learned of him, he must have come with eyes wide open and willingly," she said, her mind flashing an indelible image of Pilot's family. "A wife and two young daughters survive him. His death diminishes us. I shall send word and testimonial to Varian."

"May I add to it? Garcia entreated. "If I remain able."

"Of course," Ellis responded, the heartfelt request telling her more about the man than any Coalition dossier ever could. "Time seems against you, comandante. Do not hesitate to explain your circumstances."

"Strange and baffling they are."

Garcia labored to recount the last several days, including, to her dismay, suspicion of Ellis's involvement with everything that had gone wrong at Nadir. "My failing memory prevents further elaboration," he said in conclusion. "There may be critical omissions. My crew, five other souls, are presently worse off. I doubt we can prevail—"

"Can you transmit the relevant engineering and medical data imbedded in your mindstor?" Ellis asked.

"I am relieved you suggested it. Our facilities are rudimentary, embarrassingly so. Perhaps, with your considerable resources, you can assist us from afar."

"Zenith is well-equipped, in some respects *also* embarrassingly so," Ellis responded. "Nevertheless, I am skeptical that a resolution can be achieved remotely, and you are in no condition to attempt an arduous journey here." Ellis carefully considered what she was about to say, for there could be no retracement. "One of our two vehicles has been modified. We have the capability of retrieving you and your crew."

"You would be subjecting yourself to significant danger," Garcia protested, "both in the journey and to the possibility of an unknown peril afflicting us."

"I have no intention of leaving you in the lurch," Ellis insisted. "As for the specifics, I must defer until your data transmission is analyzed and the logistics are discussed with my staff."

Garcia thought back to the shuttle pilot's impression of her. Calm, collected, and stubborn. It was right on the mark.

"I can be faulted for failing to reach out to you sooner, Commander Ellis."

"Together, we shall remedy that fault. Expect to hear from me directly. After the upload is analyzed."

"I've never come across anything like it," Stewart said, rapidly scanning the mindstor-generated visuals of Nadir's medical records. "Not in twenty years of practicing medicine on four planets."

Two hours earlier, she and Davis had been wakened by Cooper and told to join Ellis in her quarters, where, assisted by feedback from Zenith's primary mindstor, they analyzed the critical elements of Nadir's data transmission.

The task was not going well.

"Shall we seek a second opinion, doctor?" Ellis asked, dispensing with "captain" to emphasize her vital role in the meeting.

"I was about to suggest it. Better if I try phrasing the question."

Ellis nodded.

"*Mindstor,*" Stewart said. "*Evaluate Nadir's medical records for the presence of an underlying pathology that would explain the crews' reported symptoms.*"

The mindstor's audible was instantaneous.

There is a low probability that symptoms are caused by the cumulative effects of oxygen deprivation, elevated carbon dioxide, and mental stress. Secondary conclusion. Low probability of group psychosis resulting in psychosomatic symptoms.

It was not unusual for a query to garner a "low probability" designation. Predicated on the type and complexity of the question, human input error had to be factored into the equation.

"Let's try a different approach," Ellis suggested. "*Mindstor. Evaluate subject records for possible intrusion of unclassified organism, agent, or substance into base Nadir.*"

Again, the response was immediate.

Low probability. Adequate detection and decontamination procedures are currently in place and functioning. Forty-three Standard Earth Years since the last reported foreign body detector failure.

Ellis looked at Stewart and shrugged. She was disinclined to waste time with more inquiries. To do so placed six people in greater peril—and yet. On the outer edges of her consciousness, there was an amorphous idea. "One more attempt," she said. "*Mindstor. Evaluate Nadir and Zenith files for possible intrusion of unclassified organism, agent, or substance into base Nadir.*"

Three full seconds elapsed. Davis and Ellis exchanged surprised glances at the long delay. "Holy shit," Davis mouthed.

Low probability. Adequate detection and decontamination procedures are currently in place and fully functional at both facilities. Forty-three Earth years since the last reported detector failure. Cross-reference and further review of incidents involving L. Jensen, A. Cruz, R. Allawi, and J. Ellis are indicated.

"What in hell does that mean?" Stewart demanded. "And what prompted the question?"

"Not sure," Ellis responded. "Help me put the pieces together." While Stewart searched the mindstor for the pertinent personnel files, Ellis turned to Davis. "What do you make of this?"

"Well," Davis said, taking time to think it through, "in my experience, a mindstor has never taken that long to form a response. *Never.* Perhaps we are asking it to form a conclusion based on information that is incomplete, contradictory, or without precedence. In this instance, it must be all three."

"Translation: Beyond human comprehension," Ellis added.

"It's not that arrogant," Davis said. "It does not exclude itself from being confused."

Okay, here it is," Stewart interjected. "Amanda Cruz and Roya Allawi both reacted to something in a lava tube they were exploring—Cruz's reaction was more pronounced. Their incident occurred *after* problems with Nadir's atmospherics started developing. I can only guess at why Garcia sent the record over because there was *zero* sign of a medical problem resulting from the incident. Cruz herself claimed what she experienced was an overreaction. That's credible. Her psych profile indicates she's more impressionable. Her colleague's panicked behavior most likely influenced Allawi. As for Jensen, we have a good idea of what happened there. Stress and paranoia induced her mishap. At this point, the strongest medical argument for anything unusual taking place, weak as it is, is her being without a rebreather for a long duration with no lasting ill effects. That, too, can be explained. While unconscious, her metabolism slowed enough for her to be sustained by the oxygen in Murkor's atmosphere."

"And myself?" Ellis asked.

"Aren't you the best person to answer that?" Stewart contended.

"Meditation and physical conditioning allow me to depress my heart rate and breathing—up to a point. I reached that point and went beyond." Ellis wavered. Unsure of what she was about to say, her eyes moved to the hexagonal viewport that dominated one wall of her quarters. "I briefly felt a presence. Out there."

"I believe you did," Stewart responded. "You were under a tremendous amount of physical stress, and it is not uncommon for an oxygen-starved brain to experience hallucinations."

"That does not explain similar reports made by others," Ellis said.

"A malfunctioning rebreather might," Stewart replied, "or one worn in insufferable heat for hours. Sensing something lurking over one's shoulder is to be expected on this ass-backward planet, and I can personally attest to that. The fiction feeds on itself. The mindstor just put a label on it: 'Group psychosis.'"

"That's insufficient to explain what's happening at Nadir," Ellis responded. "Or have you completely convinced yourself?"

It was Stewart's turn to waver, her turn to be drawn out to the view of a ruined planet as it slowly resolved itself in the pre-sunrise gloom. "Ghosts to God," she finally said. "People *want* to believe in things they don't see. Who is completely immune?"

"Leeuwenhoek and Higgs," Ellis fired back. "On occasion, the invisible proves to be real."

"Okay, then," Stewart said, as if conceding the point, "but what *exactly* are we trying to convince ourselves of? An undetectable entity that likes toying with humans?"

Ellis looked at Davis and Cooper. Both had refrained from voicing an opinion.

"Forty-three years is a long time," Cooper finally said. "The last so-called detector 'failure' was on *Travail*—helluva name—when a bardusaur ambled through an open hangar door. It's ten meters tall, and I don't mean the door. The sheer mass of the creature overloaded the device. There's been several upgrades since." A harsh look from Ellis and Cooper realized that he still hadn't provided the definitive conclusion she sought. What he offered next came close. "I've been inside enough of those damn tubes to feel the presence, but *nothing* can escape the detectors."

Davis chimed in. "I can't add much to what everyone has said based on any personal experience. Cooper's right about the detectors, though. On the other hand, a mindstor never takes that long to think through a response. As for Jensen, she is normally rock-solid. The long and short of it is that it would be prudent to keep an open mind."

As Ellis contemplated her next move, Murkor's indecisive sun peered over the horizon. Except for those present and a reliable tech asked to prepare the CAM-L for an extended journey, the people on base were going about the routine of their lives. Many would accuse her of aiding the enemy when informed of what she intended. Were they redeemable, she wondered? Perhaps never, or only when their self-interest was served.

"Let's move on," she said. "One thing is sure: Nadir's oxygen values are slipping below fifteen percent. From that alone, they have to be hurting. You've studied their schematics, lieutenant. Any chance of restoring their environmental support to operational?"

"Some. I've seen the configuration before. The system is outdated now. It used to be commonplace on planets with partial oxy-content atmospheres. They're paying a heavy price for not installing a fully regenerative system. Judging by their records, their engineer, Alvarez, is top-notch, but he's fixated on the newer Nexus component." Davis flashed the wry grin Ellis had come to appreciate. "He's looking for the ghost in the machine, so to speak."

"Meaning?"

"There's a fair chance he's overlooking something basic."

"You won't have much time to play the part of poltergeist," Ellis replied. "Any special concerns about the journey?"

"Other than a chance encounter with a roller, or being swallowed whole by a crevice, or getting hopelessly lost in uncharted terrain?"

"I'll request nav charts during my next chat with Comandante Garcia," Ellis offered.

"I didn't expect you to waste time on the usual 'this is risky, I need volunteers BS,'" Davis said. "Suits me. Until recently, I was getting a little bored."

"Six people in dire need of medical assistance," Stewart said, stating the obvious reason for her inclusion.

"I won't disagree with either of you," Ellis commented. She was especially gratified by the hundred-eighty-degree turnaround in Davis's attitude. Or maybe it was there all along, lost among the background noise.

"Commander?" Cooper said, feeling left out.

Ellis locked eyes on the man. "Your job, sergeant, is far more problematic. I need you to help keep a lid on this place while we're gone."

***

On his way to inspect the vehicle he would soon be piloting, Davis was waylaid in the corridor connecting Zenith's two domes.

"I hear you're going somewhere, Davis."

"Get out of my way, Kreechum, I've no time for your bullshit."

"And what are we demanding in exchange for this touching errand of mercy?" the IMC foreman persisted, deliberately blocking the way.

"Wasn't discussed."

"I'll tell you, Davis," Kreechum goaded, "no one would have thought you'd be a turncoat. Or maybe, yeah, maybe there's a bit more to it. She's not my type, but you, though—the way I hear it—"

The accusation was easier to sidestep than the bulky foreman who took up a sizable chunk of the long passageway. "If you get your head out of your ass, Kreechum," he said, "you'd realize that Nadir's CO won't object to us tapping their storage tank, returning with a hump-full." He sniffed the air and added: "Maybe you'll finally be able to take that shower you need."

"That's it?!" Kreechum spit out. "We get one lousy fucking tank of water?"

Davis placed his face a centimeter from Kreechum's, a distasteful proposition. "I've been as polite as I'm going to be. Move."

Too bad he moved, Davis thought. He would have liked to put the bastard on his ass just for the fun of it. Heading toward the dome housing the CAM-L docking station, he felt uneasy about the encounter. Why was Kreechum in the corridor? Turning around, he was just in time to see the IMC foreman quickly disappear down the far end. The man can certainly move when he wants to.

Entry to the voluminous docking station was through a pressure-sealed, verbally controlled portal. When he was five meters away, Davis issued the appropriate opening command.

Nothing happened.

The portal had an oval window providing a clear view of the docking area. Davis did not like what he saw within. Three vehicles were parked in their respective bays. The large exterior portal was fully open, decompressing the space and allowing Murkor's noxious low-oxygen atmosphere to enter. A man was lying on the floor, unmoving: Bert Imholtz. A person wearing tech garb and a rebreather was tampering with the modified extended-range vehicle. It didn't take a genius to figure out the why—the who was uncertain.

Sensing movement at the window, the tech, obviously a male, stopped what he was doing and looked straight ahead. His sole purpose was to drag out the moment. He slowly turned toward Davis. The rebreather mask did little to hide the diabolic expression on the face of Ed Anderson. "There you are, *buddy*," his sarcastic voice taunted over the intercom speaker. "Come on in. The weather's fine."

"Delighted to," Davis replied, furiously gauging the possibilities. "Just release the door interlock."

"That's way too easy now, isn't it?" Anderson replied. "You'll have to gain access the long way. Oh, yeah, don't bother yelling out an audible override. I'm way ahead of you. I've de-comm'd that, too."

Davis knew he had no time to waste, but he had to give it one more try. "Bert can't last long in there. He doesn't deserve to die. Close the outside portal. Restore atmosphere."

"Can't you see I'm busy?" Anderson said, reaching into the vehicle's guts, grabbing a fistful of bundled wires, and yanking. Grinning, he held the tangled mess up for Davis to see. "They just don't make them like they used to."

Davis quickly backtracked down the corridor until he reached the nearest wall intercom. Imholtz needed emergency medical assistance. So would he if he failed, and there was plenty of reason to believe he would. What was it that he said about wanting more excitement?

"Priority One Alert!" he shouted into the com. "Ellis, Stewart, Cooper! Man without a rebreather down in open Cam-L dock! Interior portal locked out by Anderson! No choice, I'm going in bareback!" He wasn't sure of the ramifications of what he said next, nor did he particularly care. "Oh, yeah. Confine that son of a bitch Kreechum."

Ellis would need more details, but that could wait. If he didn't act quickly, Imholtz would be dead for sure. Moreover, if he couldn't prevent the CAM-L from being completely trashed, the six lives hanging in the balance at Nadir would be forfeited.

Encountering no one, he ran to the nearest personnel portal, ironically the same one Ellis had passed through. Now, it was his chance to pull a stunt. This was crazier. He wouldn't have to jog as far as she did—the exterior docking portal was a sprint away—but it was a sure bet that Anderson wouldn't be in a receptive mood when he arrived. Damn shame that the rebreathers were safely stored on shelving in the docking area.

Except for the one Anderson was wearing.

He took several deep breaths. Saying, "Open portal," he stepped out into the thin air and blazing heat and ran. An expectant voice greeted him upon his arrival at the open docking portal.

"Take a load off," Anderson said through his rebreather mask, knowing the time advantage he enjoyed. "I expected you sooner."

"Thank Kreechum," Davis said, moving closer, hoping for a reaction.

"Was he that obvious?" Anderson responded, feigning ease but tensing at the other man's approach.

Davis kept silent. Engaging in idle chatter was a waste of breath. A glance down at Imholtz revealed that the hair on his scalp was dark and damp with blood. Option one: Drag him out of here.

"Go ahead," Anderson said as if reading his thoughts, gesturing to the exterior portal. "I won't stop you."

Should he take the bait? If he could heft Imholtz over his shoulder and carry him out, Anderson would continue to wreak havoc on the CAM-L. It would have to be option two.

Acting quickly—the terrible ache to inhale had begun—he propelled himself toward the command panel that closed the exterior portal and activated four huge ventilation ducts that purged Murkor's foul atmosphere from the dock area and replaced it with oxygenated air.

Anticipating the move, Anderson, brandishing a pipe as a weapon, ran to intercept him. The bastard was doing what Davis hoped for. Reaching the command panel counted for nothing. By the time oxygen was fully restored, he would have passed out. Game over. Stopping dead in his tracks, he spun and charged. The surprised look in Anderson's eyes told him that the timing had been perfect. Ducking under a wild swing, he dropped low to the floor and swept his legs in a wide arc that connected with the tech's shins, knocking him off his feet and sending the pipe he held clanking across the floor. For a long moment, they grappled, but Anderson managed to escape and take one step back. "Stupid move," he said, breathing heavily. All he had to do was wait while a gasping Davis suffocated.

Or so he believed.

Anderson had misjudged his aerobic capacity for the second time in two years. He had been working in the stifling heat. Perhaps Imholtz had put up a fight. Running encumbered by a rebreather and the ensuing struggle had winded him.

More importantly, during their struggle, Davis turned off a valve that controlled Anderson's oxygen supply. A facemask could not hide the look of panic as he sucked in inert gases. When he made a motion to reach the valve, Davis lunged forward, aiming a knife-hand strike to the throat, which was blocked. A knee to the groin, however, found its mark, sending the tech to the floor, doubled over in pain.

Davis let him lie.

He had neither the breath nor the inclination to inflict more hurt on the person who had once been his friend.

Davis had no recollection of reaching the control panel and entering the correct sequence of commands; Ellis, arriving barely in time to squeeze through the interlacing sides of the dock's exterior portal, found him slumped on the floor, unconscious. So, too, were Imholtz and Anderson. As the atmosphere was restored, the interior door interlock was disengaged, allowing an anxious Stewart, with Cooper assisting, to rush in and begin treatment.

Davis, reviving quickly, explained what happened. He wasted no time assessing the damage to the CAM-L and reporting the findings to Ellis. "I can mend it," he reassured her.

"How long?" she had asked.

"Five hours, give or take. With any luck, we should arrive at Nadir's doorstep before dark. We may have to return to Zenith at night. It's a concern."

"Understood," Ellis said. "I'm more troubled about what we'll find once we get to Nadir."

After being attended to in the medical bay, Anderson was interred and would stay there till Ellis decided his fate.

There was the matter of what to do with Kreechum. Acting on Davis's prior advice, the IMC foreman was "escorted" to an empty compartment, where he was placed under constant guard. After hearing the damning particulars directly from Davis, Ellis had the accused brought to her office, where he was now answering for himself. Or trying to.

"You've got nothing to make that charge stick," the belligerent foreman spouted in a grating amalgam of indignation and bluster. "What if I accidentally ran into the lieutenant in the corridor? *If* Anderson said I was involved, it's a damn lie. Has he said it? If he does, it's his word against mine."

"There's a bit more to it," Davis replied with a half-smile that no one in their right mind would mistake for amusement. "You've managed to incriminate yourself. There is a visual record of the slime trail you left behind."

"Bullshit," Kreechum said, his voice taking on a higher pitch. "There's no optics in those corridors."

"There is something almost as good," Davis replied, glancing at Ellis, her subtle nod indicating that he should remain center stage. The evidence, shortly to be dropped on Kreechum like a chunk of neutron star, had initially been her inspiration, but the lieutenant was enjoying himself far too much to interrupt.

"Mindstor," Davis vocalized, ignoring the foreman, *"review corridor wall images displayed between 0400 and 0500. Cross-reference images to archived preferences for crew member Kreechum. Using the results, plot subject's recent locations as a function of time. Visualize findings, center of this room, as a top-down 2-D image."*

In a millisecond, Kreechum's various movements, depicted by a handful of bold red lines, hovered in the air. They were an unmistakable indictment. The most telling line, also the earliest, led directly from his private quarters to Anderson's. Additional lines showed his presence in the long corridor to the dock area and the subsequent retracement to his quarters.

Although the IMC foreman kept his scowl, he could not mask his anxiety—a newly formed sheen of sweat on his face and arms gave him away.

Davis continued his pursuit. "Nothing to say?" he goaded. "Shall I have the mindstor conduct the same analysis for Anderson and correlate both of you for time and place?"

Kreechum, avoiding the question, glared at Ellis. "You'll never make it to Nadir in time."

"You'd condemn six people to die?" Ellis asked, her body tensing in anger.

In the protracted silence that followed, she waited for some semblance of compassion in the man.

When it did not materialize, she was forced to admit her own limitations: How easy it was to hate the person standing before her.

"There is a chasm between you and Anderson," she finally said. "The past is his demon, compelling him to act as he does. You're motivated solely by your greed. *You* are the demon." No longer interested in anything the foreman had to offer, she turned to Cooper and said, "Get him out of my sight."

Davis remained, prompted by a growing fascination for the woman who was willing to take on anything or anyone in the name of a *cause*. That's how he would characterize her actions since arriving on base nine days ago. What drove her? Maybe he'd never know—she tried to keep that part of herself shielded. In her admonition to Kreechum, he had seen a flash of inner turmoil in her eyes, a rare loss of serenity as she struggled to sublimate the urge to lash out at the man.

"Yes?" Ellis said, adhering to her habit of parceling words as if allotted a limited supply.

"Care to hear some unsolicited personal advice?" Davis asked, wondering how long he had been staring.

"Let it fly."

"There will always be someone like Kreechum. You can't change him. Don't kick yourself when you end up despising him."

"Worthy of serious consideration," Ellis said, again caught off-guard that Davis could read her so well.

"Should be," Davis said. "That part about not being so hard on yourself is something you once told me."

"Since you have such affinity for my advice, may I infer that *you* intend to take it?"

"Hell, no," Davis freely admitted, accompanied by his familiar grin.

After Davis left to oversee repair work on the CAM-L, Ellis considered Kreechum's and Anderson's final disposition. Their removal from base would depend on the Nadir expedition, which, in turn, might affect Zenith's near-term water crisis and evacuation plan. Some form of punishment was assured, even considering IMC's political influence. The co-conspirators had overplayed their hand by committing aggravated assault.

An unexpected visit from Schulman enlightened her on one particular. His various duties put him in close contact with personnel, many of whom he was quite willing to lend an ear to. "I have news that may elevate your spirits, commander," he began. "Assuming, that is, they require elevating."

"And the origin of this so-called 'news?'" Ellis queried.

"A statistically valid sampling of just about everyone on base—incarcerated excepted."

"Proceed."

"Few were pleased with what Kreechum and Anderson attempted; none were happy that it was to the detriment of a fellow tech. Imholtz is well-liked. There are other reasons. Anyway, commander, the prevailing sentiment on base has shifted decidedly in your favor."

"Gratifying."

"It's only fitting. As an aside, I never liked Kreechum's taste in wall art."

"Before you leave, tell me this, Mr. Schulman," Ellis said. "Why do you make no mention of our dwindling water reserves?"

"I'd be a fool to take you for one," Schulman said, deliberately looking past her, through the room's viewport, out to the menacing desolation toward Nadir. "Anyway, be careful out there."

***

Ellis's thoughts returned to the incident in the CAM-L docking station and the varying intervals the three men had spent in an oxygen-poor environment.

On cursory review, Anderson's deprivation was the simplest to evaluate. He had passed out just as ambient oxygen was restored and revived shortly thereafter. Nothing particularly noteworthy there.

Davis's case also seems to be explainable. Everything he accomplished, from the time he left via the personnel portal to when he succumbed, had consumed only a few minutes. Add three minutes for the docking bay atmosphere to be fully restored. Other than a few bruises, he showed no ill effects from the ordeal.

Imholtz's experience was, in her estimation, worthy of further study. On its face, it added to a growing mystery. Based on the principle that often the most valuable opinion is the one at variance from one's own, Ellis sought out Stewart. "How are your patients?" she asked.

"Anderson?" Stewart said, smiling. Both were acutely aware of how Davis took him down. "In shock that not only you can be a ball buster. Imholtz has a concussion. Very treatable. Light duty in a few hours. But that's not the only reason you're here."

"Have you given it any thought?"

"Sufficient consideration to tell you there is nothing here to sway me," Stewart answered. "We can only approximate the time Imholtz was lying unconscious, breathing in Murkor's low oxygen. Perhaps several minutes. What I don't know is just how much oxygen his body needed while in an unconscious state. Typically, it's less. Unlike you—and you were hallucinating—he had no sense of a presence. I asked him."

"Why would he?" Ellis said. "Like you said, he was unconscious."

"True enough."

"You find nothing strange about the disparate incidents?"

"Oh, they're strange, alright," Stewart responded. "Just not alien-strange."

Ellis persisted. *"Mindstor. Evaluate Nadir and Zenith files for possible intrusion of unclassified organism, agent, or substance into base Nadir."*

As before, three seconds elapsed.

Low probability. Adequate detection and decontamination procedures are currently in place and fully functional at both facilities. Forty-three Standard Earth Years since a reported detector failure. Cross-reference and further review of incidents involving L.

Jensen, A. Cruz, R. Allawi, J. Ellis, and B. Imholtz are indicated.

A minor victory, Ellis thought. One more name added to the growing list. Frustrated, she decided to tweak the mindstor with one more inquiry.

"Mindstor. Review last response. How many incidents are required before a high probability value is assigned to your answer?"

A very short delay ensued.

A number in excess of thirty-six, the restrictive parameter of the inquiry.

"That's the combined population of Nadir and Zenith," Stewart said, trying hard not to gloat. "In the unlikely event something out there can evade a detector, our full-body protective suits will be useless at Nadir. To save time and room, I suggest we leave such gear behind."

***

Ellis had put off updating Garcia as long as she could, hoping there would be something positive to relay. Now, even the exact time of departure was uncertain. When the comlink to Nadir was again restored, she noted that her counterpart's appearance had deteriorated further.

"I wish I had better news about the problems besetting you, comandante. We have no special insight." Great way to build trust, she thought to herself.

"I understand," a weakened voice replied.

"We also had a setback here," Ellis continued. "The vehicle capable of reaching you is undergoing

244

emergency repair. We shall be delayed a few hours." What would she believe if roles were reversed and she were told the same?

"You have taken on a lot," Garcia managed to say. "I sincerely hope it has not inspired internal discord."

"Whatever troubles we have encountered are minor compared to yours. My lieutenant will troubleshoot your ailing environmental system once you and your crew are safely in the CAM-L. If he can affect repair, the option to remain at Nadir shall, of course, be yours."

"We will be in a very bad way when you arrive—" Garcia's voice faded away, but the dire implication was clear. He struggled to begin again. "I have entries in my log acknowledging all this—one entry, in particular, you should be aware of—"

"Yes, comandante?"

"Our supply of fresh water is yours."

12 WE DON'T DIE ALONE

THE BEST A SEVERLY compromised Garcia could manage was to reduce the baffling nature of their affliction to the lesson in humility that began a millennia ago when Galileo proved Earth was not the physical center of Creation and extended to the recently discovered lifeforms on *Orb* and *BranxA*. Namely, the universe does not spin to our consciousness.

We are constantly reminded of our limitations. What humanity embraces as an unassailable fact in one age is often discredited in the next: Martian canals. Spontaneous generation. Flat Earth. The "can't-exceed-c" rule. Ideas touted by the most brilliant minds of their times now ridiculed.

Our misplaced beliefs have become more sophisticated, not fewer. Centuries ago, a widely held theory, oddly named *Goldilocks Zone*, espoused that life was restricted to a predefined "comfort zone" around a star. A theory having the same basis in reality as the fairy tale it was named after.

A frown came to his face. If hindsight is twenty-twenty, science has pointed precisely where to look.

Where was *he* not looking?

Fatigued, he pushed back from his desk, chastising himself for wasting time on another futile quasi-philosophical exercise. He was no closer to finding a solution to the life-threatening crisis that he and five other souls were confronting.

Leaving the letter of condolence to the shuttle pilot's widow unfinished, he rolled his desk chair to the viewport. For what he thought might be the last time, he gazed at the tortured landscape, absent of life and color. Several hours earlier, he had stood here unassisted. Out there were several environmental monitoring stations coated in wind-carried black grit. Those few surviving the harsh conditions registered the nearby fumaroles as abnormally active, but to Garcia, the sounds of their tumultuous expulsions were almost undetectable. Readings from a particle counter signaled a significant reduction in atmospheric aerosols. For Murkor, it was a clear day, but he could no longer see the lava field's intricate webbing of cracks and crevices.

Looking outward, he lamented, was becoming as murky as looking inward.

Not long ago, when he could still see and hear well, he had happily divided the remainder of military service into Earth days. Now, helplessly watching his and his crews' accelerating decline, time had the uncertainty and brevity of Murkor hours. A sorrowful thought seized him. Somehow, an hour had become a year on this battered planet, prematurely draining their vitality. Was this the end stage of a person's life greatly accelerated? A preview of advancing age and the inevitability of death?

He notified his fellow crew members that Ellis had, of necessity, postponed their evacuation from Nadir. With their lives hanging in the balance, the news took them down, stunned silence at first, followed by expressions of fear and a return to the suspicion of Coalition's motives that never really left. Repeating Zenith's renewed pledge of assistance, which he believed to be sincere, was of little avail: The distrust ingrained by decades of Unión-Coalition animosity could not be defeated by the mere utterance of words.

Of his crew, the least affected by the unhappy disclosure was Carlos, already inured to the worst outcome in all things related to *The Enemy*. "I wish I had been wrong," he had said, barely able to raise his head from the bed where he lay resting.

Most troubled was Amanda, desperately holding back tears, uttering, "I look old," then retreating to the solitude of her quarters without further words. Had she heard him say, "No, you shall always be beautiful?"

When two hours elapsed, and she had neither returned to the L2 common area nor responded to her comlink, Garcia took notice. Pushing aside uncertainty about the welcome he would receive (it was impossible to forget their prior intimacy), he went to her cabin, finding her draped across the bed.

"I was hoping you would come," she said.

"How are you faring?"

"Well enough," she said, the strain of speaking evident in her voice as she methodically enunciated each word. More telling was the disheveled appearance of the clothes she wore.

"Anything you need?" Garcia asked. He was the only person capable of moving freely about the base, though that luxury was drawing to a close.

"I'd like to talk," Amanda replied, patting the bed beside her. "Talk," she repeated, anticipating his hesitancy, though the fact of the matter was that nothing other than an emotional exchange was feasible.

Garcia, without reservation, sat. If he was a lousy judge of character, he could do no worse than how he had misjudged his own.

Amanda was not inherently a dishonest person. Instead, and at an early age, honesty had been supplanted in importance by vanity and pridefulness. It took her much longer to identify her poor decisions and admit that she had exploited another's weakness. "I wanted to tell you," she began, "exactly what happened when I visited Carlos in his quarters. Do you remember? It was that night I left you and Mariana—"

"You don't have to—" Garcia said, unsure what to expect, watching as she struggled to stay composed.

"Please. Let me. I must—before we all—well, you know. He turned me away. You should know why. You see, he told me he didn't want to disappoint you again."

"Again? I'm not sure I understand."

"I didn't myself at the time. I was too angry. Later though—don't you see, Carlos believes the problem with the Nexus was the first time he failed you."

Garcia shook his head in dismay, hoping that this was not the impression he gave.

"You didn't make him feel that way," Amanda responded. "Not deliberately. It was in his own mind. Eating away at him. When he understood I was only trying to use him to get at you, he refused me—even if you'd never know that's what he did."

"He said nothing about it," Garcia said, verifying that Carlos kept the incident to himself.

"He rejected me because he respects you. He didn't realize that you and I were over—perhaps we never should have started." Amanda took Garcia's hand in hers—their first meaningful touch. "I accept that now. I should have much sooner."

It was a lot for Garcia to process: A young man's respect for him evidenced by his willingness to turn an alluring and available woman away; how she, seeing the value of genuine affection, found the strength to make herself vulnerable and let him go. The three of them emotionally connected. He gently squeezed the soft hand he was holding and said, "Amanda, don't be sorry. However ill-conceived our actions leading to this junction, they have been turned into something redeemable. A fresh start."

"I would like that," Amanda replied, and then, surrendering to her fear of an uncertain future, voiced what they both were thinking. "But will they come, comandante?"

"I am certain that they will try," Garcia replied.

"You seem so sure. It's not that easy for me."

"Nor for me," Garcia admitted. "The only reasonable choice is to have faith in human nature—keeping a tight focus on the better half of it."

Amanda returned a small smile and slowly closed her eyes, acquiescing to the malady pursuing them all.

The crews' sleeping quarters, six small compartments, were on the first level. Once prized for offering a small measure of privacy, they had now turned into cells, effectively isolating them from each other. Garcia was determined to prevent that from happening. "Can you raise yourself?" he asked. Not waiting for an answer, he reached behind Amanda's back to prop her up, alarmed at how cold and listless she was in his arms.

"I was a bit shaky making it down here," she warned.

"You'll have my arm," Garcia said, helping her rise from the bed. "We should all be together when the rescue team from Zenith arrives."

What Garcia kept to himself as they shuffled to the spiral stairs leading to L2 was not the fear that Ellis would refuse to come. She would arrive too late.

***

The words "less mass, less cost," which were emblematic of Nadir's design and construction, had been repeated so frequently and with such fervor that they took on the aspect of a mantra. The same guiding principle was applied to the base's austere furnishings, including the crew's modest microfoam beds. Compressible to less than a tenth of their expanded size, they could easily be rolled and carried tucked under the arm. Spares were kept in a storage compartment in expectation of accommodating guests or visiting dignitaries who had never come.

Roya and Gustavo, aware of the dimming prospect of a timely rescue and finding themselves incapable of descending to their respective quarters, were resting side-by-side on two such beds in the middle of L2.

The cozy arrangement displeased neither of them. They had spent most of the last years trapped inside a structure the size of a large house, during which time they were at the mercy of each other's sometimes less-than-ingratiating imperfections, personal habits, and idiosyncrasies. Neither was the worse off for the imposed intimacy, developing a close friendship, and the freedom to tease each other. Brought even closer together by their incapacity, they were doing so now—each trying to comfort the other by putting on the face of courage in the face of danger.

"Care to trade?" Gustavo inquired in a raised voice. "My loss of vision for your loss of hearing?" An anomaly of the affliction they were experiencing was the inconsistent and partial effect it produced on the five senses.

"What's to be gained by that?" Roya asked.

"I won't have to hear your insults."

"Deal. With your poor eyesight, I wouldn't have to see your ugly face."

"I aim to please."

"Are you as frightened as I am?" Roya asked suddenly, turning to look directly at Gustavo, alarmed at the effort it took to accomplish the simple motion.

"Of my own face?" he remarked, trying to make Roya laugh.

"Seriously."

"Wouldn't be half as scared if I could find some meaning in this."

"As a scientist, I feel like what's happening to us is part of some grand experiment—only we won't see the results."

"Kinda like life in general," Gustavo reflected, looking up at the blur of the ceiling. "One big experiment. The final result is death."

"Nothing more?" Roya asked, responding to the skepticism. "You don't believe something follows?"

"I'm at an impasse. The devout believer devises his own God; the atheist denies a secret hope of being proven wrong." Gustavo let out a cynical laugh. "What other choice is given us? To pray?"

"Gus, Gus, I would get down on my knees in front of the whole world, not because I believe prayers are answered, I don't, but because it is *what* we pray for that defines us."

"And what would you be praying for?"

"Joy."

Roya's response had come quickly. Accepting the unexpected simplicity of the word, Gustavo faced her and said, "Then it would be my eternal pleasure to kneel down beside you."

"That would be a sight—if only we could manage." And with that, Roya, exhausted from the conversation, closed her eyes, took a shallow breath, and fell asleep. As she slept, she unconsciously shifted her body closer to Gustavo and draped an arm across his chest.

This was the touching scene encountered when, while struggling to support Amanda, Garcia alighted from L1.

"Is that you, comandante?" Gustavo asked as they approached. "Is that Amanda with you? Good."

"Roya?" Garcia inquired in alarm. There was a growing inclination to expect the worst.

"Only resting," Gustavo assured. "I tired her out by blabbing too much."

"How many beds are left in storage?"

"Three, I believe."

With great effort, a weary Garcia retrieved the beds, Amanda settling on one. In seconds, she had joined Roya in what appeared to be sleep.

"It's been a long time since I had lovely women lying on either side of me," Gustavo commented. "It's a damn shame I can't move."

"I should imagine that's a comfort to them," Garcia pointed out.

"Come back and tell us a bedtime story," Gustavo said, his eyes trying to follow the comandante as he headed away.

***

Never in Mariana Perez's exceptional medical career did she feel so utterly helpless.

Not that she hadn't lost patients before. Hazardous assignments, of which she had more than her fair share, had an unfortunate way of making casualties seem inevitable. In every instance, before a patient expired (a doctorate in interplanetary medicine helped keep fatalities to a merciful few), she had been able to diagnose the ailment and render a measure of final comfort.

And then, without pausing to look back, she carried on.

She had come to accept that there was no callousness in viewing a patient's death dispassionately. A mind might grasp, but a heart cannot hold all the hurts of the world. An indispensable lesson for a physician is that detachment should not be perceived as indifference. Emotional distance provides perspective and a measure of self-protection. Vision, she remembered a wiser colleague saying, is clearer when no tears are welling in the eyes.

Personal attachments were scrupulously avoided on the many colonies she had been stationed in. But here, on a barren planet where it was said nothing could grow, emotions had been cultivated. They had, for her, blossomed into bonds that ran the gamut from a hard-to-explain fondness for a younger, complicated woman to an easy-to-accept love for a compassionate older man.

The last vestige of Mariana's self-protection vanished when Carlos whispered that he dared not shut his eyes for fear of never opening them again. Sitting beside the bed where he lay incapacitated, she had turned her head away. Making certain that he could not see her cry.

No one must see her cry. For the most caring of physicians, crying was a sign of capitulation.

With an unsteady hand, she smeared the wetness over her cheek.

And turned back immediately.

"Carlos, I'm here," she said. "I shall stay with you." Increasing weariness had almost claimed her when he reached for her hand, his usually firm grip now feeble.

If their final hours were near, if their mutual affection meant their sorrow would be magnified, so would the solace they could share.

"What is happening to me, Mariana? To us?"

It wasn't so much a question from Carlos as a plaintive appeal, the words traveling into her semiconscious mind from an unfathomable distance. Unintentionally, she had drifted off.

With difficulty, she leaned forward, placing her mouth close to the young man's ear so he could better hear. "Do you feel any discomfort or pain?" she asked, freeing her hand to pat his arm gently. For the first time in her career, she was forced to be both a physician and patient. With a head tilt, she placed her ear near his mouth, his voice a whisper, her hearing compromised.

"No. I feel…nothing," Carlos answered.

His response was expected and, in one way, regrettable. Pain, though she did not wish it on him, could be eliminated, and its location, intensity, and type might provide valuable diagnostic clues.

The crew's lack of pain—strange in itself—eliminated the need for neuro-blockers. Similarly, the use of biostims to halt the progression from what appeared to be some form of coma had proven either ineffective or transitory. With no other options indicated or at her disposal, a lifetime of learning was reduced to monitoring vital signs. During the last hour, she had watched with trepidation and, yes, fascination as the young engineer's resting heart rate steadily decreased to below twenty-seven beats per minute while his respiratory rate, body temperature, and blood pressure sank further into the red zone. She would wager her medical license that his basal metabolic rate and electro-chem brain function had also declined, though she lacked the scanner necessary to substantiate such a conclusion.

Each member of the crew was caught in the same downward spiral. Carlos, easily the youngest of them, just happened to be the worst off.

Just happened to be—another useless entry in her medical log.

The young man took a deep breath, his chest expanding with air. Mariana timed the interval to the next inhalation, almost leaving her seat (to do what, she asked herself) when, after an excruciatingly long twenty seconds, his chest heaved once again. It was as if a series of circuits were mysteriously and prematurely switched off in response to the demands of an oxygen-poor environment. A clumsy analogy matched by the crews' wild suppositions about their affliction's identity, each harder to believe than the next.

Starting with her own: Murkor, a world so out of balance that natural phenomenon, both evident and covert, had conspired with the effects of hypoxia to alter the psychological and physiological well-being of six human interlopers. In effect, a strange group psychosis results in a group psychosomatic illness.

What had Roya speculated? Oh, yes, they were unwittingly harboring an entity of such subtlety and stealth that it could elude the advance team of astrobiologists and Nadir's supposedly foolproof detection and sterilization safeguards.

Carlos had no desire to speculate. He was sure that Nadir's concurrent and mystifying problems, the Nexus and their affliction, were part of a pair. That Coalition had developed a new class of cloaked nanoparticles and was using them to cause harm.

To her recollection, three crew members were reluctant to put forth opinions.

No, that was false. Gustavo's mischievous words came to mind. He had labeled their affliction "the devil's breath." Presumably, he wasn't being serious. She should not take him so except to the extent the metaphorical devil resides in us all.

These were the ideas that came to her. More were conjured, bizarre and half-formed, from the astronomical to the chimerical, until she drifted off, her head nodding forward, then whipping back as she resisted falling into the unnatural sleep that threatened to absorb her like a black hole.

Carlos *had* fallen asleep. If that's what it was. He seemed peaceful enough.

Her concern turned to the four other members of the crew, not seen or heard from in the last hour. Were they in need of special attention? If she didn't move, she would soon be incapable of climbing the stairs to L2.

Sight unseen, Garcia silently braced himself in the open doorway. His heart sank upon seeing Carlos so deathly still, then rose again on a wave of immense relief upon seeing the young man's eyelids flutter in response to some hidden dream. "Mariana," he said softly, unwilling to startle her. When she did not hear, he approached, steadying himself with an affectionate hand on the shoulder—a hand recognized and promptly covered with her own.

"He doesn't have much longer," Mariana lamented. "The others?"

"On L2. Resting comfortably on spare beds. All three unable to rise."

"So, this is how we're going to end," she sobbed, staring straight ahead. "One by one, falling into oblivion." Her words were filled with bitterness, almost inaudible, for she didn't want to say them. "It is said that a person is born alone and dies alone. Could that be any truer than on this godforsaken planet?"

"No, it is not true!" Garcia cried, determined to prove it false. "A newborn child is intimately connected to the mother. When we pass from this life, we carry inside us a lifetime of intimacies. It is from each other that we find comfort in an indifferent universe."

Bbrrahhuffenzellfff-kapht-tzzing!

It wasn't the first time that one of Murkor's obnoxious fumaroles inserted itself in a conversation.

The timing made Garcia take special note. "How shall I interpret *that* comment?" he said, coming around to coax a smile from Mariana. "Confirmation? Portent?"

"And, if portent, foreboding or auspicious?" Mariana wondered.

"I intend to get you and Carlos out of this room and up to L2," Garcia said, adding, when Mariana shook her head in doubt, "Perhaps I'll need a little assistance."

"I have something—" Mariana said, reaching deep into the medical bag kept by her side to retrieve two disposable stick-stim pads. "Worth a try." She had saved these last couple for an emergency. Bringing the crew together one final time qualified.

Stims were the size, shape, and color of a vanilla wafer. When adhered to the temple, they tricked the brain into releasing its natural neurotransmitters into trillions of synaptic gaps, facilitating electric signals between neurons. Although rapid, the beneficial effect on motor coordination and muscle response was fleeting.

Starting to totter, Garcia sat on the edge of Carlos's bed. Placing his hands on the engineer's shoulders, he gently shook. Unable to rouse him, he spoke sternly and loudly. "Sargento! It's Comandante Garcia! Sargento!"

A pair of dimming eyes opened. "Tired—" came back a response, low and confused.

"Drag your ass out of that bed, soldier!" Garcia persisted.

"Comandante?"

"I need to get to L2, sargento! Can't do it without your help!"

Mariana gave Garcia an appreciative nod and handed him a stim.

"… bad with stairs," Carlos responded, trying to prop himself up on two arms bent at the elbow. "Sorry… sorry… failing you—"

The apology hit Garcia hard. "No, you could never fail me. *Never.* It is *I* who have failed you—letting myself become distracted. Not making prudent decisions when time was our ally." He fastened the adhesive stim to the young man's temple, declaring, "My friend, I will always have faith in you. Who else has kept Nadir from falling apart these last few years? Now get your lazy ass out of bed. Mariana and I need your help."

Realizing that she had to act fast, Mariana held the second stim close to Garcia's face so he could see both it and the implication in her expression. "You use it," he demanded. "I'll manage—if I have to crawl every centimeter of the way."

She did not disagree. Not about the stim. "You're wrong. You did what you could," she protested. "No one foresaw."

"And no one's crawling," Carlos said, his eyes regaining focus. A moment later, he discovered the will to sit up. Then, as a silently amazed Garcia moved out of the way, he managed to slide his legs over the side of the bed, placing himself in a position to stand.

Mariana struggled to her feet, aided by the stim's jolt to her nervous system and a shaky hand offered by each man. "There's no time to waste," she said. "We have got a mountain to climb."

And so, oddly counterbalancing and helping each other, the three crewmates found the means to scale the spiral stairs to L2 and rejoin their colleagues.

***

Those already present on L2 could not rise to welcome the three arrivals, but in gathering his crew, Garcia accomplished what he set out to do. The result, however, was bittersweet—the happiness and emotional security gained by being in each other's company tempered by the realization that these were likely their final hours together.

"Mariana, carina Mariana," Roya said in greeting, the simple act of expressing her friend's name evoking a trove of sentiments: *You tried, don't be scared, lean on me—*

"I know—*I know*," came the tear-choked response, heartfelt confirmation of everything left unsaid.

The stim's rapidly ebbing effect sent Carlos, guided by Garcia, collapsing onto one of the empty beds procured from storage. It was by design that it happened to be the bed closest to Amanda, who immediately seized the opportunity, making amends for her prior behavior.

"You did right," Amanda said loud enough for Carlos to hear, who acknowledged with an understanding nod.

"Any word from Zenith?" Gustavo managed to ask.

"A status update," Garcia said, referring to the periodic progress reports Ellis was transmitting.

"'Departure imminent. Barring setbacks, ETA before Murkorian nightfall.'"

"Enough time?" Gustavo asked, the crew's survival implicit in the question.

Garcia looked to Mariana, who could only shake her head in despair. She had made a final check of everyone's vital signs before she could do no more. The readings confirmed what she already knew and everyone else strongly suspected: Within hours, they would be unconscious. Soon after, their hearts would cease beating. Death would overtake them before the arrival of help from Zenith.

Assuming they came at all.

And if they were to arrive in time, what could they do? Save them from a malady no one could identify, let alone cure? Could they rapidly restore the ESS to operation when a week's effort by their own engineer had failed? Ironically, the only contrarian news in a hopeless situation was that they were not struggling to breathe, even with oxygen levels below fourteen percent. Studying Garcia's careworn face as he knelt beside her, Mariana wondered if he had reached the same conclusion: The rescue party from Zenith would be embarking on a dangerous overland trek, jeopardizing their own lives. For what? An uncomfortable answer presented itself.

"They come only for the water?" Mariana wondered.

"I shall never believe it," Garcia said, touching her cheek.

"Then I shall not either," she responded, body sinking deeper in the bed she lay on, her words of faith nearly causing Garcia to break down. A feeble voice deflected his attention.

"Comandante."

"Yes, Carlos."

"I must leave you."

"Then rest, my dear friend," Garcia said, bowing his head to close the distance between them. "Sleep. I shall join you soon. When we awaken, it will be a brighter day."

In the end, as each of his crew drifted off into their final sleep, he noticed there was no bed for him. If fate had decided to begrudge him a little more time, so be it—the rescue party would find him where he should be. With the last remnants of his strength, he reached the nearby mindstor station, finding the words of condolence offered to the shuttle pilot's widow:

I never met your husband. I confess to not knowing his name. What little of a personal nature we shared, a yearning to return to you, his family, was communicated through the vacuum of space.

And yet, despite our vast separation, he unhesitatingly risked everything to save six souls, that of myself and my crew. It is my most profound regret that he forfeited his life in the attempt. No person can impart a greater impression upon another than he, and it is through his unselfish sacrifice that I have the honor of saying I know him well. He shall live on in my memory as a good and brave man.

I cannot hope to take away your sorrow except to the small extent of trying to address any burden you may bear in answering those who question the wisdom of his rushing to the aid of an 'enemy.' Your husband adamantly refused to be encumbered by such a divisive label. If we had the pleasure of meeting aboard his vessel, he would have learned something tangible of us: That Mariana Perez is a most excellent and caring physician, declining safer assignments and advancement in rank to be in personal contact with her patients; that Carlos Alvarez is a brash and troubled young man carrying the emotional scars of the antipathy between our respective nations; that nothing is immune from Gustavo Ramirez's humor or can prevent him from quoting his favorite author; that Roya Allawi devoted a year and a half of her life to missionary work in North Africa; that Amanda Cruz is beautiful, intelligent, and perhaps a bit self-absorbed.

As for me, I am boring. I would have too often repeated that awaiting my return to Earth is an elderly father who, disregarding my advancing years and 'lofty' title, will forever greet me by the name Mi Osito—my little bear. I long to see him as you longed to see your devoted husband. Sorrows will be joined as neither shall come to pass.

These small testaments concerning the character of my crew and myself are humbly offered as proof that although the risk your husband took was substantial, it was eclipsed by what he knew would be gained. It exposes to the doubters of the world what he understood deep in his heart: That our virtues and faults unite us. Together, let us pray that his sacrifice, his memory, will keep alive the hope that one day no barriers will come between us; that there will be a generation, perhaps your children's, that will see so far and so clear as to see no borders.

I devoutly wish for there to be solace in these meager words. If, in remembrance, they inspire tears, I hope you find that in crying, there is healing. Life is fragile, yet our spirits are resilient.

Garcia's final action was to enter the "save" command.

With eyes closed, his head came to rest on folded arms.

13 EXPEDITION

THE MASSIVE DOCKING STATION portal slowly lifted. In the sobering distance, shimmering bands of heat rose from the lava and sailed into the midday Murkorian atmosphere. Closer in, a meter-high deposit of powdery pumice was piled against Zenith's wind-facing surfaces like an incongruous drift of black snow. The embankment created was too inconsequential to be a hindrance, but its confrontational position directly in front of the formidable CAM-L caused Lieutenant Brian Davis to wonder if they were about to embark on a fool's errand. No matter, he thought. If a man's mettle could be measured by his tolerance for playing the fool, then the greater part of him was fully onboard.

It had been Davis's experience that there was typically more angst in contemplating a hazardous mission than in its actual execution. Whatever comfort he usually derived from this reflection seemed strangely absent. Ignoring his unease, he gave a self-assured nod to Ellis and Stewart (who shared navigational duties) and activated the vehicle's powerful engine. Disengaging pilot-assist, he thrust the accelerator throttles into the "forward" position, sending the heavy vehicle lurching through the open portal. It was a good show—a decisive path plowed through the snow ridge, Zenith's protective dome disappearing behind them in a towering plume of pumice.

Zenith and Nadir, positioned in the center of their abutting exclusion zones, were precisely one hundred kilometers apart. After accounting for the numerous topographical features to avoid, the distance between was much further. If Davis pressed it, and he had every intention of doing so, they would arrive at Nadir as night began to close in on them. In this, there was little margin for error.

The expedition began well enough. Several missions had ventured out in this direction, the lava tubes closest to Nadir holding the most promise of water discovery. Of aid was that the vehicle's external cameras had recorded previous forays into what had been uncharted territory, then uploaded the images to the vehicle's mindstor to produce a three-dimensional surface map. Unfortunately, the terrain-altering effects of erosion, rollers, and earthquakes often rendered these maps inaccurate.

Davis proved himself to be of value by providing navigational assistance. Having piloted the CAM-L numerous times and, on rare occasions, the larger anercrecium harvester, he had familiarized himself with prominent surface landmarks. The upshot was that Ellis and Stewart were temporarily relieved from the stress of cross-referencing the changing topography with the holo map displayed on the rendition pedestal between them. Although no one expected it to last, a relaxed mood pervaded the confines of the vehicle's pressurized cabin.

For a spell, no one spoke, the low thrumming pulse of the engine and the satisfying lava-crunching sound of the vehicle's rotating tracks prevailing. Stewart decided to take advantage of the interlude by opening a line of inquiry that could provide, if not general amusement, at least her own. Davis was the easiest of the two available targets.

"Brian," Stewart began, the three officers finding the present situation conducive to addressing each other by whatever appellation felt comfortable. "There's something I've been meaning to ask you."

Something undefinable in Stewart's tone made him immediately wary. "This can't be good," he replied.

"Come on, all I want to know is if someone is waiting for you back on Earth. Perhaps a special lady pining away with a broken heart?" Out of the corner of her eye, she watched Ellis, her next target, repress a smile—and perhaps show something more than passing interest in the lieutenant's response.

"I don't hail from Earth," Davis offered, denying Stewart the satisfaction she sought.

"And exactly where do you 'hail' from?" she persisted.

"The Ariadne Enclave."

"Are there no women there?" Stewart asked. "It only takes one, you know. Or is that too limiting for a good-looking man like you?"

"No, one is more than sufficient," Davis said. Then, under his breath: "Learned *that* the hard way."

"I see," Stewart remarked after a pause. "Shut tight as a proverbial clam."

There was an expectant silence as the unanswered question hung in the conditioned air.

"*Well?* What about you, Jen?" Stewart finally asked, using the more familiar-sounding shortening of the CO's first name to accentuate the personal nature of the inquiry.

"Terrain's changing," Ellis replied.

"If you're trying to distract me, you can do better," Stewart replied, undaunted.

"Will nothing stop her?" Davis mumbled, his attempt at disinterest betrayed by his exaggerated "straight ahead" focus on piloting duties.

"And she thinks *I'm* stubborn," Ellis added.

"You are," Stewart said. "And the word for me is tenacious. There has to be a good man for you out there. They can't *all* want to kick the crap out of you."

Davis, surprised and amused, let loose an involuntary cough and nearly sent the CAM-L careening over a ledge. Ellis flinched. She had to admit that Stewart's alluding to Lieutenant Davis and *Major Ego* Eglend in the same breath was clever, the glaring disparity between the two men almost inducing in her an emotional response, being as attracted to one man as repelled by the other. After considering, she pointed to the most prominent feature of the terrain they were approaching.

"Michele, see that giant hunk of stone?"

"The one we're trying so very hard to evade?" Stewart said with a crooked grin, the sort usually flashed by Davis.

"The same," Ellis said. "Study it closely. You stand a better chance of getting a response from it than from me."

"Think so?" Stewart said, laughing. "What I just heard, or didn't hear, says differently. If either of you had a lover, you would have said so. It's human nature to blab. One day, when both of you can put duty behind, you might find—"

"Stop," Ellis suddenly interrupted. Her words were wasted: The vehicle was already grinding to a halt.

"I see it," Davis remarked, rotating his seat to examine the odd lava formations closing in from both sides, then scrutinizing the images sent from the rear-facing camera to his command console. "Nothing looks familiar."

"The mindstor is starting to reference the nav files Comandante Garcia previously transmitted," Ellis stated. "We've crossed into Nadir's exclusion zone."

"That'll make Kreechum very happy," Davis commented.

"Problem is," Stewart noted, "the holo lacks the same degree of detail."

Davis took it in stride. Before leaving Zenith, he had the good sense to peruse the navigation file. "Nadir's crew never ventured out this far," he explained. "They never had to. All the water they ever needed was relatively close to their base. What you're looking at was transposed from their orbital planet survey."

"We'll have a tough go of it," Stewart complained. "Remind me why, with all the glorious tech we have, there's still no positioning system in place?"

"Because there is a black hole at the center of Coalition's governing body," Davis said. "Common sense can occasionally be sucked in, but it can never escape."

"That encapsulates it," Stewart said.

A network of synchronized ground-based transmitters would have allowed any vehicle or person with a receiver to pinpoint their location within a centimeter. The installation had repeatedly been postponed; the matter was stuck in an appropriations committee due to political squabbling over which company would be awarded the lucrative contract. Union, on the other hand, refused to spend public funds on a planet that was in the process of being forgotten.

Neither faction had contemplated an orbital GPS. Given the planet's problematic debris field and erratic wobble, there were legitimate concerns regarding satellite efficacy and life expectancy. Navigating uncharted territory would remain problematic until successive missions generated a detailed holo map. Of help, more so when returning "home," was the automated homing signal each base continually broadcast. A barely audible quaver could be heard when the CAM-L stopped, indicating the weakness of Nadir's signal.

"The last time I saw Nadir was well over a year ago," Davis was prompted to say, addressing Ellis. "Looked pretty rundown then. What shape is it in now?"

"From outward appearance, pretty bad. The bent mast I observed may explain the low signal."

"Will this help any?" Davis asked. *"Mindstor, overlay the direction of Nadir's homing beacon onto the holo-mapping image."*

"It'll still be a bitch to follow," Stewart said, examining the result.

"Nothing we didn't expect," Ellis said abruptly, finding a recognizable reference point. "Let's get on with it. Bearing 124.3."

As the CAM-L lurched forward, Davis decided to return a favor, concluding the best way was to prod Stewart with a hard-to-believe fact.

"Nadir is outdated construction," he began. "But did you know that centuries ago, houses on Earth were made from boards of wood fastened together by hand, piece by piece, using thousands of short, thin, steel spikes called nails?"

"Houses made of real wood?" Stewart said doubtfully, disadvantaged by the passing of centuries, the absence of forests, and having spent so little time on Earth. "That had to be expensive. How was the outside protected from the elements?"

"The top of the structure was covered with rectangular pieces of fiberglass impregnated with a petroleum product of some sort; the sides were coated with long, thin sheets of a plastic material called vinyl. Also attached with these strange nails."

"Sounds time-consuming," a disbelieving Stewart said, winking at Ellis, who decided to respond with a neutral shrug.

"What's more amazing," Davis resumed, "is that, start to finish, including completing the interior space, it took a score of workers months to complete."

"Now I know you're fooling me," Stewart said.

"Could be," Davis said. "I suggest you look it up."

"I shall," Stewart responded, helping Ellis plot a course through several complex obstructions.

They were entering an unexplored region where forward progress slowed. To port stood a long, ragged row of fumaroles spewing clouds of yellow sulfur that collected in the lava cracks at their feet; to starboard, the scarred, reddened face of a ridge pocked with the yawning mouths of lava tubes. Directly overhead, undiminished by a competing sun, cobalt-colored lightning reached down to tinge the haze a vapid blue.

On more than one occasion, Davis reluctantly altered course, sometimes backtracking hundreds of meters to avoid a deep rift the vehicle could not bridge or a jagged outcropping too high to scale. Beyond the physical demands of piloting, he appeared preoccupied with whatever thought was happening inside his head. Ellis was going to inquire when he blurted out, "Got it!" a broad smile of relief supplanting the frown of concentration he wore. "I think I figured out what's wrong with Nadir's ESS!"

"It's about time," Stewart said, not taking him seriously.

"No joke," he said. "It was right in front of me."

"How—?" Ellis demanded.

"By studying their schematics," Davis replied. "Then the process of elimination."

"If it's that simple, why didn't their specialist— Alvarez—why didn't he find the cause?" Stewart asked.

Davis attempted an answer. "Simple doesn't mean obvious. Personality comes in between. A person may want or need to find a particular solution to a problem. That said, Alvarez is a gifted engineer. He made it much easier for me, ruling out almost every conceivable possibility. He tried a few things I would never have dreamed of."

"Is there a quick fix?" Ellis asked.

"If I'm proven right," Davis said, "the offending detector can be easily repaired."

"By whom?" Stewart cautioned. "Alvarez is in no condition."

"I can talk Garcia through it," Davis countered.

"Contact him," Ellis ordered. But, after several failed attempts at communication, it was evident that Nadir had gone deathly silent, or nearly so: The persistent drone of its homing signal, once beckoning, now insinuated peril—a warning for them to stay away.

"Doctor?" Ellis said, ever sparse with words.

"Are you asking me to revisit our prior discussion?" Stewart responded in frustration, reminded that her medical opinion would be woefully inadequate. "Garcia and his crew should be physically and mentally compromised but conscious. Whatever is happening inside that base, restoring their oxygen supply, assuming it can be done, may have no benefit. Are you asking if we are pinning our hopes on a course of action doomed to fail? Maybe. We have no assurance that they are even alive."

"What are you suggesting?" Ellis challenged, believing that Stewart was losing some of her resolve.

"What I'm suggesting is that we get to Nadir ASAP *and find the fuck out!* Dammit, Davis, can't you make this beast go any faster?"

"Any faster, and we risk not getting there at all."

"You're right, of course," Stewart said. "Sorry."

"Forget it."

A new heading was entered, and the terrain changed to a high plateau strewn with rounded boulders of varying size. The largest had to be avoided, which was deftly managed. All except one, sending them lurching violently to port.

It was Davis's turn to apologize. "Sorry," he said, a grating sound from beneath the undercarriage compelling him to bring the vehicle to a stop.

"It's not your fault," Stewart offered. "I sent you this way."

"Reach behind and hand me that rebreather," Davis said. "I'll need to inspect the starboard track."

"Why? You can't repair it out here," Ellis said, troubled by the delay.

"Not likely," Davis agreed, donning the respirator, one of three they had brought onboard. "But depending on the damage, it may be prudent to kick back on speed. That, or be damn sure to avoid another hit to that side."

There was a whoosh of cabin air as CAM-L's pressure-sealed door opened and then quickly closed.

Three steps down, he was at ground level, the oppressive heat instantly confronting him. Walking to the front of the vehicle, he squatted to inspect the individual treads that composed the starboard track's loop. Made of woven bands of graphene and tridex, they were nearly indestructible, but one tread had been pushed out of alignment, accounting for the rubbing noise. Crawling beneath the vehicle, he noticed something far more disturbing. A hairline crack had developed in the housing covering the fuel cell compartment. Directly below the crack was a small, iridescent-green puddle, the first liquid the ground had seen in a million years. "Damn," Davis said before realizing he had company.

"Different circumstances from the last time I saw you beneath a vehicle," Ellis said, reflecting on the adolescent conversation she had overheard between Davis and Anderson. It was hard to believe it was only nine days ago and harder to think she was now fond of this man.

"I make a great first impression, don't I?" Davis admitted, rising to face her, trying to project confidence through the profile of his rebreather mask.

"People sometimes change," Ellis said. "You look much more worried now."

He was very much worried. "Back inside?" Davis suggested, gesturing at the cab. "Let's avoid wasting rebreather air. We may need it."

"That bad?" Ellis said.

"Bad enough. Fuel cell."

"FIDO?" Ellis stated, interpreting his meaning.

"No choice. 'FIDO.'"

It was a seldom-used military term passed down through the centuries. They both understood what it meant: *Fuck It Drive On.*

Back inside the cab, Davis ripped off his mask. Shrugging the rebreather off his shoulders, he fell into his pilot's chair. Only when they were underway did he spell out the bad news. The fuel cell had ruptured, and a significant quantity of fuel had escaped. In all probability, more would do so.

"To properly survey the extent of damage," Davis said, "requires removal of the cell's protective cowling—a time-intensive procedure in ideal circumstances, much more difficult when wearing a cumbersome rebreather in the heat. With darkness fast approaching, it's time we don't have. In the process of attempting a repair, two of the rebreathers would be depleted."

"Still, it *is* possible," Stewart insisted.

"The effort might be worth it, given the unpleasant alternative we face," Davis said. "Except alone out here, there is little chance of sealing the rupture. There's something else to consider. While I work, fluid would continue to leak out."

"Then I suggest we alter the heading to 122.1," Ellis interrupted, remaining stoic.

"And what is the 'unpleasant alternative' you speak of?" Stewart persevered, starting to grasp the urgency of the situation.

"When the fuel cell fails," Davis said, "we lose power, we stop."

Stewart glared a warning. "You're joking again?"

"There's more," Davis continued. "Cabin oxygen will be cut off."

"So why in hell are we heading away from base?!" Stewart demanded.

"Zenith is too far, even if the other CAM-L was sent to meet us. No, we have to reach Nadir."

"Where there's no viable atmosphere!" Stewart exclaimed, becoming very much alarmed.

"I can fix that," Davis said, trying to reassure.

Only the grating sound of the CAM-L's rotating tracks was heard as Stewart resigned herself to accepting the only reasonable alternative. Reluctantly, she asked, "Okay, okay, damn it, what's the chances of us reaching Nadir?"

Davis struggled with the odds when a pulsating red warning light flashed on the command panel before him. An adjacent digital meter hovered at seventy-eight percent. Last he checked, it had read four points higher. Best to switch off the alarm that would auto-activate when the fuel cell fell below half power. No need to add to the stress that he was about to induce. "On a straight-line vector, we're twenty kilometers away. Perhaps that we can do."

Stewart caught the qualifiers. She had no intention of letting them pass. *"Perhaps?!* Great, that's just great! And when we're unable to maintain a precise course, which is certain, what then?"

Davis hesitated, realizing how absurd the answer would sound, sensible only to someone with a serious death wish. He was about to reply when Ellis preempted him.

"We get out and walk."

"I don't see the humor," Stewart protested, alarmed at the sight of the somber faces that confronted her.

"It's wise to discuss this now," Ellis said. "To get our minds around the idea."

"Is there no other way?" Stewart asked, her voice low and sad.

"If it comes to it, no. We'd be forced to don our rebreathers, taking with us whatever essential items we can carry."

"If we abandon the vehicle," Stewart observed, "we lose navigational aids."

"Good point," Davis said. "Closer to Nadir, the holo images will markedly improve. I can preview and memorize the intervening topo details."

"Dehydration will come quickly. We'll need water."

"Six one-liter bottles are stored onboard," Ellis said.

"The medical kit will be heavy."

"I'll carry whatever is needed," Davis volunteered.

Stewart turned her attention back to the holo-mapping pedestal. A short time later, Ellis felt the heavy weight of her stare. Left undiscussed, for there was nothing to be gained, were the consequences of failure. Not one for motivational speeches, Ellis attempted what was, for her, the equivalent. "We will prevail in this,

Michele. By restoring Nadir's atmosphere and saving six people's lives, we save our own. Call it irony, except it's too feeble a word."

"A cynic would say we are merely attempting to save ourselves from a danger we created, by choice, for ourselves."

"Choice?" Ellis objected, facial muscles set in determination. "Coming to Nadir's aid was an imperative, *never* a choice."

It took longer than expected to travel the next ten kilometers, first negotiating a shallow, orange-tinged depression at the base of one of the stitched seams sectioning the planet's fractured crust, then skirting the rim of a vast impact crater. The terrain transitioned to a jumble of ropy and bulbous pahoehoe lava. As the number of tube openings increased, the holo nav improved in detail, thanks to Garcia having transferred data from Nadir's last water recovery mission. It was, therefore, no coincidence when the CAM-L passed in front of Tube N119, where Amanda, for lack of a better description, became unhinged. Special notice would not have been taken except that marked on the holo (and jogging Ellis's and Stewart's memory of the incident), the mysterious tag words *invisible things are the only realities* were also seen floating. Assuming the translated phrase was of literary origin, Ellis queried the mindstor, which responded as follows:

Five valid references. Most relevant short story titled "Loss of Breath," Edgar Allan Poe, nineteenth-century author.

"That takes a certain twisted kind of humor," Davis said. "Can't be sure that was Garcia's idea, but I'm gonna get along fine with whomever it was."

Contributing to the strangeness, a curling eddy of black dust appeared at the tube's foreboding entrance, brought into being by a puff of wind emanating from within. Stewart watched it rise and, just as quickly, die. "Jesus," she said with a shudder.

"Care to peek inside?" Ellis taunted. Stewart had steadfastly maintained that the only thing of subtlety within Murkor's tubes, or anywhere on the planet, were humans with overactive imaginations.

"Not funny," Stewart responded, the color draining from her face.

"You're right," Ellis admitted, angry with herself. Contributing to her crewmate's unease was a callous, stupid mistake. She wouldn't do it again.

Rapidly losing fluid, the vehicle cut a path through the mound where two rollers had collided, its wide rotating tracks flinging glittering speckles of lava glass high into the air behind. The desolate area had been labeled "Armageddon" on the holo. When the fuel cell registered nineteen percent, Davis stopped checking. He didn't need distractions, and the rate of power drain was likely to stay constant. In the unlikely event that the leaking fuel cell suddenly sealed itself, they would fall short of their destination. Exactly how short was conjecture, but if navigation errors were made, the resulting delay might prove fatal.

Complicating matters, on more than one occasion, Stewart and Ellis disagreed on an exact heading. When this occurred, the decision fell to Davis. Realizing that the fuel cell's fluid loss was a function of time rather than speed, he invariably settled the matter by risking the shortest path at the greatest velocity. It made for a rough and tense ride. Although prevented from serious harm by her restraint harness, Ellis suffered a bruise on the side of her chin from secured equipment that had been jarred loose. No complaint was raised. Every centimeter of closing the distance to Nadir lessened the hardship of trekking across the planet's surface. This last vestige of solace suddenly ended when a high-decibel alarm blared out, and a screen displayed a POWER FAILURE IMMINENT warning.

Already on edge, Stewart let out a gasp. Even Davis was startled, unaware the alarm existed. "I'm afraid we haven't much time," he said. Almost as if she hadn't heard, Ellis merely nodded in confirmation.

Finally, like a heart surrendering its last weak beats, the engine's distinctive thrumming slowly abated, becoming ever fainter until the CAM-L came to a stuttering halt. A small backup battery auto-engaged, temporarily energizing the comlink, mindstor, holo pedestal, and, more permanently, a low-power emergency locator beacon.

"Cabin oxygen will last us for about an hour or until the pressure doors are opened on exiting," Davis advised.

Without hesitating, Ellis posed a question. *"Mindstor. Calculate the distance to Nadir. Strike that. Determine the distance to Nadir that can be traversed, on foot, by a healthy adult human."*

Six point three kilometers. Margin of error ten percent.

"That sounds about right," Davis said, striking a note of confidence for Stewart's benefit. "A person maintaining a steady pace can comfortably walk five kilometers in an hour. A rebreather holds a two-hour oxygen supply. We should have time to spare—"

"Who's the doctor here?" Stewart said, cutting Davis off. "Don't you think I have a good idea of what's in store for us?"

"I imagine you do," Davis was forced to admit. "As far as any of us has." He knew the numbers he spouted were bullshit. Being out and about on Murkor radically altered the equation.

Ellis, as well, had no illusions as to their prospects. How do you assign a number to the time wasted scrabbling over jagged lava outcroppings in the oppressive heat encumbered by a rebreather? Spraining an ankle on the uneven, sharp terrain was a real possibility. Although Davis had an excellent memory, with darkness fast approaching, there was no guarantee that he wouldn't become disoriented. The mere threat of being on the surface at night would prey on their psyche. Nevertheless, she was responsible for taking them this far. At any cost to her safety, she would see them the rest of the way.

Davis took a place at the holo pedestal, where he began to scan and memorize successive renditions of the outlying terrain.

Without commenting, Ellis collected the three rebreathers, inconspicuously ensuring that she kept the one Davis had used while inspecting the vehicle's damage and giving him hers, which was slightly less depleted. The third rebreather, fully charged, went to Stewart.

To this point, progress updates had been periodically transmitted to both bases; Nadir, of course, had been silent, Zenith reacting with heightened concern. With the disturbing inference that it might aid a future recovery team, Ellis transmitted the entirety of the CAM-L's external camera feed. In the unlikely event that base-to-base contact was restored (meaning someone had survived at Nadir), Davis sent a message describing how to repair the ESS.

With these tasks hurriedly completed, a last communique to Zenith was necessary—a duty naturally falling to Ellis. Before departing, explicit orders on how to proceed in her absence had been entered into the record. Still, she felt uneasy about the heavy burden assigned to a subordinate.

"How goes it, sergeant?" she said in greeting.

"Commander," Cooper said in welcome. "Perhaps you should see for yourself." As he spoke, the camera angle widened to show the entire room. Every available space was filled with base personnel. She could make out most of the faces—in addition to the service personnel under her direct command, Bert Imholtz, Lori Jensen, and several other IMC techs were present.

Front and center was Daniel Schulman. "More folk wanted to crowd in," he said. "I reminded them you didn't have much patience for idle chat, especially when you had somewhere to be."

"You have me pegged, Mr. Schulman," Ellis said. "I almost regret not inviting you along."

"Ah, ha! Next time, commander."

"We wish you three intrepid souls *and* Nadir well," Cooper added, the sentiment echoed from behind by comingled voices spontaneously raised in agreement. Several hands were raised high and signaling "thumbs up."

"You couldn't have answered 'how fares it' any better, sergeant…all of you," Ellis, temporarily at a loss for words, managed to say. "I trust our next contact will be from Nadir. Be well. Out."

Terminating the link, Ellis stripped down to the sport's bra beneath her shirt, slid into her rebreather harness, attached two water bottles to her pants belt, and then impatiently waited for her colleagues to finish their preparations.

Davis, rebreather already secured on his back, helped the less-experienced Stewart into hers. The doctor had filled a large haversack containing the medical items she considered indispensable: a portable blood analyzer, stim pads, and six syringes filled with her entire supply of a short-duration injectable oxygen compound. "Wish I had better," she said.

Davis hefted a heavy sack filled with diagnostic tools and slung a searchlight over his left shoulder. "Here's some advice," he said, "from someone who's been out and about far more than either of you. Keep to a steady pace. Easy, even strides. Move too fast, and the heat will bring you to your knees."

"Take the lead, then," Ellis replied, a penetrating stare lending double meaning to her following words. "You best know the way."

With an understanding nod and emblematic grin, Davis affixed his breather mask. Stewart and Ellis did the same, adjusting the clear, pliable plastic to form a tight seal over the nose and mouth. The CAM-L's pressurized door slid open, releasing, with the vehicle's occupants, the last precious remnants of their cabin oxygen.

The outside air was brutally hot and perfectly still. Low in the sky, a mud-brown sun awkwardly rushed to its inconclusive set. Stewart, unaccustomed to the abusive temperature and the least physically fit of the three, was given a few moments to acclimate. Ellis and Davis assured themselves that the rebreathers were functioning at peak efficiency, checking and rechecking gauge readouts of gas mixture and regulator pressure.

One critical value, tank oxygen, was displayed as a percentage, with Stewart's gauge reading ninety-nine percent, Ellis's ninety-two, and Davis's ninety-seven. On this occasion, the lieutenant noticed Ellis had donned the rebreather he had worn previously. Although the differences were minor, he became suspicious. Unwilling to call undue attention to the matter, two words were exchanged: "Cute," uttered by the lieutenant, followed by an innocuous "What?" from Ellis.

Once underway, Davis applied himself to maintaining an even pace, stopping for water breaks (all three were sweating profusely) and to confirm bearings. When the terrain made it challenging to keep abreast of one another, Ellis intentionally lagged, attentive to

Stewart's labored progress. An early indication that the doctor struggled came when thirst forced her to drink while walking on uneven terrain. Removing her rebreather mask, she began choking on water, then gulped in rarified air, causing her to panic briefly. By the time Ellis was at her side, she had fully recovered and, after a nod to acknowledge the CO's concern, continued as if nothing had happened. There could be little talking, with each retaining their private thoughts.

Forward progress came at a high price. Lava, hot to the touch, began to burn their hands. Shoulders, straining under the constant pressure of rebreather harnesses, began to ache. Conveyed by wind and perspiration, fine pumice entered and irritated the eyes. The only good news was the absence of bad: Rollers, those few spotted, stayed in the distance.

They came to a high abutment requiring mutual assistance to scale. Ellis used the opportunity to compare oxygen values again. Hers, eighty-one percent, came as no surprise; Davis, expending extra energy carrying the heaviest haversack, had dropped to seventy-four—no cause for alarm. Stewart's number, however, had plummeted to fifty-six. Anxiety and lack of physical conditioning had increased her respiration rate. The tank would be depleted before reaching Nadir. Broaching the subject without further unsettling the doctor would be difficult.

"You once said you prefer hearing the truth," Ellis began. "No matter how unpleasant."

"I've been dwelling on something *you* said," Stewart responded, "On how to calm the mind."

"And?" Ellis asked, comprehending that Stewart had anticipated her concern.

"I still can't do it."

"Keep practicing," Ellis said. Turning to Davis, she asked, "How far?"

"Approximately halfway."

"See that?" Stewart said, staying positive. "No worries. I shall do better."

"I believe you will," Ellis said. She reflected on not having told Stewart the whole truth. Nor could she. No matter. They had lied to each other, and they both knew it.

Shortly after, Davis and Ellis had a brief opportunity to speak privately.

"Don't be mad," Davis said. "We're not halfway. Seeing her struggle—well, I thought it best."

Ellis reacted immediately. "Soon, I'll be ordering—asking—something of you. Don't argue the point—please."

"One foot in front of the other," Davis responded vaguely, saying no more as Stewart came up alongside them.

With every step, the terrain and heat fought them. By outward appearances, Murkor had won, their clothes soiled and torn, hair soaked and stringy, black particles clinging like a million ticks to the surface of bare skin. All three had superficial bruises and abrasions. Davis favored a swollen knee caused when he suddenly lost balance climbing a jag of lava and elected to protect the haversack he carried. Despite rationing, all water had been consumed. Symptoms of dehydration— muscle cramps, confusion, and dizziness were taking their toll.

Emotionally, they were faring no better. Dusk, allied with exhaustion, deceived the mind into changing the bleak landscape into formidable and intimidating shapes. Lava outcroppings rose to become stone-cloaked specters, haunting them as they moved amid a graveyard of despoiled burial chambers. Hanging back in the half-light, Ellis wondered what, if anything, she could have done differently. "We shall fail!" she unwittingly cried out. Peering ahead, she perceived two shadowy figures hovering in the gloom. Neither had heard. Good. No witnesses to her pang of doubt. Or was guilt stabbing at her, this compulsion to be absolved for a past mistake, no matter the consequences? She should be condemned if two more lives were shed in vain. If only she could have pursued this path alone…

"Commander!" Davis shouted. Equipped with a searchlight, he had forged ahead. "You need to see this."

The steady incline they were on had finally crested at a grooved ridge. Below lay a smooth basin. On one side, stretching as far as they could see, a line of noisy fumaroles added their foul contribution to the atmosphere. The lieutenant pointed to a far-off smudge of artificial light originating from a shape that did not belong. Nadir. "An hour, max," he said. The look in his eyes told the rest of the story. "What's your tank reading?"

"Fifty-nine," Ellis responded.

"Damn, you gotta teach me how to do that," Davis said, encouraged by the number, then reading his rebreather gauge. "Forty-three."

"Twelve," Stewart volunteered, futility and fatigue causing her to sit.

"Get up," Ellis ordered, standing over her. "We'll stop when *I* say. Only when your rebreather reads low single digits."

Stewart struggled to her feet.

Moving onward, Ellis once again played it out. Stewart, who was laboring, would require a second rebreather. The decision had to be postponed until the doctor's tank was nearly empty. Trying to reach Nadir using injectable oxygen was discarded, for to do so would diminish everyone's chance of survival.

Within a half kilometer, Stewart's rebreather read three percent. Barely enough to accomplish the exchange.

"Off with it," Ellis said.

"No," Stewart said.

"Off!" Ellis threatened, stepping toward her.

"El—," Stewart said. She, too, had been thinking it through. But seeing Davis's resolute expression made it clear this would be an argument she could never win. "El—no—"

"*Commander,*" Ellis insisted, somehow injecting firmness in her voice, taking a final step forward and clutching Stewart's rebreather harness.

"I'll goddamn carry one of you," Davis senselessly implored, despair written on his face.

"You know the reality," Ellis reasoned. "You're both needed if Nadir is to have any chance. I'm expendable. We're wasting breath." Moved by the distress on her colleagues' faces, her voice cracking, she tried once more. "Brian—Michele—Please—"

"Do it!" an angry Davis directed, staring at Stewart, furious for feeling so helpless.

With his assistance, the exchange was made. Relenting, safely wearing Ellis's rebreather, Stewart fought back tears.

Davis shook his head in disbelief as Ellis, facing Nadir, sat in the lotus position. "Leave me," she pleaded, wanting to save them the pain of seeing her suffer.

"I'll return for you," Davis exclaimed, kneeling before her. "I swear it. I—"

"I know you will," Ellis breathed, lightly caressing his face. "Go."

Rising, Davis seized Stewart, who seemed determined to stay, by the arm. "Bravest damn thing I ever saw," he said, leading her away.

Watching her crewmates disappear, Ellis closed her eyes and waited.

Accompanied by the sounds of fumaroles exhaling their noxious mixture into Murkor's dreaded darkness.

"Brian," Stewart whispered. They had been walking for some time. "Keep close. My imagination—I feel something—"

"It's okay. Almost there," he answered, directing the searchlight to illuminate the path in front of them. "We're gonna make it."

14 DOWN PAYMENT

CIRCUMVENTING A SEQUENCE OF interlocks allowed speedier transit through Nadir's partial-pressure decon room. What appeared to be a blatant disregard for safety protocols made complete sense: Detection/sterilization procedures, a week ago tolerated as a mandatory nuisance, were now a waste of precious time. If an agent or entity hazardous to human life lurked inside, impossible as that seemed, it had gained entry long ago.

Exhausted and critically low on oxygen, Davis and Stewart staggered into the base's lower level. A visual scan revealed a drab, compartmentalized interior. Ambient lighting had been subdued either through malfunction or by design. Somewhere inside, due to unknown causes, six people were lying dead or nearly so.

"Hola! Hay alguien a saludarnos?" Stewart said, shouting their arrival. She did not expect to be heard.

"Thirteen percent oxy," Davis said, multi-meter in hand. "No noxious compounds. The air temperature reads high. Feels cold after outside."

"Rebreather masks stay on," Stewart ordered. "Remove it, you won't be thinking clearly. In a minute or two, you'll pass out."

Davis nodded in affirmation. "They abandoned this level," he said, stopping at the environmental system compartment.

Shrugging his shoulders, he let the heavy haversack fall to the floor. Removing his diagnostic equipment, he pushed the lightened bag to Stewart.

"You'll want these," she said, reaching inside for the self-injectable oxy. "It's pointless to use them on myself or whoever remains alive here until you've restored the atmosphere. The closer to an artery, the better, and remember to breathe out every few minutes to remove carbon dioxide in your bloodstream."

No reason to argue, Davis thought. Stewart did seem calmer now. Finally freed of the stifling heat and no longer scrabbling over lava, she wasn't struggling as much. Most likely, their rebreathers would be depleted at about the same time. He directed the searchlight at the glow originating from the stairwell. "Scream if you need me," he said, grimacing at his warped humor.

"When you're done here, *mister*, you know exactly what you have to do," Stewart said, putting him in a tight embrace, then resolutely pushing him away. Davis wondered if it was a final goodbye as he watched her scramble up the spiral staircase leading to Nadir's second level.

Gazing at the daunting array of wiring, piping, ductwork, gauges, and assorted controllers of the ESS, he had to fight off a sudden wave of panic. How in hell did Alvarez keep this mess functioning, let alone adequately balancing essential gases? The repair would take longer than anticipated. Visualizing 3-D schematics in your head was one thing; seeing it in person was quite another.

The first task was to find the central air plenum, which distributes conditioned air throughout the base. No problem, located straight ahead, but to reach it, he had to navigate a jumble of intervening ductwork while hampered by a rebreather, an armful of instruments, and an aching knee.

Precious time now wasted, he found himself staring disbelievingly at the metal sides of the plenum. Secured thereto were five identical sensors, each monitoring the concentration of a specific gas and then sending the data directly to the Nexus for evaluation. *None were labeled.* Alvarez must have memorized them by their relative position. Locating the carbon dioxide sensor would require removing each cover individually to identify the circuitry inside.

Cursing what had been the schematics' lack of detail, he methodically started loosening, of all things in the bloody Universe that might wind up killing them, the first set of small retaining screws. The first sensor exposed was a nitrogen detector. Focusing on the next, he lost track of time, and then a loss of manual dexterity caused him to fumble the tool he was holding, sending it to the floor. A quick reach for it made him lightheaded. If he needed something else to worry about, the strain of accessing the plenum had caused him to drain his oxy cylinder prematurely! Discarding the rebreather, he grabbed an injectable tubule and firmly pressed it against an exposed spot on his chest, sending a flood of oxygen-impregnated lipid microparticles into his bloodstream. The jolt would last approximately five minutes, depending on the level of physical activity. He resumed work, finding the absence of breathing unnatural and unnerving, the body and mind out of sync. A trivial nuisance compared to what may come should he fail.

"Carbon monoxide," he groaned, exposing the complicated guts of the second sensor. He stared at the three remaining, frightened that he'd run out of time. "Which one?!" he screamed aloud. Which damned one?!" An instant later, the answer came with certainty. He had failed to see the obvious. He shared a brief moment of empathy with Alvarez. The poor bastard must have repeatedly removed the carbon dioxide sensor's cover—*in the process wearing and abrading the tops of the retaining screws*—each time failing to see the defect hiding in plain sight.

He managed to remove the cover in good time. As expected, nothing inside *appeared* amiss. Nothing indicated the device was transmitting impossibly low carbon dioxide readings to the Nexus. By bridging two circuits, the defective sensor would revert to its emergency default setting, compelling the Nexus to adjust its errant thinking and reactivate the carbon dioxide scrubber and oxygen concentrator. Handily accomplished with a small soldering gun and a short piece of solder—a crude fix until a replacement part was installed. He hoped.

Leaning over his work, a drop of sweat fell from his damp brow onto the hot electrical repair. Fascinated, he watched it sputter and hiss, evaporating its tiny water content into the air. Water and air. Why was this microcosm so mesmerizing? On the verge of passing out (the lipid microparticles in his blood had ceased releasing their oxygen content), he was left with no choice. He stabbed himself with a second injectable. The seconds slowly ticked by as he waited to hear a telltale hum followed by a whoosh—the sounds of oxygenated air flooding the base—and that he might live to see another Murkorian day. He had been this scared once or twice in his military career, but it was only for himself on those occasions.

When the sound finally came, he was already on the move, shouting, "On my way!" up to Stewart, though he knew she could no longer reply. He tried to absolve the guilt of abandoning her by calling to mind her last words, for which there was no mistaking. In retrospect, it dawned on him that she had more than one reason for handing him all the injectables. She understood that he, like her, hated beyond bearing the thought of the commander being left out there in the dreaded darkness.

Alone.

Wincing in pain, he hobbled out into the terrible heat. Powering up Nadir's CAM-L, he quickly confirmed what Garcia had communicated, that the vehicle had discharged its limited capacity of pressurized air shortly after completing its last mission. The cab was useless as a temporary place of sanctuary. There was no time to do anything about it now. He estimated the time it would take to retrace their path, then weighed the chances of finding her alive, thinking if anyone had that chance, it would be her.

The vehicle's powerful hood-mounted floods fought to beat back the enveloping murk of the planet's deep night. When Nadir became obscured somewhere within a shroud two thousand meters behind him, he stopped. Utterly exhausted, he plunged a tubule into his chest. In a heightened moment of awareness, the haunting sounds of fumaroles came from somewhere in the unseeable distance. Farther away, a roller's vicious march across the surface created a barely audible *hiss*. A terrible feeling of defeat almost overtook him when a small, solitary shape nearby caught his eye.

At the edge of darkness, sooner than conceivable, he saw her, pathetically slumped to one side, no rebreather in sight. There was no way to determine if she was unconscious or dead. Overcoming disbelief, he jumped onto the hard lava. Ignoring the self-inflicted pain, he ran to her. Feeling for a pulse meant nothing other than a useless delay. Turning Ellis onto her back, he pressed the oxy tubule to her chest.

And then he looked into the impenetrable Murkorian sky and mouthed one word:

"Please."

"Brian—"

"I'm here."

"You—look worried."

Overwhelmed with emotion, Davis gently cradled Ellis's flushed cheeks in his hands and said, "If this life's worth living—"

And then kissed her on the lips.

She did not resist. To do so would have been a lie.

"Blame oxygen euphoria," Davis said, the wry grin she loved returning to his face as he moved to support her. "Quickly now. Hold on to me. We have just enough tubules to get back."

"How did—Stewart—the others—?" Ellis asked, managing to gain her feet as the injectable began its work.

"Captain Stewart's there." If she were alive, he could not say. Stepping up into the vehicle, he extended an arm and pulled Ellis in. "Nadir's oxygen is being replenished as we speak."

"No longer expect the worst."

"Because of what happened to you out here?" Davis asked, confused. By no means did he know what took place. Nothing made sense.

"All of it," Ellis replied, hesitating before adding, "In some strange sense, I believe we are being protected."

"You'll owe me a better explanation," Davis said. "I don't believe in ghosts."

Reaching across, she firmly squeezed his arm, letting him know that, at the very least, she was solid.

During the short journey back to Nadir, both said no more of the matter, preferring to advance the conversation only after seeing what additional revelations awaited them.

***

"El!" Stewart exclaimed, laughing in amazement at the living, *breathing* sight of her, having been certain that the commander knowingly forfeited her life by relinquishing her rebreather. No, *certainty* could no more be applied to her than the planet she sojourned on. "Are you even possible? Is there no limit to what you're capable of?"

"Ahem," Davis coughed, standing by with his big grin, then enjoying his second embrace of the day and assurance from Stewart that she would soon attend to his swollen knee. Their own needs would have to wait. Nadir's second level had taken on the aspect of a morgue. There were six lifeless bodies stretched out on the floor.

"I found them exactly as you see," Stewart began to explain, watching the distressed look on her crewmates' faces. "They wanted to be together to the very last. Quite touching. I found the handsome older gentleman, Comandante Garcia, collapsed at his desk. He had been writing a eulogy. Imagine that. I wanted to make him comfortable, so I found bedding and moved him. No easy feat."

"*Comfortable*?" Ellis asked, confused, seizing on the word to bolster her wish that all could still be well despite every indication to the contrary. Crouching down, she studied Garcia's noble features, her voice becoming melancholy and subdued. "So peaceful in repose—"

"No—he is alive!" Stewart said, regretting the false impression she had given. "They all are! I, too, mistook the poor souls for dead, their hearts and respiration low enough to make them appear so. I retain hope for their full recovery. I've already seen signs of improvement as oxygen levels increase. See?! Look there! A small hand movement!"

Fascinated, Ellis took Garcia's hand in her own. "Cold. As if waiting at death's door."

"He couldn't stay on this side indefinitely," Stewart said. "Eventually, cells require nourishment, even at greatly reduced metabolism."

"Cause?" Ellis asked.

"I'll have to get back to you on that," Stewart replied. "Hopefully, blood and tissue samples will reveal more."

"Can we discuss *you* for a moment?" an impatient Davis demanded. He had needed multiple injectables to survive during the time Stewart had none. Even now, they were having some difficulty breathing, the air not yet returning to the twenty-one percent oxygen content to which humans were accustomed. "Why aren't you hypoxic?"

"No secret there," Stewart contended. "As I began focusing on my medical duties, I relaxed. My respiration rate decreased. When my rebreather finally registered zero, I was pleasantly surprised that I had a few minutes of residual air."

"A small discrepancy between the gauge and what's in the cylinder," Davis said. "It can happen. Keep going—"

"By then, you had performed *your* miracle. You could have been quicker about it," she teased, kneeling beside a young man she knew to be Carlos.

"So that's it?" Davis asked. "Nothing more to it?"

"My, you're exuding skepticism," Stewart observed, deliberately drawing out her explanation. She resumed monitoring Carlos's vitals, nodding in satisfaction. "The truth is, I nearly passed out. I couldn't respond to your shout." She pointed to a metal grid at eye level on the nearest wall. "Not when standing on my toes with nose smashed against that air vent."

Laughing, Davis looked at Ellis and said, "Your turn."

She was contemplating a response when Garcia flicked open his eyes and tried to speak.

"Cómo están—how are—?"

"Your crew is well," Ellis replied, with Stewart coming alongside to watch with interest as Garcia's mental processes kept pace with his rapid physical recovery.

"Commander Ellis—or only my delusion—" Garcia said.

"In the flesh and gladdened to see you. Now rest a little while longer. At least until Doctor Stewart permits you to move about freely."

Leaving Stewart to assist with Nadir's crews' revival, Ellis and Davis descended to the communication hub, where they reestablished contact with Zenith. An ecstatic Sergeant Cooper, also shocked upon seeing his crewmates' dreadful appearance, was provided a summary of what had transpired. Many of his concerns were left unaddressed, including how and when they would attempt the return journey.

Returning to L2, Davis and Ellis discovered the comandante standing solidly on his feet and four of his crew attempting to rise. Stewart advised that discussions concerning all but the most pressing topics be postponed until everyone was lucid enough to participate.

Carlos, the first to be held in the clutches of the unnatural sleep, had the distinction of being the last liberated from the throes of the mysterious affliction. He did so abruptly, discovering three strange, grit-covered faces hovering over him. Any of the three would have suited his purpose, but the closest was Ellis. Startling everyone, he lashed out with one of his heavily muscled arms, coming within a centimeter of grabbing her by the throat.

"Easy there, big guy," Davis said, tightly wrapping his hand around the meat of Carlos's forearm, forgetting that his English words might be misinterpreted. "Commander Ellis may look unimposing, but she can kick serious butt—mine included."

"*Ellis*?" Carlos spat out, hatred returning with his five senses. "Aquí para robar nuestra agua."

"Sólo con permiso, y sólo un vaso pequeño," Ellis quickly replied.

"Para ti? Nada!"

"Carlos, enough," Garcia ordered.

Everyone wisely backed away to allow the comandante, whose recovery had accelerated, a chance to intervene. He chose his next words carefully, for they were intended as much for Carlos's benefit as for Ellis. "Your Spanish is excellent, commander. You extend great courtesy to us by speaking it here. We will be as comfortable speaking your language. As for water, you will have all you want, including unlimited showers. There is little else we can boast of at Nadir."

"Accepted with gratitude," Ellis replied, appreciative of how Garcia handled a difficult situation and his calming effect on his youngest crew member.

"I am glad to see *you*, comandante," Carlos interrupted.

"And I, you, my friend."

"Restored?"

"Yes, Carlos, oxygen restored," Garcia replied, patting the engineer's shoulder. "Though I still don't know how." Rising, he turned to his Zenith counterpart. "Nor do I have an explanation for the bruised condition of these courageous people. You appear to have suffered much, and we are exceedingly anxious to hear the details. Perhaps together we can also make sense of the puzzle that confounds us. But first! To your own detriment, you have attended to our needs. I must insist you allow us to reciprocate. While my crew collects themselves and celebrates their good fortune, I shall escort you to facilities adequate to accommodate your requirements for personal hygiene, nutrition, and basic medical care—in whatever order you see fit."

***

They had made it, Ellis reflected. And yet, an old, badly worn idiom came to mind: *The end justifies the means.* She had risked two lives. Two to save six, with uncertainty skulking on both ends of the equation. Where does a responsible person set the boundary between what might be gained and what might be lost? And, to confound, what if the ethics of arriving at and executing a course of action are obscure, or worse, in opposition to one's values? If she (as commander), through moral paralysis, could not find it in herself to make life-or-death decisions, then those decisions would be made by others.

History has shown that armies of less discerning people are willing and waiting.

And yet…

The decision *she* made on Diverna cost people their lives. Today's fortunate result did not exonerate her from a self-imposed debt. It represented a small down payment.

Beneath a restorative shower of glistening water, she began scrubbing off the layer of abrasive pumice clinging to the residue of her sweat.

Tilting her face up, she gazed at a million splintering sparkles of liquid light. Splashing on her naked body, they elicited a feeling of déjà vu. Reality striving to emulate a recent, almost forgotten dream.

Wandering alone on the Murkor's surface also had a dreamlike quality. What happened to her out there? The eye sees a small slice of the electromagnetic spectrum; likewise, the mind avows only a fragment of reality.

Dream or reality? Who would believe that what happened to her fell somewhere between the two?

Sticking out her tongue, she caught warm droplets in her open mouth.

Was it the mystical, life-giving quality of water that inspired these reflections?

More the reality of luxuriating in Nadir's shower.

Clutching a soft washcloth, she smoothed soap over her breasts, flat stomach, and legs.

Slippery and wet.

There is also a sensual property to water.

In a heartbeat, her imagination fixated on Brian Davis.

A few minutes later, as she toweled dry, she pondered making another tough decision.

She seriously doubted she'd have the willpower to reassign him.

15 THE SYMBIONTS OF MURKOR

NINE PEOPLE WERE CROWDED around a table designed to seat six. No one was complaining, especially Amanda, who made a point of sitting close to Davis. On at least one occasion, her leg brushed up against his.

Without drawing attention, he carefully moved out of harm's way.

There was a second round of introductions. The first, which haphazardly took place when Nadir's crew was still basking in the overwhelming joy of each other's unexpected recovery, hadn't quite stuck.

"So, you've now seen Nadir," Gustavo said, striking up a conversation with Davis. "What do you think?"

"Have you been to Stigel V?" he replied.

"Can't say I have."

"Good. Then there's no harm telling you Nadir's worse."

"Well, *I've* been there," Roya volunteered, exaggerating a scowl. "Stigel's a freakin' armpit."

"Oh, shit," Davis said. "There goes détente." It was an easy laugh, made more enjoyable in the context of antagonists meeting for the first time.

Other bilateral exchanges were in progress. Ellis noted Mariana Perez, Nadir's physician, animatedly engaged with Stewart, comparing medical terminology in each other's language. She heard the word "estasis" used repeatedly and with questioning inflection. Amanda Cruz had been friendly with Stewart and certainly with Davis, who, for his part, seemed more intent on swapping stories with Gustavo. Good. Jealousy is the ugly word for what she might have felt otherwise. She never suspected a woman could be overly lovely.

In turn, she found herself speaking at length with Garcia. *El Comandante.* From the start, he had been especially loquacious and charming. She wondered if the relaxed atmosphere that pervaded Nadir was due to his easy manner or some specific instruction on decorum privately relayed to his crew—in either case, the positive effect was the same.

Only Carlos, absorbed in thought, remained distant. Accordingly, she prepared for a confrontation, verbal or otherwise. The moment came early on.

In consideration of their guests' continued thirst, someone had set the communal table with a large pitcher of cold water and several tall drinking glasses. Reaching across, intent on pouring herself some of the tempting treat, Ellis discovered her hand roughly pushed aside. Carlos, of course. Noticed by all, the affront needed to be addressed in some unequivocal fashion. An unpleasantness best left to Garcia, Ellis decided, withdrawing her hand. A quick read of his icy stare told her the prospect was inevitable, but he was prevented from taking action by what transpired next.

"Let me," Carlos offered, seizing the water pitcher by its handle. And then, with all eyes on him, he slowly refilled Ellis's glass.

Ellis habitually rationed words. Now, they had gone completely AWOL. By the time she thought of "thank you," Mariana had chosen to prod Carlos with a few words of her own.

"What's got into you?" she said, half-jokingly. "I'd love to check your oxytocin and serotonin levels."

"Yeah, full of surprises," Roya added. "You never pour me water."

"Have any of you looked out the east viewport?" Carlos replied, enjoying the attention.

"Why bother? Can't make out much in the dark," Mariana replied. "What did you see?"

"It's what I didn't see, even using the infrared scope. No vehicle. There's an unimpeded view out to the bluff. That's four kilometers. You know what that means? It means they walked at least that far. At night. If nothing else, that deserves some respect."

"Commander Ellis?" Garcia asked, unable to decide which was the greater marvel, Carlos's change of attitude or the distance Ellis and her fellow officers had covered on foot. "Is this true? Is it even possible?"

"Oh, it gets better," Davis interjected.

"True, with a few clarifications," Ellis said. Then, with Nadir's crew listening in fascination, she recounted how, when, and approximately where the CAM-L broke down. Their struggle to walk in the insufferable heat. The inadequacy of their rebreathers. How, on arriving, Stewart persevered until Nadir's ambient atmosphere was breathable. Fittingly, she let Davis explain his clever repair of the environmental system. To his credit, he spoke with considerable tact and modesty. Having succeeded where Carlos failed, it would have been bad form to embellish his ego at the expense of another's.

Davis, however, didn't need to tread quite so carefully. Carlos knew precisely how the repair was made and had used the knowledge to come to terms with himself. Cleared for duty, prompted by curiosity and suspicion, he had immediately investigated how the ESS was, in his estimation, "tampered with." The process might have consumed hours, but he concentrated on the most logical subsystems and where he found the tools Davis had hurriedly left behind. His eye caught the carbon dioxide sensor protective cover and the screws that had not yet been replaced. He quickly deduced the rest.

Stunned, he spent several minutes staring at the faulty relay. He was forced to conclude (at considerable damage to his pride) that he had overlooked the blatantly simple cause of the ESS's malfunction. The revelation was easier than accepting *why* he had been so blind, a leap that entailed re-evaluating the three chancros in their midst. Learning what they had to endure en route to Nadir helped push him in the right direction.

Garcia needed less proof of Ellis's good intentions. "Commander…captain…lieutenant," he said, deliberately addressing Zenith's officers individually. "You jeopardized your lives coming to our assistance, which also brings to mind the Coalition transport pilot who lost his. Obligations such as these are too dear to be repaid but permit me the satisfaction of trying. Ask anything—"

"Then I ask for the one commodity Zenith presently lacks," Ellis said, surprising everyone before adding, "Your friendship."

Garcia laughed. "Ahh, you choose well. It is something that enriches us both. Be assured, you already have it—but, no, I am too selfish to let you off that easy. Give me time. I will think on it further."

"Commander," Mariana began, seeking Ellis's attention. "I'm interested in the time you spent alone on the surface. Details are missing. Am I sensing a reluctance to relive the experience? If so, I shall desist. I do not want to press you. Shall we focus our energies on solving the medical mystery confronting us?"

"I intentionally omitted details," Ellis responded, "because I believe they should be part of the same inquiry."

"I don't follow," Mariana responded.

Ellis looked at the tired faces ringing the table. "I felt a presence," she said, earning a gasp from Amanda, who turned ghostly pale as she recalled her encounter in Tube System N119.

"Wow," Roya said in a whisper. She, too, had felt the presence. Days afterward, she proposed an outlandish connection: A mystery agent, "X," had been disturbed in the lava tube, then somehow infiltrated Nadir, intent on slowly killing them. She glanced at Gustavo. She shouldn't have.

"El aliento del Diablo," he said, repeating the words he had blurted out what seemed like a lifetime ago. "¿Dónde estás?" he added, waving his hand as if to sample the air they were breathing.

Of the laughs elicited, a few were genuine. More were nervous.

Garcia faced Ellis, the welfare of his crew foremost in his mind. "What *exactly* happened to you out there?"

"It may be useful if I relate the unusual nature of a prior, somewhat similar, experience," Ellis said, then described how she circumnavigated Zenith without a rebreather.

She didn't have to wait long for the expected rebuttal.

"May I interject?" Stewart asked.

"I'd be disappointed if you didn't," Ellis responded.

"My medical opinion is that Commander Ellis was aided by the strict physical and metaphysical regimens she practices. That and a healthy dose of adrenaline. As for this so-called presence she felt? Most physicians would diagnose it as a hypoxia-induced hallucination."

Garcia looked to Mariana, her ambivalent shrug doing nothing to help him form his own conclusion.

"May I inquire, Commander," he asked, "why you took such a risk in the first place?"

"Primarily to distract a sizable complement of disgruntled mining techs."

"Disgruntled?"

"Cessation of the anecrecium mining operation. Water rationing."

"That bad?" Garcia asked.

"Evacuation plans are in place," Ellis said, choosing to reveal the truth for no reason other than to assess the comandante's reaction. "A small contingent will remain to keep Zenith viable."

"An unfortunate development," Garcia replied, his expression convincing Ellis that the sentiment was genuine. "This is a topic I'd very much like to pursue before you leave here. But please continue your story."

"However you try to explain my ability to persevere outside Zenith," Ellis resumed, "it motivated me to pick myself up and continue towards Nadir, keeping sight of its light and the one Lieutenant Davis carried. By then, he and Captain Stewart were far ahead, my progress hindered by a late start and the difficulty of walking in near-total darkness. Calling out to them, drawing attention to myself, would have served no purpose."

"Your rebreather registered three percent oxy," Stewart pointed out. It was a point she would have to make often. "My own experience tells me it likely held more."

"Which does nothing to clarify what followed," Ellis replied. "When the rebreather ran out, an odd feeling came over me. Have you ever felt that someone was standing behind you when nothing has overtly disturbed your senses?"

"That feeling is easily explainable," Mariana said. "The human body has subtle ways of revealing itself. We emanate heat, raising the local air temperature a fraction of a degree. Pheromones are exuded. The space we occupy alters air currents. Weak electromagnetic fields are generated. The moisture from exhalation causes a minuscule increase in humidity—"

"There's molecular outgassing from the clothing we wear," Amanda added, drawing on her knowledge of chemistry.

"Fair points," Ellis said, undeterred. "Now expand the concept to those forces science is reticent to recognize: The *ch'i* of Chinese culture. *Prana* in Hinduism. *Auras or life force* in Western culture. The universe holds many unrecognized or misunderstood phenomena. When detected subliminally, the intellect recoils from the lack of understanding. Relate this to what I and others have felt on Murkor. Only it's more than the feeling of someone or something lurking behind you. It permeates space—though, admittedly, the instinctive reaction is to turn around." Ellis looked directly at Amanda, who remained uneasy. "I can see where the sensation might be frightening. It doesn't have to be." She stared at Garcia. "And I believe what I am describing can go undetected when a person is in a secure environment, distracted, or sleeping."

"Or, conversely, the feeling intensifies when alone," Roya volunteered.

"Doubly so when in a lava tube," Amanda had to admit.

"Yes, I would imagine so," Ellis acknowledged.

"The feeling is pronounced when you're alone," Stewart objected, "simply because people tend to be more frightened when they're alone. Nothing more to it. Sorry. Continue."

"Somewhere along the way here, I ditched my depleted rebreather. My respiration became extremely labored but settled as I forged ahead—"

"—a few hundred meters before collapsing where Lieutenant Davis found you," Stewart said, interrupting again.

Ellis shook her head. "No. The light he held had vanished, though I retained the hope that you both made it inside Nadir. By my estimation, I had walked more than a kilometer."

"No one can last on Murkor's surface that long," Gustavo chimed in. The protest was halfhearted. "Can they?"

"Coincides with where I found her," Davis said.

"Come on, lieutenant," Stewart protested. "I seriously doubt you were in any condition to judge distance accurately."

Davis made a motion to disagree when Carlos, eyes fixed on Ellis, spoke up. "I know exactly where your rebreather lies. I spotted it when looking for your vehicle. Can't say how, but you almost made it here."

"Thanks for that, sargento," Ellis responded. "I knew I was close, but I was too exhausted to go on. I sat down, gradually losing awareness." She turned to Davis.

"Lieutenant, how much time between when I ordered you and Captain Stewart to continue without me and when you found me?"

"Somewhere north of seventy-five minutes," Davis said. "Pretty damned astounding, if you ask me."

"Part of that time you were unconscious," Stewart asserted, although, on hearing, the explanation seemed woefully inadequate.

"I didn't succumb to hypoxia," Ellis said. "I prefer the word you found applicable to Nadir's crew. *Stasis.* Imperfect, but it's a better fit."

"Wait a second," Garcia demanded. "This word describes our physical condition when you found us?"

"Possibly," Stewart said. "In the short time I monitored your vitals, they stabilized. Unfortunately, your rapid revival prevented knowing this for sure."

"A minor inconvenience we'll just have to live with, no?" Garcia said, smiling. "For the moment, let's assume our vitals held steady. What then?"

Stewart considered carefully. "If Nadir's internal and external atmosphere equalized at nine percent oxy and the ambient temperature remained relatively constant, maybe you survive a few months. Lack of water and nourishment being the limiting factors."

"You mean hibernating?" a skeptical Carlos asked. "Like six bears slumbering through the long Murkorian winter?"

"Something like that. A possibility."

"What I'm still not hearing is *why*," Roya asked. "What could cause this?"

"Want speculation?" Stewart asked.

"We've heard little else," Garcia replied.

"You, your crew, were profoundly affected by the psychological and physical stress of coping with an environment where oxygen was known to be diminishing to the point of lethality. This untenable situation, occurring over a prolonged period, caused a group psychology to form. As the available oxygen decreased, somatic and psychosomatic symptoms increased. Each of you was affected slightly differently, with symptom onset inversely related to age: The youngest of your crew and most impressionable, first to succumb; the oldest and least impressionable, last. Ultimately, a self-defense mechanism kicked in. The mind shuts the body down to protect itself against asphyxiation.

"There is an analog, though a poor one, I must admit. It's called the mammalian diving reflex. There are instances of children surviving after more than an hour of submersion in frigid water. Breathing stops, heart rate slows, and blood is diverted from the extremities to the brain and body core."

Stewart, wondering if she had convinced anybody, looked around the table. "There you have it, folks. Medical conjecture of a sort, wrapped in a nice tidy package."

"A portion of it sounded plausible. Ellis said. "It doesn't explain what happened to me."

Garcia agreed. "We've taken another detour, Commander—as you seemed to have anticipated. I'm quite willing to be intrigued. You're implying some common agent affected us both?"

"Not implying," Ellis, undaunted, responded. "I'm stating it outright. And at least one other person, Laurie Jensen—she's one of our techs—should be included."

Garcia and his crew had not been privy to Ellis's prior effort to find a common denominator for the strange events on Murkor. She recited Jensen's harrowing incident inside lava Tube Z784C, including the odd presence she felt that had left her shaken but otherwise unharmed. When finished (Stewart was obliged to offer cogent counterpoints), Ellis sipped her water, leaned back, and braced for the reaction her next remark would provoke.

"It's evident our lives were intentionally spared."

Gustavo's voice rose above the others. "Spared? Not from my point of view," he declared, exaggerating the sentiment by slouching in his seat and tilting his head straight up. "You know—flat on my back—staring up at a ceiling I could no longer see."

"That's where we'd still be if it weren't for Commander Ellis," Roya reminded, diplomatically acting as her crewmate's apologist, her eyes misting upon recalling what was believed to be their last moments together.

"You see, Commander," Gustavo said, looking at Roya with fondness. "We thought our lives were over. I meant no offense."

"None taken," Ellis said. "What I'm suggesting is a hard thing to accept given the mysterious origin and seeming finality of your incapacity."

"Let's assume we developed a myopic mindset," Garcia said, speaking on behalf of his crew. "To suggest that our separate experiences, yours *and* ours, are connected is one thing—to claim it was intentional is quite another. And what happens now? All of it strains credulity. Nevertheless, Commander, I can see by your expression that you're in earnest, and I, for one, refuse to dismiss any idea out of hand. Please state your case."

"Look no further than yourselves. Six humans among the two hundred billion who ever lived. Seven millennia of recorded history. And yet Zenith's mindstor cannot reference a single medical profile that equates to yours. As for myself? It is impossible to last more than a few minutes on the surface. Yet that is what I did. For more than an hour. These seemingly unrelated events, obscure in isolation, resolve when viewed together. Although the specifics differ, our assured survival is identical— accomplished, albeit imperfectly, when our bodies adapted to the varying amount of oxygen available. Captain Stewart characterized it as a form of stasis, but I disagree that it was self-induced. To encompass all our cases demands the active intercession of an outside agent."

Roya finished the thought. "An entity exemplified by an aura or life force you postulated earlier?"

"Yes, I believe so."

"Your argument would be more persuasive," Amanda said, "if there were a chance of something evading our detectors. It just doesn't happen."

Ellis glanced at Davis. "They're Tarsier V's," he confirmed. "State of the art."

"The only thing on this base that is," Carlos added.

"It can only detect what is within human experience," Ellis replied. "What lies outside our comprehension is far greater."

"And the astrobiologists' reports?" Amanda asked.

"Same answer," Ellis said.

"Lieutenant Davis," Garcia said. "Care to weigh in on this? Assuming it exists, how would you describe this entity?"

Davis looked beyond Garcia and through the dirty viewport to where sporadic lightning diffused blue energy into the late-night murk. When he finally responded, he did so absently. "I'd say it's struggling. In retreat. On a world sterilized of most life, it would seize every opportunity to perpetuate itself. It's motivated to keep us alive. It requires us. A mutually beneficial association develops. A form of symbiosis. I'd call it a symbiont." The reasoning sounded pretty good. Did he believe it himself? More importantly, Ellis appeared— what? Amused? Pleased?

More than Garcia would have expected, Davis's idea resonated. So, too, with almost everyone else present, judging by the flurry of questions: Is the entity intelligent? Could it be a form of pure energy? Are they still harboring it? The ideas, suggestions, and concerns were entertaining to muse over—all predicated on an underlying premise that remained very much in doubt. Finally, unintentionally, the spell was broken.

"This entity is a selective one," Stewart observed. "I give you Ed Anderson—one of our hard cases. He tried to decommission the CAM-L that brought us here and also accessed your mindstor. Anyway, hypoxia took him down. He went stone-cold unconscious after being exposed, sans breather, on the planet's surface. When I revived him, there was no mention of anything like— what should I call it—a visitation?"

"He shouldn't have been," Carlos said, half-joking. "Revived, that is."

"I, too, passed out from lack of oxygen," Davis said. "Nothing else. Proves little. It was different circumstances. Should we expect a total unknown to surrender its secrets so easily?"

Another interval of back and forth followed, after which they were nearer to exhaustion than the truth.

"To sum up," Garcia had to concede, "we have competing and unprovable speculations. What other tools can we bring to bear?"

"Comparison of blood and tissue samples taken before and after you and your crew revived," Mariana said. "Interpreting the data will take time."

"Gustavo and I can update Nadir's mindstor," Davis said. "Gus suggested that we establish a crosslink with Zenith's primary mindstor, allowing inquiries to be filtered through the thought processes of both. It's a good idea, though I suggest we manage our expectations."

"In that case, Commander," Garcia said, "I recommend we reconvene at 0900. The lateness of the hour wears on us. My crew and I have had an unnatural sleep while you and yours have had none."

"Agreed," Ellis said.

"Good," Garcia said, pushing back his chair.

Drezzzergghhhfahtaa! *Glusssherverjenpencalfist! Mipfigmipfignahdah!*

"How do you put up with the incessant noise?" Davis asked Gustavo as they walked through Nadir's pitiful surroundings to temporary guest accommodations on L1.

"You'd be surprised what can be tolerated with time—just look around, my friend. *Es un lugar mierdoso.*"

"You have to help me out with that one, Gus," Davis said.

"Shithole."

***

The following day, there was something of a setback for Ellis's theory—her Symbiont Theory, as designated by Davis and adopted by all. Carlos decided the best way to prove the existence of the elusive entity was to venture "bareback" onto Murkor's scorched surface and go about the business of breathing. He was accompanied by Gustavo, wearing a rebreather, only because the engineer threatened to go it alone. The experiment ended when Carlos, choking and turning a darker shade of Murkor's lightning blue, had to be dragged back inside.

The morning's meeting started fifteen minutes late, Garcia's tongue-lashing of both men taking that long.

Test results on blood and tissue samples shed no light on the medical mystery. Changes in blood chemistry observed in pre- and post-revival specimens, notably differences in oxygen and carbon dioxide saturation, were to be expected. Furthermore, samples showed no abnormal or unidentifiable substances. The absence was expected but supported Stewart's theory that the crews' stasis had been self-induced.

The linked mindstors proved to be slightly more enlightening. Before proceeding, Davis warned that the AIs were of different human templates. Unmatched, the unity, for better or worse, would be subject to inevitable vagaries. Accordingly, he began with a simple question.

"*Mindstor, report—*" Davis caught himself. Glancing at Garcia, who was smiling, he resumed: "*— English language response preferred—report the current status of the link.*"

Completed. Working. Overdue.

Gustavo, raising an eyebrow, commented, "A curious way of phrasing it. *Mindstor, please explain 'overdue.'*"

The answer was instantaneous.

Earlier establishment of a two-party link would have decreased the probability of undesirable consequences for both bases' inhabitants.

"*Cite examples,*" a curious Davis asked.

Increased probability of preventing Anderson's unauthorized intrusion into Nadir's mindstor; increased probability of an earlier resolution to Nadir's environmental system malfunction; increased probability of breaking the chain of events resulting in the head injury to Zenith's Imholtz; increased probability—

"I get it," Davis said, forgetting the phrasing necessary to end communicating with any mindstor.

—of breaking the causal chain of events leading to the death of Coalition shuttle pilot—

"Mindstor, end response," Davis, irritated, commanded.

"Sounds like we're being lectured to," Amanda said.

"Deservedly so," Garcia said. "Let's get on with it. May I? I prefer to keep this simple."

"The best approach," Ellis answered.

"Mindstor," Garcia said, *"Has an unknown or otherwise unidentified organism or substance intruded into base Nadir?"*

Low probability.

"Mindstor. Was the medical condition resembling biological stasis observed in Nadir's crew self-induced?"

Low probability.

"Posit an explanation for this unusual event."

Unable. Insufficient information.

"Is there a correlation between what affected Nadir's crew and the inordinate time Commander Ellis spent on the surface without a rebreather?"

Yes. Both events occurred on Murkor; Commander Ellis's sojourn on the surface directly resulted from Nadir's need for assistance.

"As I feared," Garcia said to the humans assembled, "we're getting nowhere. Anyone else?"

Everyone took a turn. After several fruitless minutes, Ellis said, "I'll give it one last try: *Mindstor, characterize this impasse.*"

Inability or refusal to pose the right question.

"*And what, exactly, would that question be?*" Ellis asked.

Are technology and science presently competent to explain all that transpires on Murkor.

"*And the answer?*"

Unequivocally, no.

"I didn't think that mindstors had a sarcastic sense of humor," Gustavo said.

And that, too, got a laugh.

***

"When you're that close to something," Davis said, "it's hard to see." He and Carlos were sweating beneath Zenith's broken CAM-L, making final repairs. Two hours earlier, they had ridden out together, taking components borrowed from a nearly identical vehicle Nadir had long ago been forced to abandon, along with several rebreathers essential for the task at hand.

"She really whipped your ass?" Carlos asked, referring to Ellis.

"Can and did," Davis responded.

"Impressive. What's the lubed torque setting on this bolt?"

"One hundred fifty Newton meters," Davis said. "They say it's hard to keep a good woman down."

"Not saying anything's going on, but you got a thing for her?"

"Not saying," Davis offered, his transparent rebreather mask making it hard to hide a smile.

"Uh-huh," Carlos mumbled, knowing when to let it go. "Try backing off a little on that aon regulator. The flow will actually increase by half a percent."

"Didn't know. Good tip."

For a spell, the two worked in silence.

"I know someone like you," Davis finally said. "Hand me that—?"

"Impetometer. Is this where you say remove my head from my posterior?" Carlos asked, self-deprecation being a newly minted talent.

"This mate of mine is in the brig right now. He couldn't get beyond the hatred. Couldn't change. From what I see, you've made a start. Of course, your recent Lazarus-like resurrection may have something to do with it."

A short while later, Davis, piloting the repaired vehicle, followed Carlos back to Nadir. As they labored prepping the Cam-L for its return trip to Zenith, Roya went about fulfilling Garcia's pledge, filling the hump with water from Nadir's on-site storage tanks.

"Are you departing too late?" Roya asked.

"If we delay much longer, yes," Davis answered. "The return trip will be much easier, however, the path between us having been plotted and stored by the CAM-L's onboard nav."

"I left my sergeant in command," Ellis added. "He reports all is well, though I'd prefer to relieve him of duty ASAP."

"And Zenith is lacking a physician," Stewart said. "I should be there."

"Then we shall get you on your way," Garcia responded. "But first, am I correct in assuming you'll again pass in proximity to N119, more specifically, the location where Amanda and Roya had their, uh, shall we say, *uncomfortable* experience?"

After receiving affirmative nods, Garcia had one more question, his voice suggesting that he had a pretty good idea of the answer.

"Roya, please inform us about the quantity of water in that lava tube."

"Sorry, comandante, I can't do that. Amanda and I siphoned three thousand liters without any sign of drawdown. The observable water level remained constant."

"And I assume you'd prefer to avoid the inconvenience of conducting a full hydrogeological study?"

"Go back? ¡Dios mío, no!" Roya protested, eyes rounding in feigned shock, a sentiment echoed by her crewmates.

"I see," Garcia said, slowly stroking his chin in contemplation. "It would seem that I have both a mutiny and a useless lava tube on my hands. Well, then, there is a possible solution. Commander Ellis, you must unburden me of this liability. You are welcome to N119 and the water it contains. Unlimited access."

"Yes, please, take it," Amanda said. "We insist."

"Of course, if, for whatever reason, you're unwilling to enter *that* tube," Gustavo teased, "I'm sure we can find something more suitable. Perhaps something even closer to Zenith."

"It is more than generous," Ellis responded, stirred by the magnitude of the offer and the affable manner in which it was presented. "I am, however, hesitant to accept."

"You must," Garcia entreated. "As a favor to me. My obligation to you—no, our friendship, requires it."

"I foresee much trouble in this for you," Ellis responded. "Ultimately, you will be censured for your largess. Unión will demand it."

"Speaking plainly, Commander, there may be a problematic order or two of yours to consider. Something about subjugating partisan advantage to protect an adversary's welfare. I will construe your silence as an ascent." Garcia shifted his focus to encompass Ellis's fellow officers. "The three of you have endured tremendous hardship and risked your lives. My crew and I believed our lives were lost. What do any of us have to fear from the displeasure of our superiors? Please rest easy concerning my future. I can assure you it is the least of my worries."

"You are very persuasive, comandante," she said. "On behalf of a grateful Zenith, I accept—on one small condition."

"Small or large, name it."

"Any water rights Nadir grants to Zenith will be contingent upon both parties entering into a collaborative venture." Ellis looked questioningly at Davis. She didn't have to ask.

"Anecrecium output—and profits—will triple over IMC's original projections," the lieutenant volunteered. "Too bad," he added, smirking, "Kreechum won't see any of it."

"A partnership," Ellis continued, "entitling Nadir, and therefore Unión, to a significant portion of mining profits. There will be details to sort out. I would expect you to drive a hard bargain."

Contemplating the proposal's potential ramifications, Garcia broke into a broad smile. "I accept your 'condition.' May it go well beyond resolving the trivial problems you and I face. An opportunity to bridge a divide—"

"Oh, I can guarantee you'll make fast friends," Stewart said. "Just as soon as the IMC techs learn of their good fortune."

"An open invitation is extended to you and your crew," Ellis said.

"I look forward to the opportunity," Amanda commented. She had wisely given up on snaring Davis, but a new watering hole populated with male techs meant her personal drought would likely be over.

"Perhaps Unión will be embarrassed into letting me overhaul this disaster," Carlos said, envisioning the changes he would make to Nadir.

"In a few months," Gustavo agreed, "who knows what will be possible? You might replace your Cro-

Magnon bags of rocks with proper weight-training equipment."

"*That's* what they were for," Davis said. "Clever."

"My, we're an agreeable bunch this morning," Roya observed. "Must be something in the water."

The jest inspired a lighthearted groan—and a curious bit of reflection.

"Mariana, I regret leaving you with a medical mystery," Stewart said.

"If not us, who will solve it?" Mariana wondered.

"Allow me—" Garcia said, trailing his words as if he had handily unlocked the puzzle.

"Comandante? Seriously?" Mariana asked.

"Yes, and with minimal difficulty, simply by using the evidence hiding in plain sight. I have witnessed a pronounced change in our behavior during the last several days—a tendency to support each other emotionally and physically as the trying circumstances dictated. I can personally attest to this behavior blossoming in my crew. Clearly, Commander Ellis, the same sentiment took possession of you and yours during the perilous journey to Nadir. Based on what you have been kind enough to disclose, the same altered state of mind seems to have taken hold at Zenith. Is that so?"

"It is," Ellis answered.

"Even more remarkably," Garcia continued, "and it goes to the heart of my revelation, there is the favorable interaction between us: On your part, and accomplished at considerable risk, the timely restoration of our atmosphere; on our part, providing the water resources necessary to sustain your crew. Water for oxygen, with each of us contributing an essential constituent for life. For *human* life. Strange behavior indeed coming from adversaries who, much to their own detriment, have more often acted like they belonged to two entirely different species."

Garcia paused briefly to let the thought sink in.

"And so, with due respect to you, Captain Stewart, the evidence supports Commander Ellis's and Lieutenant Davis's opinion that an organism on this planet behaves symbiotically. I know this with certainty. For it is *we* who are the Symbionts of Murkor."

"Contemplative silence can be a sign of appreciation," at last, someone said, "Do you hear that?"

Except no one did.

Which was precisely the point.

Even the fumaroles were quiet.

***

"Nicely done, comandante," Ellis complimented, stepping into the CAM-L.

Garcia maintained his usual modesty. "I merely tried to put an agreeable gloss on a valid disagreement." Then, as the others said their goodbyes, he leaned in and whispered in Ellis's ear words only she could hear: "I expect you'll be proven right."

With final plans and promises made, Zenith's crew headed away, leaving Nadir's pyramid to be swallowed in the murk behind them.

Ellis reflected on all that transpired. She had come to Murkor with a single-minded purpose and had gained far more. She had no reservations concerning Garcia. He would follow through. As a symbiont, it was in his nature.

A glance at Davis and Stewart showed them to be smiling. She allowed for a feeling of satisfaction: The down payment to fulfill a commitment made long ago might be more substantial than previously imagined.

More than she could have reasonably hoped.

Verging on a future of self-forgiveness.

How soon, she wondered, would everyone realize she had help?

16 THE BEST OF ALL POSSIBLE WORLDS

LIPS PRESSED TIGHT, EYES narrowed, corners turning down into a vaguely menacing squint. There was no mistaking his intent. He would respond to the provocation.

"We'll have to be quiet," Ellis said, aroused by the danger. Of all the people in the world, she alone knew what to expect.

"Good luck with that," Davis replied.

They were side by side on the bed. On the brink of touching.

Self-denial can be a most exquisite form of torture.

"Don't move," he threatened. "I'm going to take my sweet time." Propping his head up with one arm, he began tracing a circle around the outline of her nipples, watching as they stiffened beneath a sheer chemise that barely covered her hips. Grabbing a spaghetti strap, he forced it down over the smooth roundness of her shoulder, revealing the fullness of her breast.

"Put it in your mouth," she pleaded.

He shook his head, choosing instead to caress her unexposed nipple through the gown's thin, silken fabric. Not fair, she thought, loving him for it. Swallowing hard, she reached over, freeing him from his shorts. Wrapping her fingers, she began to stroke, drawing excitement from the feel of hot skin.

"No," he said, his voice hoarse, moving her hand away. "Today, *I* give the orders. "Flip. On your stomach."

As she complied, he jammed a pillow beneath her hips. "Something for you to hump." It was more of a command than a statement, and she didn't need a playbook, enticing him with the fluid, undulating motion of her back. She was incredibly supple. A lifetime of yoga gave her a physicality with some decidedly pleasurable benefits. "You're beautiful," he whispered, softly kissing the nape of her neck, then slowly moving down the curvature of her spine, lingering there with a teasing flick of the tongue.

"I want you inside me," she said in a moan, raising her hips.

"Say it."

"Fuck me—please."

Pressing his lean body against her, he delayed the inevitable.

"Again. Say it."

"Fu—shhh—wait—I hear something. *"*

"Ignore it," Davis pleaded, knowing she wouldn't.

What mother could? While waiting to be fed, one-year-old Carlie Ellis Davis started crying in the next room.

Hurriedly adjusting her nightgown, Ellis gave her spouse an affectionate peck on the cheek. "Sorry. Rain check for later?"

Curious. Only upon returning to Earth did he hear expressions using the word "rain."

"I did say I'd take my time," he responded, frustrated but in good humor. "Ten hours isn't exactly what I had in mind."

"You'll be at the Institute that long?" Ellis said, referring to IHI, the Institute of Hybrid Intelligence.

"I think we're on the verge of a minor breakthrough."

"Excellent. Still meeting me later? In time for his address?"

"Wouldn't miss it," he shouted after her as she headed for the adjoining room. "Not for the world."

"How long has it been?" she shouted back, saving 'since you've seen him' for Davis to figure out.

"Almost three years." Discounting holos, it was the last time he saw Garcia, not since having left *both* commanding officers behind on Murkor. Entering the shower, he began to reminisce.

He had stayed on four months after Garcia cut a lucrative mining deal on behalf of Unión. When he said his last farewell, the means to increase anecrecium production were firmly in place. Six months later, traveling interstellar, he found himself back on Earth.

He remembered the conversation with El before departing (he had always referred to her as *commander* when in uniform), informing her of his decision not to re-up. A position awaited him at the prestigious IHI. It was a perfect opportunity to develop a budding idea. "We can do this, you know," she had insisted. What she meant was continuing to keep their hands off each other.

Maybe. Except *if* it was true, it was only because he had refused to compromise her. "I'd be making this move whether you plan to return to Earth or not," he had said. "But if you do return, I intend to make it impossible for you ever to leave."

Many long months later, having completed her tour of duty, she had appeared at the Institute. They blew right past the preliminaries. One fine morning, not long into their marriage, she looked him in the eyes and simply said, "Tick-tock." Always the wiseass, he had stared back at her and said, "The sound an old timepiece makes?" Soon after, she was pregnant.

Making him happier than he had the right to expect.

A beautiful daughter—hmm, no longer crying in the next room.

"Do my back?" Lieutenant Colonel Jennifer Ellis Davis said, stepping naked into the shower.

"I'll do more than that." Brian Scott Davis, a civilian, responded.

***

Back on Murkor, things were going well. Three extended-range CAM-Ls with increased water storage capacity were placed in service, along with two spanking new harvesters. At long last, a land-based positioning system was installed, greatly aiding surface navigation. These and several other improvements increased anecrecium production beyond the wildest expectations. Garcia had re-upped for one more year. Under Ellis's and his tenure, the "boondoggle," known as Zenith, came to be regarded as one of Earth's most profitable off-world mining ventures. Sufficiently so that the Coalition politicians who previously went subterranean could poke their heads above ground and appraise the weather. Seeing it balmy, they reemerged like so many overwintering insects to take credit.

However, concessions concerning the involvement of others had to be made. Ellis, for one, had something to do with this vastly improved state of affairs. So, a public ceremony was held. Speeches were made. A shiny commendation was awarded. Looking below the surface, she recognized the gestures for what they were: Splendid PR opportunities for politicians.

More importantly, her reassignment request had been granted. A month later, she assumed command of Coalition Sector 4, the expansive, arid, and equally problematic region that shared a thousand-kilometer common border with Unión. Aided by a no-nonsense, straightforward manner, her outreach efforts to local civic groups had begun to reduce cross-border tensions.

Returning from one such visit, she entered an old adobe mission repurposed as a field office. Although several hundred years old, its half-meter-thick exterior walls, built from clay, silt, and sand, acted as an effective low-tech heat sink, absorbing the scorch of the daytime sun and radiating it into a starry night. There were few windows, and her staff closed them to enjoy the retrofitted air conditioning. They hadn't been to Murkor, where the simple pleasure of opening a window did not exist. She lifted a creaky sash and inhaled desert air scented with the golden blooms of sweet acacia.

Ellis's publicly touted success off-world and accomplishments in Sector 4 had unexpectedly made her a public figure with a fair degree of political capital. The notoriety had come with a few perks, including a rapid rise in military rank—first to major, then to lieutenant colonel. Her good fortune was instrumental in transferring a lower-ranking officer so that he fell under her command.

It was an excellent opportunity to handle a matter overdue for redress.

"Sit down, Major."

Major Eglend sat down.

Ellis stared at the man. In the months before her reassignment, stories of his misogynistic behavior had filtered up to her. None were actionable until now.

"I am relieving you of command responsibilities."

Eglend, recovering quickly after being taken aback, dared to flash a confident grin. "I see. Right to the point. On what possible grounds?"

"Section A15-8. Conduct prejudicial to good order and discipline."

"Who made this ridiculous charge?"

"A civilian brought the complaint to my attention. A man."

"A man?" a surprised Eglend repeated. "I don't follow."

"Husband to the woman you were having an affair with," Ellis said. "Very angry. He had her under surveillance, so there's no question of documentation."

Eglend sat silent for several moments, processing his predicament. The stratagems used on Varian could not help him now: Not the intimidation of women subjected to unwanted sexual overtures nor the coercion of junior officers into providing an alibi.

And certainly not the blind-eye indulgence of an immediate superior.

"You deliberately had me brought here from Varian," he growled, losing his composure, along with a good portion of his self-confidence.

Ellis let her silence be the answer.

"I won't go down easy," Eglend threatened.

"You did once, and hard, major. How long did it take for that broken nose to heal?" That remark had to be Davis rubbing off on her, she thought, repressing a smile.

Eglend's face turned reddish pink, closely matching the adobe's exterior walls. "Your action is subject to review."

"I'm counting on it," Ellis replied, knowing the more attention drawn, the better. "In the meantime, pack your kit. I'm sending you to Langemak."

"Never heard of it."

"A helium-3 mining operation on the flip side of the moon. A small colony known to be desolate and utterly devoid of female inhabitants."

"There's a word for women like you," Eglend said.

"Careful, major. You're one word away from insubordination. Now get out of my sight."

Major Eglend left.

Quietly. And after saluting.

Would this put an end to Eglend's reprehensible behavior? Ellis wondered. When word got out that he was vulnerable to censure, the aggrieved women would be less reticent to come forward. She sent a concise update to Stewart, who had decided to remain on Murkor: *Major Ego transferred. Look up Langemak when you get the chance.* Despite the long transmission delays, they had stayed in contact. The doctor's messages were a reliable source of scuttlebutt, such as the relationship between Schulman and Nadir's Allawi and Amanda's most recent conquest of a Zenith mining tech.

It was also gratifying to learn the IMC techs now thought highly of her. Maybe it was because they had become exceedingly wealthy, even with their tiny productivity percentages. All, that is, except Kreechum and Anderson, interred on Varian for one year and five years, respectively. Anderson was said to regret his actions. Kreechum's remorse was strictly monetary in nature.

In concluding the day's business, Ellis looked ahead to attending Garcia's speech and the dinner that followed. An auto alert sounded as she packed the evening gown she would change into en route.

Message from HealthScan is available.

Those who could afford it had a subcutaneous micro device/nanoinfuser programmed to send encrypted medical reports to one's mindstor.

"Play message," Ellis said.

Pregnancy detected. Term: Ten days. No level two genetic abnormalities.

"Gender?" Ellis asked, her heart racing.

Male.

"Implement Family Planning Protocol FP1."

Implementation in progress.

If all went well with her pregnancy, a near certainty, she would conceive a second child.

Reclining in the AirCar that would take her to Coalition's capital, she made an important decision.

To forego the chardonnay she planned on having with dinner.

***

Half of IHI regional headquarters' seventy-four levels were underground. Thankfully, Research and Development occupied five top floors, affording Davis a stunning view of Rivière des Prairies as it meandered past central Montreal's silver-blue spires.

He did some of his best thinking while staring out of windows. Those thought processes, aided by crucial contributions from Gustavo and several others, were beginning to bear fruit.

Or so he hoped, for there remained a great deal of uncertainty in the groundbreaking territory they were charting.

The many ways human intelligence was approximated and amplified—from circuit boards processing strings of binary code to quantum computers and subsequent iterations—had, a generation ago, been outmoded by IHI's development of the mindstor. It accomplished this by infusing a molecular hydrocolloid with the "circuitry" of the left frontal lobe of the cerebral cortex, specifically that area of the brain associated with reasoning, problem-solving, logic, and speech. The results were revolutionary—an exponential increase in information processing and a corresponding reduction in energy usage and heat production. Original thinking (some would say imaginative), however, was still primarily the purview of the human brain. The mindstors utilized on Murkor were fitting examples of AI's limitations.

IHI gave Davis free rein to pursue a different, additive approach. Why not, he suggested, supplement a mindstor's hydrocolloid with the brain's intuitive, creative, and, importantly, meditative thought centers? The way to proceed, he reasoned, was when a human subject, a mentor, was experiencing the psychophysical effects, or state of mind, of deep meditation.

And so, with a sticky mat and duffel in hand, Ellis arrived at IHI. Greeted by Davis, she was guided to an R&D room on the seventy-first level. There, she changed from a military uniform into loose yoga clothing. A team of technicians fitted her with the "skullcap" necessary for the infusion process to proceed.

Unfurling the sticky mat, she assumed the full lotus position: Back straight, bare feet tucked on opposite thighs, hands resting on knees, thumbs and index fingers touching to form an "O," the hand *mudra* of choice. Sprouting Medusa-like from her head, a tangle of wires connected to banks of softly glowing electronics. It was an image of striking contrasts, her lithe form and ancient pose, and the modern trappings of science and technology.

Although the experiment occurred months ago, the researchers were still struggling with the results. Aware of the diversion it would create, Gustavo suggested that a fitting test of the mindstor's capabilities would be to pose a series of inquiries deemed either deliberately obscure or unanswerable. Davis recalled two favorites among many:

Q: Mindstor, is there a God?
A: If you want there to be.
Q: What is the meaning of life?
A: All.

It almost seemed that the mindstor could outsmart them, Gus had remarked.

Wasn't that precisely the point of it all? Davis had responded, suggesting they move forward with a new inquiry.

The inquiry. Held in abeyance, it had been their primary motivator.

Nearly four years had passed, and the root cause of the strangeness on Murkor remained a mystery. There had been no further incidents. Not even Ellis, who was the first to reenter Nadir's inexhaustible Tube N119, felt anything noteworthy.

Disappointingly, there had only been the initial and abbreviated attempts at closure, principally by a science team dispatched from Varian. The same investigators refused to suspend transit to and from the planet, perhaps because they were made to understand that restricting planetary access would negatively impact mining operations.

The eroding property of time made it easier to claim that what took place on the planet was merely the fertile imaginings of the human psyche. And so, the matter remained an unfinished chapter in the lives of those directly or indirectly affected. Of them, only Davis and Gustavo had found a way to pursue a resolution.

Davis understood the odds of succeeding were stacked against him. The first task was ferreting out and transferring to Mindstor II all data related to humanity's tenure on Murkor. Much of it, however, was out of reach within Unión mindstors on Nadir, Varian, and Earth. To address this hindrance, he petitioned IHI for project assistance in the capable person of Gustavo Ramírez. The granting of the request was a tangible sign of the developing thaw between rival superpowers, but for Gustavo, the politics did not matter. He came willingly based on his former association with Davis and personal interest.

The two had worked well together. After speaking with Ellis, they agreed on how to phrase the initial inquiry, deciding that simplicity was best.

"The only time I was this anxious about a response," Davis commented, "was when I asked El to marry me."

"Really? I always thought you and Commander Ellis were a sure thing."

"What?!" Davis said in surprise.

"Relax. Mariana clued me in. She's got a sixth sense about those things."

"Great. So, how sure are you about this?"

Gustavo always had Edgar Allan at the ready. "I have great faith in fools—self-confidence, my friends will call it."

"And we are the best of friends," Davis pointed out. "But here goes anyway: *Mindstor, access and research all available records pertaining to Murkor. Determine the probability of an unidentified organism or substance existing on the planet.*"

Unable to comply. The parameters of the inquiry are too limiting.

Davis flashed Gustavo a disappointed look. It seemed like more of the usual BS. Or maybe, his gut told him, there would be more to it this time.

"Mindstor, continue dialogue. Explain."

There is a high probability that the entity is both an unidentified organism and an unclassified substance.

"Maybe we're on to something," Gustavo said. "Keep with it."

Davis, restraining his excitement, thought for a moment. Continuing with simplicity, he asked:

"Offer further proof."

A statistically significant correlation exists between reports of an entity's presence and false positives issued by the Stanton Model 16xvb and AquaStatt Model 18xvb Sniffers used to detect ambient water molecules in parts-per-trillion.

"We had the Stanton with us most of the time," Gustavo said. "I can confirm the false positives."

"Same with the AquaStatt," Davis replied. "The mindstor must realize they function using two entirely different operating systems—"

"Which makes false positives in both exceedingly unlikely," Gustavo said, completing the thought.

"But what the *hell* are we dealing with? An entity that's all water? No way is that possible."

"Ask."

"Mindstor. Is the entity water?"

No.

"What, then?"

A mimic capable of rearranging subatomic particles to replicate water's chemical and molecular properties.

"For what purpose?"

Concealment.

"Was the biological stasis observed in Nadir's crew induced by the entity?"

Probable.

"Why—strike that—to what aim?"

To perpetuate the life of the affected humans.
"For what purpose?"
Unknown.
"Mindstor, is the entity on Earth?"
Unknown.

And so it went. A score of additional inquiries were made, and just as many "unknowns," including how such an entity could alter the physiology of a human. For the present, they could get no further down the path they had embarked on.

"We've created a greater mystery than when we started," Gustavo finally said.

A pensive Davis retreated from the table where they had sat for the last hour and stood at a west-facing window. Scattered sunlight had painted the sky orange; the spires' shiny sides mirrored the reflected sky's color. "We have at least set the wheels of further inquiry in motion, my friend. Among the suppositions, there is one hard fact a scientist can latch on to."

Gustavo nodded. "Yeah, curious as to those sniffers. I must admit, though, you have to ask to what extent the mindstor reflects the wishes, dreams, and imagination of one Jennifer Ellis Davis?"

"El!" Davis exclaimed, turning from the darkening sky. "Look at the time! We're going to be late!"

"Forty minutes transit to New Detroit," Gustavo said. "It *will* be tight."

***

When Garcia returned to Earth, he was gratified to see that his aged father, retired from politics, retained much of the influence and craftiness his time in public service as ranking member of Unión's *Cámara de los Deputados* could bestow. When an opportunity arose to fill a vacant position in that prestigious legislative body, the father, driven by filial pride and force of habit, decided to convince his son to run for office.

Although reticent at first, Garcia had to concede that the arguments put to him were as persuasive as the man making them. Foremost, he had culminated a long and honorable military career on a high note. The hugely profitable venture on Murkor was viewed through the prism of national pride as primarily his doing. His father also knew that when his son was thrust into the public eye, they would like what they saw: A distinguished, exceedingly handsome man who looked the part of a leader. It did not hurt *El Comandante's* chances that he was intelligent, well-spoken, and had the full backing of his politically savvy father. The election wasn't even close.

Beholden to almost no one, Garcia set about trying to make a difference. Drawing on his experience on Murkor, he hit upon what he believed to be the right idea at the right time. Hopefully, the speech he was about to give would further that cause. The venue was a large lecture hall crowded with luminaries, dignitaries, and Coalition politicians. He had been accepted into what many in his home country would call the enemy's camp. It helped that the topic of discussion, *Economic and Sociological Disruptions Due to Climate Change*, respected no boundaries.

Sitting to both sides of him at the dais were the evening's other speakers: Coalition's vice president (who had just given the keynote address), a climatologist, a renowned sociologist, and representatives of three of the world's largest multinational corporations. As he listened to himself being introduced, he spotted El in the audience, sitting a few tables back and looking radiant in a bright green evening gown. Next to her were two empty chairs. Making eye contact, he watched her shrug, then beam, when Davis suddenly approached: All imposing two meters of him, running cover for the much shorter Gustavo. Taking a seat next to his wife, he flashed Garcia, now moving to the podium, a sly grin, a sympathetic wink, and a "thumbs-up" sign. The crowd, they knew, would have to be won over.

"Thank you for the invitation and the kind words," Garcia began in a forceful, clear voice. "Considering just how far I am from mi casa, I hope not to change the graciously expressed positive sentiments."

Scattered laughter broke the silence and tension. What would this Coalition audience expect of him, Garcia wondered? He had composed his short speech quite literally 'on the fly' from Unión's current capital, Bogotá.

"We are gathered here compelled by extreme circumstances to become enlightened students of climatology," he continued. "For those who struggled through history, an anecdotal story comes to mind.

"A man in an expensive, well-tailored suit sits alone on a dome. All around him is water and the tops of a few important-looking buildings. Eventually, a boat appears. 'Hello!' its concerned captain shouts. 'There's room on board! I shall come alongside and get you safely off there!'

"'You shall not,' the man on the dome shouts back. 'I am quite content to remain exactly where I am.'

"'But, my good fellow, you shall be at the mercy of the rising water.'

"'Nonsense, the water shall recede, the land will return.'

"'Untrue,' the boat captain says, humoring the man, 'and this is low tide.'

"'Well, then, I shall wait for the sun to dry this nuisance out.'

"The captain was beginning to understand the stubborn nature of the person he was dealing with. 'Have it your way,' he says. 'If you change your mind, I shall send another boat tomorrow.'

"'Don't trouble yourself,' the man on the dome says. 'I never change my mind.'

"'Yes, I can see that," says the resigned captain. "By the way, what is that building under you?'

"'Why, you damn fool, it is the Capitol, home of the Senate. I'm out here to get a bit of fresh air. My colleagues are still in session.'"

After an awkward pause, half the audience began to laugh politely.

"Exactly *which* capital and senate," Garcia continued, "I shall leave to your choosing, but looking back, we know governments never fully embraced the urgency of climate change or did so belatedly. None had the political will to make the hard individual concessions that collective action required. We, our planet, are dearly paying the price.

"Now, let us look to the future. Let us do so with guarded optimism that we are on the threshold of a global change in the political and social climate, this time for the better. We only need to look to Murkor for proof. Through the heroism shown by Coalition citizens—two, I am gladdened to say, are in attendance tonight—I witnessed affirmation of our better nature. It seems a wellspring of goodwill was born from that encounter—and, not incidentally, a fair amount of wealth was generated for our two nations. Is this a harbinger of the great things we can accomplish together, or will we squander the opportunity this example personifies?

"I come before you with the well-intentioned consent of my government and the people it represents, holding a branch from an olive tree. But an olive tree will wither and die without fertile, irrigated soil to grow. And so, within the year, Unión Latino will commence construction of a desalination project sufficient in scope to provide the freshwater needs of the entire Pecos River Valley, the Lower Rio Grande Valley, and the Ojos Negros Region—areas impacted by drought and the subject of acrimonious water rights disputes between our respective nations. Unfortunately, the entirety of the massive project cannot be accomplished unilaterally. We propose a collaborative venture with your government—the construction and operation of facilities extending water distribution mains to farmlands within the jurisdiction of both nations.

"For too long, we have exploited natural resources with one nation's gain achieved through the other's loss. Policies dictated purely by self-interest have led to our undoing. The social disruption and strife caused by climate change are sad proof. I ask, is it not common sense to see our Earth as common ground?

"The answer is for us to join together, providing what the other lacks while mindful—even prideful—of those attributes of ethnicity and national character that allow us to excel. In doing so, we shall make each other exceptional.

"If we dream this now, we will one day awaken and find a better place. A verdant planet where each person flourishes within our shared humanity. We will transform our home, this Earth, into the best of all possible worlds."

"Well done," Ellis commented as Garcia joined her, Davis, and Gustavo for dinner. "I believe you won over more than a few people."

"Agreed," Gustavo said, surprising his former comandante by filling his glass with Torrontés, a bottle of pleasing white wine he had hidden for the occasion. "But I am curious. How'd you get the desalination project funded?"

"I threatened," of course. "I said that the only way to avoid disruption in anecrecium production—and the free flow of funds into Unión coffers—was to allocate a sizeable portion of those funds to the project. It wasn't a hollow threat. With your help, Commander

Ellis, I've cultivated the contacts I previously established on Murkor—both Unión *and* Coalition."

As they were dining, the Coalition Vice President approached. After a brief exchange of pleasantries, he turned to leave, saying, almost as an afterthought, "The president appreciated your anecdote. He asked me to tell you all—his exact words—he's 'onboard.'"

"That was quick," Gustavo remarked when the VP was out of earshot.

"Does he have a choice?" Garcia commented. "The offer I made is part of the public record. Refusing to participate means withholding irrigation to the southwest region, alienating a sizable portion of his party's power base."

"I see you've acquired some interesting skills while in office," Davis said.

"I have to credit my father," Garcia responded.

"¿Cómo esta tu padre?" Gustavo asked, lapsing into Spanish.

"Very well. Seeing his only son in politics has invigorated him."

"Any recent news from Murkor?" Ellis asked.

"Nothing from Roya. Mariana is coming to visit me next month. Amanda seems content to stay on the planet—at least for now. Carlos became bored after upgrading Nadir. He 'turned civilian' when his term of service was up. Purchased a small farm not far from where his parents had a place. The owners' family was among the few who had refused offers from the big corporations."

"He'll do well when water comes to the area," Davis observed.

"That's an astute observation," Garcia responded. "Land values will double. Before going public, to avoid any hint of impropriety, I told only those with a good reason to know about the proposed project."

Something about the way Garcia spoke led Davis to believe that the constraint did include Carlos. He let the thought go. Instead, he addressed his wife, saying, "The lessening of border tensions will make your assignment easier."

"Possibly," Ellis said, patting his hand. "But only for the next eight months or so."

"Something to tell me?" he asked, staring at her unfilled wine glass.

"You're going to have a son."

"¡Qué buena suerte!" Gustavo and Garcia blurted out, slapping Davis on the back. They tried but couldn't get close to Ellis. She had disappeared in her spouse's massive hug.

When the congratulations had subsided, Gustavo caught Davis's eye. "Hey, papá, Mindstor II's your other baby. I'll let you tell her."

"A surprise for me?" Ellis asked.

"It's preliminary stuff," Davis said. "Mindstor's suggesting an alien presence."

After the explanation, Ellis had a comment.

"Is it not strange that the fortuitous events of the last few years seem to trace back to what happened on Murkor?"

"Coincidence or something more, time may tell," Garcia said. "For now, I propose a toast."

Four glasses were raised. One filled with life-giving water.

"To the continued health and happiness of the expectant mother—and to our belief in each other."

17 A QUESTION

"MUH-THA," CARLIE DAVIS ASKED, "why do people fight?"

"There are lots of reasons," Ellis said, avoiding the question. "Sit up straight at the breakfast table, sweetheart." From the corner of her eye, she watched her husband, relishing the *caldo de costilla* made from a recipe Garcia had sent them.

"Nice deflection," he said, hoping to remain an interested spectator. "One reason will suffice for now."

"No, I want *two reasons*!" Carlie emphasized with all the innocent charm that a four-year-old could muster.

El pondered the reason for her brief hesitation. She wasn't the type to hide the world from their two children. The trick was making sense of the insanity. "People fight, sweetheart, when they get really mad at each other. Sometimes, it's because one person takes something the other one wants."

"Like when Lyle grabs my toys?"

Hearing his name, Lyle Pilot Davis, barely two,

ceased wiggling in his chair. He rested his chin on the table's rim and peered over the plateau. Absorbing all, he said nothing.

"Not exactly," Ellis said. "Your brother's a little person. He doesn't know any better—"

Ellis immediately realized her mistake. Hubby did, too, forming a slight smile.

"Aren't big people *suppost* to know better?" Carlie protested.

"Yes, they are. That's what makes it so sad. Now Daddy will give you a second reason."

"I will?" Davis said, pretending to be put out, but he already knew his answer. He wasn't overly protective of his kids, either. "It's because they're afraid, sweetheart," he said, tidily rolling a thousand reasons into one.

Carlie tilted her head, squinted her eyes, and twisted her mouth, simultaneously contorting her face into a frown and a scowl to make it crystal clear that she thought what her father said was crazy.

Davis liked stretching his kids' boundaries. "When people are afraid, they don't *always* hide. Sometimes they want to hurt. Want to know what makes them afraid? Sometimes, they're afraid because someone else looks or acts a little different. They can't look past that to see they're very much alike. Never be that kind of afraid, sweetheart."

Lyle, taking special notice, raised his head off the table. "Me too?" he suddenly asked.

"Especially you, little man."

Gary Tarulli holds a B.A. in Literature from the State University of New York at Oneonta. He is the author of the science fiction novel *ORB* and the social satire novella *TOO BIG*. He currently lives in Long Island, New York, with his understanding wife and an eighteen-pound pooch named Maggie.

Praise for Gary Tarulli's novel, Orb

There's intelligent life in this SF yarn—a smashing beach read. --Kirkus Reviews

"Orb is highly satisfying for a first novel. The scientific questions raised are not cliché and the author deals with them in a mature but entertaining manner. Recommended for anyone with a thirst for good character study or deeply speculative science fiction." -SFRevu

"A story of close quarters and the psyche, "Orb" is an intriguing pick for those who like science fiction with a psychological edge." -Midwest Book Review

"I think what kept me hooked the most was the element of suspense woven seamlessly throughout the story. There was always the question of 'What next?' in the back of my mind." -Red, Red Reader Reviews